new relationships to the series. Fans of Lucy Arlington's 'Novel Idea' mysteries may want to enter the writing world from another angle."
—*Library Journal*

OF MURDER AND MEN
"A Colorado widow discovers that everything she knew about her husband's death is wrong... Interesting plot and quirky characters."
—*Kirkus Reviews*

A STORY TO KILL
"Well-crafted... Cat and crew prove to be engaging characters and Cahoon does a stellar job of keeping them—and the reader—guessing."
—*Mystery Scene*

"Lynn Cahoon has hit the golden trifecta—Murder, intrigue, and a really hot handyman. Better get your flashlight handy, *A Story To Kill* will keep you reading all night."
—**Laura Bradford**, author of the Amish Mysteries

"A Colorado widow discovers that everything she knew about her husband's death is wrong... Interesting plot and quirky characters."
—*Kirkus Reviews*

TOURIST TRAP MYSTERIES
"Lynn Cahoon's popular Tourist Trap series is set all around the charming coastal town of South Cove, California, but the heroine Jill Gardner owns a delightful bookstore/coffee shop so a lot of the scenes take place there. This is one of my go-to cozy mystery series, bookish or not, and I'm always eager to get my hands on the next book!"
—*Hope By the Book*

"Murder, dirty politics, pirate lore, and a hot police detective: *Guidebook to Murder* has it all! A cozy lover's dream come true."
—**Susan McBride**, author of the Debutante Dropout Mysteries

Books by Lynn Cahoon

The Tourist Trap Mystery Series

Guidebook to Murder * Mission to Murder * If the Shoe Kills * Dressed to Kill * Killer Run * Murder on Wheels * Tea Cups and Carnage * Hospitality and Homicide * Killer Party * Memories and Murder * Murder in Waiting * Picture Perfect Frame * Wedding Bell Blues * A Vacation to Die For * Songs of Wine and Murder

Novellas

Rockets' Dead Glare * A Deadly Brew * Santa Puppy * Corned Beef and Casualties * Mother's Day Mayhem * A Very Mummy Holiday

The Kitchen Witch Mystery Series

One Poison Pie * Two Wicked Desserts * Three Tainted Teas * Four Charming Spells * Five Furry Familiars

Novellas

Chili Cauldron Curse * Murder 101 * Have a Holly, Haunted Holiday * Two Christmas Mittens

The Cat Latimer Mystery Series

A Story to Kill * Fatality by Firelight * Of Murder and Men * Slay in Character * Sconed to Death * A Field Guide to Murder

Death in the Romance Aisle

A Survivors' Book Club Mystery

Lynn Cahoon

LYRICAL PRESS
Kensington Publishing Corp.
www.kensingtonbooks.com

LYRICAL PRESS BOOKS are published by

Kensington Publishing Corp.
119 West 40th Street
New York, NY 10018

All Kensington titles, imprints, and distributed lines are available at special quantity discounts for bulk purchases for sales promotion, premiums, fund-raising, educational, or institutional use.

Special book excerpts or customized printings can also be created to fit specific needs. For details, write or phone the office of the Kensington Sales Manager: Kensington Publishing Corp., 119 West 40th Street, New York, NY 10018. Attn. Sales Department. Phone: 1-800-221-2647.

Lyrical Press and Lyrical Press logo Reg. U.S. Pat. & TM Off.

First Electronic Edition: September 2023
ISBN: 978-1-5161-1117-6 (ebook)

First Print Edition: September 2023
ISBN: 978-1-5161-1118-3 (Print)

Printed in the United States of America

To my husband, the Cowboy, who still makes me laugh after twenty-plus years.

Chapter 1

The Tuesday night Survivors' Book Club was starting in less than thirty minutes, and Sam Aarons still hadn't shown up with the treats for the meeting. Rarity Cole, bookstore owner, texted her friend for the third time after she saw Shirley Prescott coming into the shop. Besides Rarity, who'd started the club, Shirley had been the first member, and she considered herself second-in-command for the club, especially surrounding the treat portion of the night. Shirley looked like the group mom or grandmother. With her gray hair pulled into a bun at the back of her head, no one could stand up to her bulldozing her way into their heart. Rarity tucked her phone away and smiled, hoping Shirley was in a good mood. "Good evening, Shirley. How's George?"

"He's fine. Grumpy as usual." Shirley glanced back at the treat table that currently held only coffee and lemonade. "Was it my turn to bring treats for this evening? I can run home and get something really quick. Sometimes I'm so forgetful."

"Sam's bringing cookies tonight. I talked to her earlier. I'm not sure why she's late, but she'll be here. I've got a few things to finish up before we start. I'll meet you by the fireplace." Rarity walked over and set up the *We're Open, so Yell if You Need Help* sign. She didn't think it was necessary, but she didn't want people to think that just because the book club was in session, they couldn't buy a book. And she still hadn't seen the need, or the income, to hire someone to cover the register while the club was in session. She was more focused on setting up additional book clubs. At least now that her first employee, Darby, had put in her notice. Rarity grabbed Killer's lead and took him out front to make sure he wouldn't need to go while they were talking.

Killer was a tan Yorkie she'd taken in as a foster for a few weeks until they'd found out that his former owner had been killed. Then he'd just stayed and became Rarity's dog. Constant companion. Confidante. Okay, she treated the dog like he was her kid. But she wasn't going to change that. She adored the little guy. A lot of people thought he was a Pom. Or at least a lot of people who came into the bookstore said that. He sniffed at several spots on the artificial-grass yard—okay, a few squares—that she'd set up in the front. He had a second place in the alley at the store for when she was working while it was closed.

Rarity saw a glimpse of herself in the window of the closed door. The darkness outside with the streetlamp made it look more like a mirror than a window. Her curly dark hair cascaded over the side of her face, hiding the worry she felt that must have been apparent to everyone else in the room. She put the negative thoughts away and turned to the right and to something she could actually fix tonight.

Sam's crystal shop was next door to the bookstore. Rarity could see Sam on the phone through the window. She waved at her, hoping to catch her gaze, and she did. Sam nodded and pointed to the phone. Apparently, that meant she'd be over as soon as she locked up her business and finished the phone call. Rarity nodded and hoped that Sam hadn't forgotten cookies, because if she had, Shirley would leave the meeting and run home to whip the group up something for a treat.

Shirley was a big believer that when two or more shall meet, there should be food. Feeding people was her way of serving others and showing her love. With her husband in a memory care facility, Rarity knew Shirley needed to feel needed. Shirley still hadn't told many people that George wasn't living at home, but that was her secret to tell, not Rarity's.

Killer was ready to go back inside, and he whined at her feet. He'd done his business, now he needed a treat.

She returned to the register and took a sip of the water she'd poured earlier. The ice had already started to melt. She must have been busy researching her next book order and had let drinking it slip. Drinking more water to stay hydrated in the desert air was one of Rarity's personal goals. But it wasn't working out. Maybe she should try another tactic. Just having water nearby didn't mean she'd drink it. Rarity needed to trick herself into actually consuming the liquid. But that was a worry for another time. She got a dog treat out from under the desk and praised Killer for his good work.

Then she headed over to start the meeting, hoping Sam wouldn't be too late. She took her spot at the front of the group circle, where she could still watch the front door for customers.

"Good evening, everyone. Why don't we gather 'round, take our seats, and find out how everyone's doing this week." Rarity saw Shirley's hand shoot up. "Oh, and Sam's running a little late with the treats, but we'll take a short break when she comes in to keep you all from starving to death."

A chuckle ran through the group, but the announcement had worked. They didn't need to worry about the food; it was on its way.

"First up, I wanted to let you know about Darby, in case you haven't heard. She's attending school abroad this year in Scotland, so we won't be seeing her until the spring term ends. We're having a bon voyage party over at her place on Thursday night before she leaves on Saturday. She's asking that we don't bring presents, but I'm sure she'd take cards and money. College students are always short on money. Especially when they'll be studying in a Scotland castle." Rarity swallowed a sigh. She wasn't going to be sad about Darby's great news. But she'd miss her first employee at the bookstore. She glanced over to her right and kept going.

"Now, I've got some local good news in case any of you have kids or know any random kids." The chuckle came back again, this time louder. "The Next Chapter is starting another book club—hopefully, four —for our younger Sedona residents. I've hired a couple of college students to run the events here at the bookstore on Saturday mornings. Each age group will meet once a month. That way, they'll have time to read the books before the next meeting. Flyers are over on the register counter, so please take a few and get the word out. I'd like to introduce two new employees of The Next Chapter, Janey Ford and Caleb Thompson. Janey will be running the elementary school–age club and doing Mommy and Me book readings for the preschool group every Wednesday afternoon. Caleb's handling our middle school club and working with the local high school library to set up events."

Janey and Caleb stood as Rarity introduced them. Then Janey quickly sat down. Caleb grinned at the group. At six feet plus, he looked like an adult version of a popular kid wizard, with dark hair and smoldering eyes. "We flipped a coin to see who would talk, and I lost. I'm always losing the coin flip. I'm beginning to think Janey has a rigged coin. Anyway, she and I are excited to meet the residents of Sedona. If you're looking for a recommendation for a gift book, we'd be glad to give you some tips there as well. I read high fantasy, and Janey, well, she's in love with love."

Janey blushed at that introduction. Her long, straight blond hair and bright blue eyes made her look like many of the heroines in the books she loved to read. "I have to admit, I am. It's a guilty pleasure, but I'm also boning up on kids' books, so just reach out if you need anything."

Rarity stood as Caleb sat. "I'm so excited to learn more about Janey and Caleb. They'll be attending our book club until they get comfortable in their new roles; then we might not see them again. At least not in the Tuesday night group. So let's get started talking about our newest read."

Sam came in about twenty minutes late, her face flush with either exertion or excitement. She had a stack of cookie containers from Annie's Bakery. Malia Overstreet, one of the regular club attendees, was listing off all the things she hadn't understood in the book. And the list was long.

Rarity smiled at Malia and held up her hand. "Since refreshments have arrived, let's put a pin in your list and return to let the group chime in after a few minutes. Maybe someone else had some of the same issues with the book?"

Malia glanced around the circle at the others. "I'd like to hear what other people think about her personality. I just didn't get her. At all."

"Malia, you never get characters who are the slightest bit different than you. You expect everyone to act the way you would." Holly Harper, another member of the group and Malia's best friend, stood and walked over to the treat table. "Sam, can I help open the oatmeal chocolate chip container?"

"I do not think everyone should be like me." Malia had followed Holly to the treat table. "Hi, Sam. Nice to see you. And don't give her the cookies. She just wants to eat them."

Rarity smiled as she watched the exchange. Shirley hadn't gotten up for cookies. Instead, she was still crocheting a pink afghan. She saw Rarity watching her, and she paused.

"No cookies?" Rarity asked.

"My doctor says I need to cut out sweets. I'm not going to waste my sugar allotment on Annie's cookies when I have a batch of my peanut butter drops sitting at home waiting for me to take over to the home tomorrow. They're George's favorite." Shirley went back to her project.

Rarity went over and sat next to her, Killer on her heels. He always seemed to know when someone was hurting. "How's George doing?"

Shirley wiped her cheek with the back of her hand and pulled out yarn to keep from losing her stitch. "He's fine. Calmer now that I'm not mother henning all the time. You know they asked me to limit my time at the home to evenings."

Rarity nodded. "That must be hard on you."

"I was a stay-at-home wife for years. When the kids left, it was me and George. Besides my volunteer stuff, my life was making George happy. Now I don't even do his laundry. What am I supposed to do with my time? My doctor doesn't want me baking cookies." She locked gazes with Rarity. "It's hard not to be needed anymore."

Rarity reached out and squeezed her shoulder. "You're needed. You just need more structure in your life. I told you to come work for me. I need someone a few days a week, even with hiring Janey and Caleb. It would give you something to do."

"I don't know. I love books, but do I want to make what I love my job?" Shirley chuckled. "You're trying to solve my problems, and I'm complaining. Sorry about that. Let me think about it, and I'll let you know soon. I need to get some more coffee now and stretch my legs. Sitting is the new smoking, you know."

Rarity watched as Shirley moved to the back, greeting other club members as she went. Killer whined from where he sat on Rarity's lap. She ran a hand down his back. "I know, buddy. Shirley's sad. But people get that way sometimes. We'll just have to watch her."

"Watch who?" Sam bounced into the chair next to Rarity. "And who are you talking to? Killer?"

"Sometimes he's the only one around to listen. So why were you so late? Did you get a big order?" Rarity asked.

Sam ran the crystal shop next door, and she knew a ton about the different types of stones. She turned the stones into jewelry for people to clean their chakras or bring some energy into their lives. Sam had made Rarity a necklace when she went through chemo, and she still wore it, mostly because she loved the way it looked.

"No, not an order. I'm still working on getting stock ready for the Fall into Sedona festival next week. It's better than that." Sam giggled and bounced in her chair. "My brother is coming to town tomorrow. Actually, he's already here. He's staying at the hotel at the end of town. He's coming by the shop tomorrow. I haven't seen Marcus in years. And the best part? He's thinking about moving here. He works from home, so he can work anywhere. Isn't that amazing!"

Rarity didn't know a lot about Marcus except that he went away for college and never came back to Arizona, not even for his parents' anniversary party Sam held last year. Oh, and he did something in computer software development. But Sam was happy. Rarity didn't want to be that friend who rained on everyone's parade. "That's wonderful. I hope to meet him."

"Of course you will. I'll bring him over to the shop. And he can come to Darby's party. It's going to be amazing. I hope Drew likes him. Being a cop, he has a certain standard. Marcus can be a bit unconventional." Sam pursed her lips, as if she was thinking about the differences between her brother and her boyfriend.

"And on that note, it's time to finish up this discussion." Rarity stood and clapped her hands. "Let's get back together and finish up with this book. I've got a new one I want you all to consider for the next open slot. I've also got next month's book ready to purchase at the front counter."

They continued discussing the current book, a domestic thriller. Malia allowed that maybe some of the reasons she didn't like the character were her personal bias, but several other members agreed with her that the main character let herself be victimized, then whined rather than taking control of her life. Anytime the group read a book where the main character didn't deal with the cards she'd been given gracefully and full force ahead, the book got slammed in the meeting.

Rarity thought it was probably because many of the Tuesday night group were cancer survivors. They knew life wasn't fair. They'd lost friends during their journey. Now, they took their lives into their own hands. And, mostly, didn't whine about their circumstances.

After they'd finished the meeting, Rarity was ringing up a purchase for Holly when Janey and Caleb stopped at the register. They looked like they were heading back to Flagstaff, where they lived by the college.

"Thanks for coming tonight. I wanted to give you a flavor of what a book club might be like and have you meet some of our patrons. Of course, your clubs will be kids, so it's probably not comparable."

"I loved being here. My mind is filled with ideas for my clubs." Janey pointed to the treat table. "Do we have a budget for food? I'm thinking about finding a kids' book about a certain food; then we can taste it at the end."

"I hadn't thought about a food or supplies budget, but yes. Just let me know what you're spending, and we'll figure out a reasonable budget for both groups." Rarity handed Holly's credit card back to her. "I suspect you're off to work?"

"Yeah, I'm still digitizing records. Now I'm working with the electric bureau. It's a ton of fun. Not." She turned toward Janey and Caleb. "Make sure you check the boxes about being willing to travel when you meet with the career counselors. Or you could wind up stuck in a little town like this."

Janey's eyes went wide, but Caleb laughed. "Believe me, my only requirement for a long-term career plan is to be in a city that actually has more than two stoplights. Not that I don't appreciate working at your bookstore, Rarity. I just want to have a place where I can explore and meet interesting people. Like New York or LA."

Janey shook her head. "No way I'd go somewhere that big. I want a job where I can make a good living but also have a great life. I guess I'm looking for the picket fence kind of world."

Rarity thought she saw a shadow cross Caleb's face, but it changed so fast, she wasn't sure she'd even seen it. "It takes all kinds. That's why the store has an entire frozen food case just for ice cream."

They laughed, and the three headed out the door. As Rarity watched, Caleb's hand gently touched Janey's back as he held the door open for her. A friendly gesture or more? Rarity would need to watch her new hires to make sure an office romance didn't get in the way of getting the work done.

Archer Enders came in the door as the last club member headed out. Sam hadn't stayed long, wanting to see if her brother would meet her for drinks. "This place cleared out fast. Usually, I have to kick people out so I can walk you home and get some dinner in you. I've got a chicken salsa stew on the stove at your house."

Archer was an amazing cook, the local hiking expert and tour guide, and Rarity's boyfriend. He had a key to the house and had started going over to her place after he got off work on Tuesdays so he could cook dinner for her and have it waiting at nine when she got home. He wasn't bad to look at either. His blue eyes, blond hair, and tanned body made the customers at Enders's Tours treat him like some Indiana Jones character. And he played the part well.

Rarity was just glad he was also sensitive and smart, and he liked her. And the good cook thing. That was important too. She picked up Killer's food dish, put the contents into a ziplock bag, and tucked it under the counter. Then she started cleaning up from the book club. "Would you lock the door and then dump the coffeepot? I'm starving."

By the time they got the bookstore in shape, the streetlights had come on. They walked the few blocks from her store to the little bungalow she'd bought mostly for the pool in the back.

She leaned into Archer's shoulder and sighed. "It's a beautiful night."

"It is." He adjusted her jacket to cover her shoulder. "We're going into winter, though. I might have to come get you in the truck soon."

Rarity took in the starry night sky and got lost in the grandness. "I hope not too soon. This is amazing."

He kissed the top of her head. "I'm not complaining, but what has you so happy tonight?"

She grinned up at him. "Sam's brother is coming into town. She's so excited to see him. I guess it's wearing off on me."

He squeezed her shoulders as they walked onto the porch and into the house. "I'm glad you're happy for Sam. I'm happy for Sam. But sometimes, family can disappoint. I hope this isn't one of those times."

Chapter 2

Wednesday after lunch, the doorbell rang. Sam and a tall, muscular man walked into Rarity's bookstore. She waved at them from the register, where she'd been working on a list of current and classic elementary-aged books for Janey to look through. Right now, Janey was sitting on the floor in the children's books aisle, reading what they already had. Rarity had to admit, Janey was taking her new job seriously and getting ready for her first book club in two weeks.

"Hey, guys, what's going on?"

"Rarity, this is my baby brother, Marcus." She pulled him toward the register counter. "Marcus, this is my best friend, Rarity. And don't hit on her. She's in a relationship."

Marcus held out his hand. "All the good ones are. Nice to meet you, Rarity. This is a great shop. I've always wanted to run a bookstore, but IT pays a lot better. Or at least that's what I've heard."

"Since I used to do marketing for a large firm, and I know IT paid more than what I was making there, I think your sources are sound." She shook his hand. Strong, quick, but warm. "On the other hand, there's a lot to be said for work-life balance. I run my shop; then I go home and swim or take a hike. And if I want to head out for a day, I close the shop and leave. No one is telling me what to do, and I'm not punching a time clock. Of course, my paycheck is based on what I do, not my position."

"You're making self-employment sound more attractive." He pointed toward the thriller section. "Mind if I glance through what you have? I need some reading material to keep me busy at night. I'm on vacation, and it's killing me not to open the laptop and just work. Especially at night."

"And that's why you should come to Darby's party tomorrow night." Sam stared at me, waving her hand to get me to invite him as well.

"That's a great idea. You'll meet a ton of people from here. My boyfriend, Archer, will be there, and you can ask him about the hiking around here." Rarity pointed to another section of bookcases. "We've got a ton of tourist and hiking books about the area. Oh, and Drew Anderson should be there too. He's your sister's beau."

"And one of Rarity's friends. They share a love of dogs," Sam added.

"I'll think about it. But I do need some books." Marcus excused himself and went to the other side of the store.

"What's that about?" Rarity turned to Sam. "He doesn't want to meet your friends?"

Sam shrugged, staring after her brother. "I'm not sure. I know he just got out of a relationship. Maybe he just needs some alone time."

"Well, if he's going to be moving here, there will be plenty of 'alone' time. He needs to figure out if Sedona is the right fit. Living in this small of a town isn't for everyone," Rarity reminded her friend.

Janey came up from the other side of the store. "Sorry to bother you, but do you have that classics list? I think some of the books are shelved wrong."

"That's quite possible. The kids pull them out and put them back or don't. I'd rather they didn't, but I haven't figured out a way to stop them." Rarity reached down to get the sheet she'd printed out, when she saw Marcus come back with four books he set on the counter. "Oh, Janey, this is Marcus. He's Sam's brother."

Marcus grinned at Janey, and Rarity could feel the heat between the two immediately. "Janey, so nice to meet you."

"Looks like you're going to be curled up in your room reading for a few weeks. I'm doing the same. I hate getting behind at the beginning of a term. And unlike undergrad, graduate students don't get an easy year in the program. I can't believe they want me to take stats." She took the paper from Rarity.

"Is that what you're reading now?" Marcus pointed to the paper.

Janey laughed and held it out so he could see. "Nope. I'm immersing myself in elementary literature for the book club I'm running in a couple of weeks. And there will be no math books for the club. Unless the kids outvote me."

"I got As in my stats class. So if you ever need help studying, I'd be glad to help. I haven't been away from college so long." Marcus smiled at Janey.

Rarity felt like she and Sam were invisible.

"That would be great. I better get back to work. Lots to learn." Janey nodded at me, then turned to Sam. "Nice to see you again, Sam. I guess I'll see you tomorrow at the party?"

"Yes. I'll be there. I'm trying to convince Marcus to go as well." Sam punched Marcus lightly in the arm.

"You should go." Janey waved and disappeared into the stacks.

The trio didn't talk at first. Then Sam asked Marcus, "So you're coming to the party?"

He stared at the spot where Janey had disappeared into a row of bookshelves. "I think I am."

* * * *

Thursday morning, Rarity and Killer were on their way to the store when Drew Anderson pulled up beside them in his truck. Drew was a local police detective, Sam's boyfriend, and the reason Rarity had Killer.

She leaned into the open window on the passenger side. "Hey, Drew. What's up?"

"I was wondering if we could have coffee this morning. I have a dilemma." He reached over to open the door. "I'll pay, and we can sit outside at the tables so Killer can come too."

"If you're buying, we're coming. Did you know Annie's started making dog treats too? Killer loves the peanut butter wafers." Rarity picked up Killer, and after tucking her bag on Drew's floorboard, lifted Killer up onto the seat, where he ran to greet Drew. Drew was one of Killer's favorite friends. The feeling was mutual. She shut the door and put on her seat belt. "Killer, come sit by me so Drew can drive."

Killer reluctantly obeyed, and Drew drove them to Annie's Bakery on Main. He climbed out and met Rarity on the sidewalk. He locked the truck since he had his police laptop inside, and, Rarity surmised, he probably also had a firearm. Drew was never completely off duty.

She stayed outside enjoying the pleasant morning while Drew went into the shop to get coffee. Killer watched people walk by on the sidewalk while he sat near Rarity's feet.

Since it was early, it was a little cool, and Rarity was glad she'd worn a jacket to walk to the shop. Later in the day, she wouldn't need the jacket. Sometimes she'd have two or three at the shop she'd forgotten to take home. Tonight, she'd run home after work, change into a dress, and grab a quick sandwich before meeting Archer at Darby's house for the party.

Killer would have to stay home tonight. She brought him as much as she could, but a party was just a little too much stimulation.

Drew came back with two large coffees and a bag of something that smelled sweet. He sat down, then leaned over and held out a doggie biscuit for Killer. "It's pumpkin something. Annie said you've had them before."

Rarity laughed. "You know you live in a small town when your dog's bakery order is available for anyone to get."

"Sedona's a great place to live. Sure, we don't get four seasons, but we can go elsewhere for that. I enjoy the heat." He opened the bag, set a napkin on the table, then a peach scone in front of Rarity. "Annie said she got the peaches from Georgia this summer."

"She's always making something new. I'm surprised these don't have chilies in them." Rarity lifted the scone, then saw Drew's face. "These aren't hot, right?"

"These ones aren't, but she did have some with green chilies. How did you know?" Drew took the second scone out and flattened the bag to use as his plate.

"It's Arizona. Everything seems to have a bit of spice in it. My palate has changed since I left St. Louis. But I have to be careful what I offer Killer." She took a sip of coffee. "So why the early morning chat? What do you want?"

"Who said I wanted anything? We're friends, right?" He glanced around the empty café tables. "Okay, I'm worried about Sam's brother."

"Besides, you said you had a problem. Okay, are you worried he won't like you?" Rarity hadn't seen Drew this way before. He'd been hesitant to start dating Sam, mostly because he wasn't sure he was ready for something serious. And he hadn't wanted to mess up a relationship that might be his forever partner. Drew thought way too much about things. It was a bad habit they had in common. "Or something else?"

"He seems a little entitled. Like he's still the captain of the football team and Sam's just another groupie. He shouldn't treat her like that." Drew sipped his coffee. "Or am I just seeing things that aren't there?"

Rarity thought about her one and only encounter with Marcus. He did seem confident, but it appeared that he really cared for Sam. Of course, that could be a total act. Rarity saw the concern in Drew's face. "I'm not sure. I've only met him once and I didn't have the same reaction that you did. But maybe he's better with women. Some men can charm women, but there's something with their male friends that doesn't work. I guess we'll just have to reserve judgment until we get to know him better. You know he might be staying around."

"Another reason I'm not exactly thrilled about this. I don't know, maybe I do feel threatened. Sam's really happy he came to visit. Maybe I should just go with the flow." He finished his scone. "I'm trying to talk myself out of running a background check."

Rarity pointed out the flaw in his idea. "You don't have any reason to run one, so that wouldn't be ethical, and you know it."

Drew's lips flattened, but then he nodded. "You're right. There's a reason I asked you to breakfast. Mostly to talk me off this edge I worked myself onto."

"Invite him for a beer. Or take him hiking. Maybe doing something with just the two of you would ease your mind." Rarity squeezed Drew's hand. "I know all you want is for Sam to be happy."

"I guess I'll see him tonight at the party. I've got a late shift tomorrow. I'll ask if he wants to go hiking." Drew leaned back and rubbed the top of his head. His hair was buzz-cut short this month. It made him look like a GI Joe doll in a police uniform. It wasn't a bad look for him, but she could see how Marcus and his too-long hair and casual jeans was his total opposite. Hopefully the men could bond over something they both agreed on. Or at least agreed to disagree for Sam's sake.

They talked about a few other things, but soon, Rarity glanced at her watch. "I need to open the store. Thanks for coffee. I'll see you tonight?"

"Thanks again for talking me off the ledge about Marcus." Drew reached down and gave Killer a rub. "I take it Killer's grounded tonight?"

"Yeah. Darby wouldn't mind if I brought him, but he doesn't like to be around a lot of people, so I'll keep him home." She stood, and Killer stood with her, ready to follow. "Don't worry so much, Drew."

He shook his head as he walked with her toward his truck. "You don't get it. That's my job. I'm supposed to worry and see things other people miss."

As Rarity walked the couple of blocks to the store alone, she wondered about Drew's last words. Was there something Marcus was hiding from Sam and his new Sedona friends? Why had he decided to move home? Rarity knew there was more to moving than just a breakup. She probably would have stayed in St. Louis if she hadn't truly felt she didn't fit in at her job anymore. And without a significant other with her to tie her to the area, she had made the leap. So what was Marcus's reason for making a life change? That was the question.

Usually, Darby worked on Thursdays, shelving books and entering them into the bookstore inventory. But last week had been Darby's final days at the bookstore. At least until she came back from Scotland. She needed the time away from Sedona. Time to grow as a person. Time to find out who she wanted to be as an adult. Rarity didn't begrudge her employee's new experiences, but she was going to miss having her around. Tonight would be a hard goodbye.

After opening the store, Rarity focused on getting the week's book order ready for customers. Several books were set aside and not put on the shelves. She called their new owners and let them know the books had arrived. Rarity loved having just the right book tucked away for her customers. And when they ordered the first book in a series, she always ordered a duplicate as well as the rest of the series. Word of mouth could sell a book faster than a good ranking in an online store. She'd found a loyal following for the bookstore after being open for over a year. Now, she just had to continue to cater to what the customers needed.

Like the Mommy and Me readings that would start next week. Janey seemed like the perfect coordinator for the series. They had a starting book already chosen, and Janey was supposed to give her a flyer by the end of the week. She had better digital art skills than either Rarity or Caleb, so Rarity thought Janey might take over those tasks for the bookstore. At least if she wanted the hours.

Working with college students tended to be hit and miss. When she found someone like Darby, Rarity didn't mind working around their school schedule or activities. If, like Darby, they could commit and show up for a certain number of hours a week. For some she'd interviewed, they'd wanted so few hours, it didn't make sense for them to drive from Flagstaff or for her to schedule the hours that would change on a weekly basis or, sometimes, on a whim.

She hoped Janey and Caleb really wanted the jobs. She couldn't pay a lot or give them benefits, so they had to love working with books. Like Rarity did. Typically, she'd been recruiting from the English department, but Janey was a teaching graduate student. She taught for one professor, one class, and needed more to do. She'd explained in the interview that she liked keeping busy, but parties and college dorm activities didn't fill her well anymore. She'd spent four years in a sorority, but now that she lived off campus, she wanted something more substantial to do. Something that would earn her money as well as teach her new skills.

Rarity wasn't sure this would fill Janey's well, but she was willing to give her a chance.

Caleb was a more traditional hire. He was also a graduate student, but his professor didn't want him teaching; he wanted help with grading the papers and the admin work. So Caleb was excited to be able to work with the book clubs for kids. And he'd also suggested an adult sci-fi club once he'd proven himself.

Rarity shelved the last book and walked through the aisles, wondering what she was missing. She paused at the romance section. It shared shelves with what she called beach reads, and as she scanned through the offerings, she realized she had a lot of contemporary romance but not much in historical or fantasy. Unless she had those shelved in the wrong area.

"Hello? Rarity? Are you in here?" Janey's voice called from the cashier's desk.

"I'm here. I was just seeing where we were short in what we offer. And then you arrived. Do you have a few hours to work?" Rarity talked as she walked through the bookshelves to the back of the store.

"That's why I'm here. I got off class early and thought you might need some help with the store, since the party was tonight." Janey smiled as Rarity came around a bookshelf. "Although you seem pretty quiet in here."

"There's lots to do when it's quiet. I think you can help me with something." Rarity took Janey over to the romance section. "I think this needs to be beefed up. Who are some of your favorite authors? Are they here? Am I missing any popular trope or subgenre that we should be stocking?"

Janey's eyes got wide. "That's a lot of questions."

"Well, you hang out here. You're on the clock from now until five when we close up shop, and then you can come with me to my house while I get ready for the party." Rarity glanced at Janey's jeans and college tank. "Did you bring anything to wear?"

Janey's smile widened. "I found the perfect dress a few weeks ago and bought it on a whim. Now I'm glad I did. It's in my car."

"Okay, then you can drive me and Killer home and get ready at my place." Rarity paused. "If that's all right? I don't want to be pushy."

Janey took a notebook out of her backpack. "You're my boss. You're supposed to be pushy."

"Yeah, but this is a party, not work." Rarity watched as Janey answered her phone.

"Hello? Come on, please stop this. It's annoying." She hung up the phone.

"Everything okay?" Rarity didn't want to pry. "If you have to be somewhere else rather than the party, it's fine. This is just a going-away party. You can meet Darby when she comes back."

"Oh, no. I want to come to the party. I've just been getting some random calls. I know someone's there, but they don't say anything. It's creepy. It doesn't matter if I pick up or not. In fact, it's worse if I ignore them. They just keep calling until I forget and pick up the call. Once I do, they don't call back for a few days." She glanced at the phone, then tucked it into her tote. "I'm thinking about getting a new number. One that's not listed with the campus. But I've had this for years. Campus security thinks it's just prank calls. Maybe a frat joke. But it's not just during the school terms."

"That's scary. How long has it been going on?" Rarity didn't like the sound of this at all.

"Just since last December. Just before term let out." Janey dug out a pen. "Don't worry about it. I'm handling it. I think I'm going to get a new number, though. I'll let you know as soon as I do."

"Sounds good." Rarity wondered if Drew Anderson could help Janey. Since she lived in Flagstaff, technically, it was out of his jurisdiction, but maybe he had some ideas. She'd introduce him to Janey tonight and see if he could give her some suggestions.

Janey pulled a stool closer to the bookshelves. "I'd love to see where you live. And I have to change somewhere. So it's either the bathroom here or your house. You pick."

"Let me know when you have an ordering list. I'll show you how to put it in the software." Rarity left Janey alone to work as she went back to work on the schedule. Book people were always the best. She thought Janey was going to fit in nicely.

Chapter 3

By the time they got to Rarity's house, changed, and got Killer set up, they were already late for the party. She'd convinced Janey to leave her car at Rarity's since the parking would be limited at Darby's. "We'd probably have to park just as far away in the other direction." Rarity's phone rang while they were walking over to Darby's. She glanced at the display before answering. "Archer, we're a few minutes away still."

"Sorry, did I get our wires crossed? Was I supposed to pick you up?" His voice sounded warm and caring, and Rarity smiled as she listened.

"No, we're just running late."

"Okay, then..." He paused. "Wait, you're not bringing Killer, are you? The party's already going, and he's not going to like all the people. I'll run him back to the house when you get here."

"No, I'm not bringing Killer. He's safe at home. I turned on *Harry Potter* for him to watch while we're gone." She smiled at Janey, who had been trying not to listen, but Killer's movie preferences had her grinning. "Janey's with me. One of the new bookstore hires. We decided to walk over together."

"Oh, okay. Hey, Drew's waving me over. Come find me when you get here."

She tucked the phone away. "It's nice having people concerned about your whereabouts, but sometimes, it's a little too clingy. That was Archer, my boyfriend, wondering where I was."

"Sorry I made you late. I could have changed at the bookstore and met you at the party." Janey glanced around at the houses. "I didn't even know this subdivision was back here. I've only driven through Sedona on my way down to Tempe."

"It's a good neighborhood. Lots of snowbirds, so we don't have much traffic. Although people are starting to rent out their places when they're not here." They turned onto Darby's street while they talked. "I love my cottage. Of course, it was the pool that sealed the deal. I'm obsessed with swimming. It's a good stress reliever."

"I take dance classes. Sometimes an exercise-dance mix, but I always have a dance class scheduled. Tuesday, I start a barre class. So I can't work late those nights. Just a warning."

Rarity laughed. "No problem. I've got the book club that night, and most of my regulars are either in the club or know to stay away while it's going. I don't think I've had a walk-in on Tuesday night for months."

"It must be hard running your own business. You don't have family around Sedona?"

Rarity shook her head. "No. I moved here because of Sam Aarons, the woman who owns and runs the crystal shop next door. She's my best friend. We met in college and stayed close. Then I was diagnosed with breast cancer. After the cancer treatments were done, I moved here to start a new life. One where I wasn't doing marketing projects and trying to quantify the results to my bosses."

"Now, you're the boss." Janey was a great listener and easy to talk to.

"True, but that has fewer perks than you would think." They spent the final few minutes before they reached Darby's house talking about Rarity and the store. Before she knew it, they had arrived. Music flowed out of the open front door, and people were standing and sitting all over. Rarity had been right about the cars. There were parked cars on both sides of the street as far as she could see. "And we're here. Let's go find Archer, and I'll introduce you to some of my friends."

They made their way through the crowd. Rarity recognized a few people, but no one she considered a friend. Darby must have invited a lot of her college classmates, as Janey knew people they passed that Rarity didn't. It took a while for them to finally find Archer. When they did, he was not only with Drew but also Sam and Marcus. Drew and Archer were talking about local football teams, and Marcus looked bored. Sam brightened when they came up to the group.

"Rarity, I'm so glad you're here. Now, maybe we can talk about anything but football?" Sam gave Rarity a hug.

Drew pulled Sam closer. "Sorry, hun. That last game was killer. Rarity, good to see you again. And this is?"

"Sorry, this is Janey. She's my new Darby. Although Darby will be so missed, I had to hire two people to replace her." Rarity reached over and gave Darby a hug as she came up to the group.

"I'm sure that's not true. Hi, Janey, nice to meet you. I hear you're handling the little kids' events for Rarity. I'm glad someone is, because that wasn't something I wanted to do at all." Darby handed everyone a champagne glass from a tray the server held who'd followed her through the crowd. "Rarity sponsored the first round of drinks, so you guys better get one before everything's gone. More people showed up than I expected."

"Well, these are for your toast, so let's get that out of the way." Rarity whistled, and the crowd settled around them. "Good evening. Thank you all for coming. I just wanted to wish Darby an excellent school year in Scotland. May you learn a lot and enjoy your time in the castle. And if you fall in love, remember us fondly back home if you decide to stay." Everyone laughed, and Rarity held up her glass. "To Darby, have fun and stay safe. We'll see you in a year."

"To Darby," the crowd repeated.

They took a sip, then Archer gave Darby a hug. "Be sure to send me pictures of the trails. Maybe I can get Rarity to step away from the bookstore, and we'll come visit you."

"Maybe." Rarity gave him a hug as she turned back to Darby. "Are you all ready to go Saturday? Do you need a ride to the airport?"

"Malia and Holly are taking me. They're staying over tonight and tomorrow to finish packing what I need to get shipped. Then we'll close up the house. Drew, you'll check on it while I'm gone, right?" Darby asked.

"Of course. Leave a key with me, and I'll do a walk-through every couple of weeks and make sure everything's working. I'd hate for your heater to go down and burst some pipes," Drew offered.

Darby pulled a notebook out of her dress pocket. "I'll put 'drop a key off' on my must-do list. Seriously, keeping this going is insane. I'm sure I'm going to forget something."

"If you do, just call. We'll take care of it," Rarity assured her. "Or ship it to you."

Darby nodded, then waved at another group. "I need to keep making the rounds. Thank you all for coming, and, Janey, good luck with Rarity. She can be a pill of a boss."

After tossing a wicked grin at Rarity, Darby hurried over to the next group.

Rarity shook her head. "Children are so ungrateful these days. I'm an amazing boss."

"Sure you are, honey. Keep telling yourself that." Archer pulled Rarity into a hug and kissed the top of her head. "So, Janey, tell us about yourself. What made you decide to work for this monster?"

They talked as a group for a while, then Marcus asked Janey if she wanted another drink. The couple walked away as the other two couples watched.

"Uh-oh," Drew teased Sam. "I think your brother isn't going to be at your beck and call anymore."

Sam elbowed him. "They're just getting a drink. But that would be nice if Marcus found someone to hang around with. I think this last girlfriend kind of messed with his head a bit. He seems a little wary of jumping into the dating pool again."

Archer snorted. "He doesn't seem wary at all. I would have been scared to death to ask a girl I'd just met to go get a drink. He's got smooth moves, that one."

"You just don't know him. He's all cool and confident on the outside, but inside, he's jelly." Sam turned to watch Marcus and Janey get their drinks, but instead of coming back to the group, they headed out to the patio and pool area.

"I can see he needs so much hand holding," Drew deadpanned.

"Come on, guys, stop teasing Sam." Rarity sipped her drink. "I hope Darby has fun this year. If I was going to study abroad, it wouldn't be in Scotland. Isn't it cold there?"

"Darby's going to be fine. Man, both of you need to rein in your mother hen genes. Let the kids fly." Archer glanced around. "And we all need a second drink. Drew, come help. And bring your wallet. I didn't realize this was a cash bar."

"Then I guess you and your date are drinking water, right?" Drew punched Archer playfully in the shoulder. "Besides, I can see the outline of your wallet, dude."

"That doesn't mean I actually have any money in there," Archer teased as the men walked toward the bar to get beers for the foursome.

Sam was still watching the now empty doorway where Marcus and Janey had disappeared.

Rarity stepped closer and snapped her fingers. "Earth to Sam. Why are you so worried about your brother?"

Sam bit her lip, then shook her head. "It's nothing. Water under the bridge, I guess. So Janey worked today? What did you think?"

"She's smart, catches on quickly, and has killer ideas. I'm happy. Caleb's working on Friday afternoon, then they both are coming in Saturday to run a mock book club. We should have the first elementary club up and ready to happen the next weekend." Rarity set the empty champagne glass on the tray and picked up a shrimp skewer. "I really lucked out on hiring both of them."

"You need to knock on wood somewhere." Sam grinned as she glanced around the room. "Was Caleb coming to the party?"

Rarity scanned the room. "I thought he was, but maybe he got held up on campus. I don't see him in the crowd."

The men returned to the group and handed off the drinks. Archer leaned next to Rarity. "Drew has a great idea. After this beer, we should go to the pub and grab dinner before all these kids decide it's a clever idea too. We can get the early bird special."

"That sounds good to me. I'm starving." Rarity glanced over at where Janey disappeared. "Janey's parked at my house, but I'm sure she could find her way if I left. Let me text her the address and tell her I'm leaving in a few minutes. I don't want her to think I ghosted her here."

"Not sure if that's the correct usage of the word, but we'll give you an A for effort." Sam looked up at Drew. "I know you and Marcus aren't exactly seeing eye to eye, but I appreciate you being nice to him."

"I just don't like the way he talks down to you at times. I get that family's different, but there's also a respect level that I expect. Especially to your sister. Joanna would punch me if I talked to her that way. Even after all these years." Drew pulled her closer. "I'll give him some leeway for a while, but if he does stay around, we're going to have a talk about his manners."

Sam reached up and stroked the side of Drew's face. "My knight in shining armor."

Archer held up his hand. "And his trusty sidekick, Sir Hikes-a-lot."

"What about Sir Mountain Tamer?" Rarity added as the foursome moved toward the door, where Darby was saying goodbye to some of the guests. "Sounds better and less like a Monty Python character."

"I don't care what you call me as long as it's not late for dinner." Archer squeezed Rarity's side. "Are we ready to blow this popsicle stand?"

"We have to say goodbye to Darby; then we can go eat." Rarity set her empty glass on a side table. She'd call tomorrow and see if Darby needed some help cleaning this place before leaving. And with that thought, she waited in line to say goodbye, hoping she wouldn't cry.

* * * *

Saturday came early, and Caleb and Janey were there as soon as Rarity arrived. Caleb had stopped for donuts and coffee at Annie's. "Breakfast of the gods. At least the college gods, especially after a Friday night frat party. Sorry I missed your friend's going-away party. I know some kids who went that said it was epic."

Rarity laughed as she opened the door and let Killer inside as well as her new employees. "I think we left before it turned epic. Old people need their dinner and their sleep."

"You're not old, and neither are any of your friends." Janey headed to the back to drop off her jacket and tote. "Thanks for the introduction, by the way. Marcus is interesting."

"You two seemed to be hitting it off. Are you going to go out?" Rarity followed her into the back room and filled Killer's water dish.

"We went to dinner last night, and he's coming to get me tonight after work. Then tomorrow, we're going to hike into this amazing quarry lake." Janey was rattling off the details so fast, she didn't see Caleb's eyes flash. Rarity did. *I thought there was something there. At least one-sided.* Rarity decided changing the subject would be a good thing. She didn't want Caleb to be hurt any more than he already seemed to be. "Let's jump into designing the book clubs. I'd like to do this as a group exercise, so if one of us is gone, someone else could fill in that day. That's why I had you attend Tuesday night's club."

"Those women are amazing." Caleb had turned off whatever sadness he'd been feeling over Janey's new dating plans. Maybe it was for the best. "I'll run that group anytime you need me to."

"Unless she asks me first." Janey grinned. "I'm here. I'm not invisible, no matter what some professors seem to think."

"I had professors and work peers that did the same thing." Rarity shrugged. "I guess it's a male thing."

Caleb held up his hand. "Just because some guys go all alpha and forget to look around to see who's actually in the room is no reason to paint us all with the same brush. I'm sensitive. Just ask my mother."

Rarity laughed and nodded. "Okay, no male-bashing permitted. And if we do talk about incidents, we'll talk about that specific person who made us feel less because of our sex."

"Now, was that so hard?" Caleb set up the flip chart on the stand. "I'll take notes. Let's start with the elementary club and build up? Will that work?"

They worked all morning, with Rarity taking breaks to help customers, but by the end of the day, they had an excellent plan.

"Okay, so next week, Janey, you're scheduled on Wednesday and Caleb Thursday. Then you're both here Friday and Saturday. If you can't be here at opening, just call and let me know when you'll be here. I'm really excited about our new clubs."

They said their goodbyes, and Rarity closed up the store.

Archer was outside waiting to walk her home as she locked the front door. He took her bag and Killer's leash, then put his arm around her. "Good day?"

"Great day," she agreed, and they talked about food and the future while they were walking.

* * * *

Early Sunday afternoon, her phone rang. "Hey, Drew. What's going on? Are you and Sam coming over for a game night?"

"No, Rarity, this is a business call."

She took in a breath. "Not the bookstore."

"No, not the bookstore." He paused for a moment. "Maybe I should just come over."

"It's not Sam, is it?" Now fear had started to set into her head. Drew was being too cryptic. Something horrible was wrong. "Just tell me."

Drew sighed, then said, "Rarity, it's Janey. A hiker found her out at the quarry. She's dead."

Chapter 4

Sam and Archer arrived at Rarity's house right after Drew's call. She let them inside, and they all sat around her dining room table drinking coffee. Rarity felt numb. "I just saw her on Saturday. She was so happy. She and Marcus were going on a date, then going hiking at that quarry the next day." Realization hit her as her eyes widened, and she looked at Sam. "Tell me Marcus is alive. They weren't both killed in some freak accident, were they?"

Sam glanced at Archer. "No, Marcus is at the hotel. Drew's over there talking to him now. He's supposed to call me as soon as I can go over."

Killer stretched his front paws onto her leg, and she reached down to put him on her lap. Rarity stroked his warm fur and felt her heart rate drop just a little. "So do we know what happened? I can't believe Janey's dead. She was so alive. So happy."

"Drew's being very closemouthed about this." Archer stood and refilled Rarity's coffee mug. "I was at Annie's when I got the call to go get Sam and bring her here. I think Drew wants the two of you out of public. Just in case."

Sam wiped tears off her cheeks.

Rarity still didn't get it. She looked from Sam to Archer. "Seriously, what does Janey's death have to do with us?"

Archer looked over at Sam, then took Rarity's hand. "They're questioning Marcus about the murder. He was the last one to be seen with her."

Sam let out a little moan, and Rarity stood and wrapped her arms around her friend. "I'm so sorry, Sam. I'm sure he didn't do it. Or if he did, it was an accident. Drew just needs to rule him out."

"Drew hates Marcus. Why would he rule him out? This is the perfect way to get him out of my life," Sam muttered as she pushed up off the chair and out of Rarity's hug. She started pacing the room.

Killer, who'd been returned to the floor, followed her, keeping away from her feet. He sat by the French doors to the patio and whined as she continued pacing.

Finally, Sam took a deep breath. Then she sat back down. "Look, I know in my head that Drew's not going to frame my brother for this. But there's something in Marcus's past that might just look bad now."

Rarity was about to ask what, but a knock on the door stopped her. She hurried over to the door to let Holly and Malia inside. "What are you two doing here?"

Holly reached down and picked up Killer as they moved into the kitchen to join the others. "You're kidding, right? One of our own has a problem. We're here to help. We heard about Janey's death on the news, so we came to see what the SBC group is planning."

"The book club? SBC?" Archer shook his head. "No wonder Drew wanted me over here. I'm probably supposed to keep all of you from going off and searching for a killer. With all your specialized book club skills."

"Archer, that was rude." Malia added a chair to the table and pulled out a box of cookies from Annie's. "If you don't want to know what we're doing, you're free to leave. We'll tell Drew you were here the entire time, and we watched *Persuasion* on television."

"I didn't mean to be rude, Malia." Archer ran his hand over the top of his head. "I just hate that you're getting into something you don't know anything about. It's dangerous."

"So is having a murderer running around Sedona killing young women. It's in our best interest to be involved," Holly responded. She took one of the cookies and used it as a pointer to emphasize her words. "Oh, and Shirley's on the way with updates for our murder books."

"And probably something to eat for dinner." Rarity smiled over at Archer. "We're set up for these things. We're here for each other when bad things happen."

"Like when Darby went through that bad patch." Malia frowned. "Holly and I dropped her off at the airport yesterday afternoon. We went out to the pub last night, and now, this starts up. It's like Sedona wants us to be busy so we don't have time to miss her."

"You realize Janey was a real person, not just a way for you to keep busy," Archer pointed out.

"Malia's a little direct. We know Janey was a real person, Archer. It's just our way of dealing with something so horrible." Holly glanced over at Sam. "I hope you don't think we're insensitive. If so, we can wait for the meeting on Tuesday to start talking about this."

Sam ran her finger over the top of her coffee mug. "Honestly, I'm not sure how I feel right now. I know one thing. Marcus didn't kill anyone, so if this gets his name cleared sooner than Drew and his police techniques, then I want to help."

"We'll have to list him as a suspect in order for us to clear him. Are you okay with really looking at his alibi? I know this might be hard. When we helped Darby, she was the person with the most to lose, but she wanted us involved. You're trying to prove your brother didn't do it. What if he did?" Rarity stopped talking and stared at Sam, waiting for her to make a decision.

Sam looked at each of the people at the table. "I'm probably going to be a pain in the butt calling out Marcus's innocence, but we need to find out who did this. If it's Marcus, and I know it's not, but just to say, *if,* then he needs to pay for the crime. But if it's not, he shouldn't be labeled a killer just to close a case."

"Drew wouldn't do that." Archer rubbed Sam's shoulder. "You, of all people, should know that. If Marcus is innocent, Drew's going to see that and find the real killer. We don't want to have a killer running around free. It's not a good draw for the town festivals."

Malia laughed, spitting out her coffee. She wiped it up with the arm of her hoodie. "Okay, now all I want to do is make up festival mottos. Come to Sedona's Halloween night party—chances are, you won't be the one found dead in the morning."

Rarity saw Sam smile at the joking going around. But her eyes still showed her fear about her brother's fate. "Okay, let's get some thoughts, which aren't about marketing mottos, on the whiteboard. What do we know?"

They talked about everything they knew about Janey. As they were listing things off, Shirley arrived at the door with the promised notebook updates and a handful of pens.

She gave Rarity a hug. "I didn't know if you'd have enough. Archer, be a dear and bring that Crock-Pot in. Be careful, it has hot soup inside. And I brought rolls we can warm up in your oven."

Shirley's magic power was in feeding people. Making them feel included was just a side effect. They got settled with potato soup and warm rolls and continued working on what they thought they knew.

At five, Sam got a call from Marcus asking her to come over to the hotel. Archer volunteered to drive her there. The rest of the group broke up as well, promising to bring anything else they'd heard about Janey's death to Tuesday's club meeting. Rarity helped Shirley wash her Crock-Pot and pack it and the extra packets and pens into her car.

Shirley paused before getting in the car. "This is going to be hard on Sam. Even though she says she wants the truth, I don't think she really believes her brother could do this. Right now, he's Drew's best suspect."

"I know. I don't know how to help her. She's going to be crushed if he even accidentally killed Janey. I need to go over Janey's job application and see if she left any emergency contact information. Of course, Drew probably already got that from the school. I guess I'm just a little rattled."

Rarity had Killer on a leash outside with them. He was wandering through the front yard, looking for smells.

Shirley glanced at her watch. "I need to go see George. I think today's the first day in a long time I haven't been sitting in the car in front of the home waiting to be allowed inside. They're going to think I've lost my mind."

Rarity watched her drive off and waved until Shirley couldn't see her anyway. It was great that Shirley was involved in something that had taken the pain out of losing her husband to a terrible disease. The only problem was that Janey had to die to keep her busy. Maybe they needed to have a Sunday brunch at her house to keep Shirley at least a little occupied. She'd talk to the group about it. Shirley was part of their family. And you did what you needed to do for family.

The thought made her shiver as she considered Marcus and Sam's newly renewed relationship. Rarity paused at the front door and looked over at the house next door. Terrance Oldman, her neighbor, had gone on a cruise with some of his old navy buddies and their wives. He'd be gone until next Saturday, and then Rarity planned on having him over for dinner so he could show off his pictures and tell her about the trip. Archer had already agreed to attend, and she'd invite Shirley as well. Just to keep her busy.

Rarity and Killer went inside, and after turning on a movie, she cleaned the house and started laundry. If she got enough done, she'd celebrate by swimming a few laps before taking something out of the freezer for dinner.

Rarity liked being alone. As an introvert, living alone gave her time to recharge. Archer was the same way. He liked his quiet time. They'd been finding that recharging worked just as well when they were doing it together. He didn't need a lot of attention while she read or worked on marketing ideas for the business. He'd watch a movie or a game while she puttered in a different part of the house or stretched out beside him, reading on the couch.

Shirley needed people to recharge. She was a true extrovert. And she'd lost her partner in life to a memory care home. Rarity just needed to find ways to keep her friend busy.

* * * *

On Mondays, Rarity didn't open the shop until noon, so she finished the few weekly chores she hadn't completed yesterday as well as swam in her pool just before it was time to get ready to leave. She had a system. And she liked her systems. Tomorrow night, she'd keep the store open late for the book club. Then Wednesday, they were supposed to start the Mommy and Me club. She had too many people signed up to cancel, even though they'd probably understand since the woman she'd hired to run it had been killed. She'd ask Shirley to step in. She'd been talking about volunteering at the store. This way, Rarity could pay her for her time and keep her busy. And Shirley adored her grandchildren, who all lived way too far away. At least that was Shirley's story.

Rarity picked up the phone before she left the house. Shirley answered on the first ring.

"Hey, it's Rarity. Could you do me a huge favor?"

"Of course. You want me to bring treats for Tuesday, don't you? I knew it was your turn, and with this whole thing, you're probably swamped." Shirley rattled on about a cookie recipe she'd found.

"Actually, no, that isn't it. But you're right, it is my turn. If you could bring something, that would be awesome. I was calling about our Mommy and Me book club we were supposed to be starting on Wednesday. Since Janey's gone, can you handle it until I get another person hired? I can give you the book Tuesday night, if that would be enough time to read it. I don't think Janey was planning on doing an activity with it, but you could do whatever you want."

"Oh, dear. I'd love to. What's the book? I'll see if I can plan a fun activity to supplement the reading." She giggled and then apologized. "I'm just so excited about this. The best part of being a grandma is reading to the kids."

Rarity gave her all the information and let her know she'd be at the store in a few minutes if she wanted to talk more about the job. Then she got herself and Killer ready for work.

They stopped at Terrance's yard and picked up his morning paper. Rarity put it on the floor of the deck under the table by the door. Terrance had warned her that even though he'd put in a vacation hold, the paper delivery person seemed to just keep delivering. She didn't have to pick up his mail, just keep the papers from piling up and announcing an empty house.

When she got to the bookstore, Caleb was sitting outside on the bench, waiting for her. His eyes were red, and he looked like he hadn't slept.

When he heard her steps, he stood. "I didn't know if you'd heard or not. They announced it at school. They're doing a vigil for her tonight. I can't believe she's gone."

"I'm so sorry, Caleb. If you don't want to work Thursday or Saturday, I understand. Just let me know." Rarity reached out to squeeze his arm, but he shook off her gesture of comfort.

"I'm fine. I'll be here to work. I just didn't know if you'd heard." He nodded, then stepped past her and went to get into a bright green Jeep.

She watched him leave while Killer sniffed around the front of the bookstore and the artificial grass she'd put in for his personal use. Caleb was hurting. She wondered if he'd even known he was falling in love with Janey. Having her talk on Saturday about dating Marcus must have hurt. Rarity felt bad for Caleb. He'd lost something he'd never admitted needing, and now he'd never have the chance to let her know how he felt.

Sometimes, losing the possibility of love was harder than being dumped or love growing cold. There was a saying about that, and Caleb was definitely in the "never loved at all" category. Or maybe the saying meant something else. Her head was starting to hurt.

Rarity went inside and turned on the lights. Monday was a slow day, and the only reason she even opened at all was to work on accounting for the week before. That way, she knew the books and the deposits would get done. She liked systems. Especially around things she hated doing, like math and spreadsheets.

She booted up her computer and, after making a pot of coffee, sat at her counter and started going through the income and expenses since last Sunday.

Rarity was just finishing up when a customer came in.

He smiled as he approached the register. "I didn't think you were open. When I drove by this morning, I thought I saw a closed sign."

"We're open on Monday afternoons." Rarity held out her hand. "I'm Rarity. How can I help today?"

"Josh. And I'm looking for something in the spy craft or thriller category. Lone wolf type heroes that do it all themselves and still get the girl, at least until the next book?" He shook her hand, grinning. "I'm here on a job for the next few weeks, and I'm afraid I've read all of the stash I brought with me."

"Not a bad problem to have, at least not for your local bookseller. Thrillers are over to the left on the other side of mysteries. I keep a good supply since they're always popular sellers." Rarity pointed toward the correct section. "What type of job are you doing?"

"Just some scouting. Really boring stuff. The client wants a feeling of what the town's vibe is, at least in my opinion." He nodded. "I'll be done before closing, I promise."

"No hurry. I still have a few days' of receipts to update." She turned back to her notes and almost immediately heard the bell again. She sighed as another person came inside the store. "Good afternoon. How may I help you?"

Archer grinned and held up a cup from Annie's. "Salted caramel double shot. Just for you."

She grabbed at the cup and finally wrestled it out of Archer's hand. "Stop making me fight for it. I need the caffeine today."

"You shouldn't stay up so late. For a lark, you sure have owl tendencies." He set a white bag on the table. "And here, just in case you need a sugar high at three."

"No-judgment-allowed zone, sorry. Thanks, there's a reason I love you." She leaned over and gave Archer a kiss. "Have you talked to Sam or Drew today? What's going on with Marcus?"

"I talked to Drew last night, and there's not enough to arrest him for Janey's murder, but he's convinced they know their suspect. I can't change his mind without evidence showing Marcus was somewhere else. And the guy is hiding something. I can tell. He's always had shifty eyes, at least the few times I met him."

"Again, don't let Sam hear you talking about her brother that way. She's convinced he's innocent." Rarity smiled at the customer, Josh, coming up behind Archer. "I can ring those up if you're done. Did you need anything else? I can order anything you didn't find and the book would be in on Wednesday if I get the order in by five."

Josh set the books down and shook his head. He met Archer's gaze and nodded as he pulled out his wallet. "Hey, man, how's it going?"

"Hey." Archer nodded back at the customer.

"Actually, these will get me through," Josh said to Rarity, "and since that top one is a series, I can just come back for more of those if I run out of material. Thanks."

Archer tapped the counter and turned to Rarity. "I'll pick you up at five, and we can drop Killer off at the house before we go to dinner."

Mondays were now a standard date night for them, especially since Rarity worked late on Tuesday nights, and weekends could be iffy based on their schedules. She pulled the books closer. "I'll see you then."

After Archer left, Josh handed her his credit card. "Well, I figured it was a long shot."

"Finding a specific book?" Rarity looked up at him, confused.

He laughed as he picked up a pen to sign the charge slip. "No, me hoping that you weren't seeing anyone. I was trying to get up the nerve to ask you to dinner."

"Yeah, sorry, I'm involved." She put the books into a bag. "But thanks for stopping in. I hope you come by next time you're in town. Or if you run out of reading material."

"Definitely. I like this town. Maybe I'll have to check into moving here. I hate the snowy New Jersey winters." He took the bag.

"Our winters are the best part of Sedona. Lots of hiking around here. Archer, my boyfriend, he runs a hiking tour company, if you have some spare time." She handed him one of the bookmarks she had with the list of Archer's favorite hiking books. She had several different partnerships with local businesses for bookmarks, and she rotated them into purchases based on people's interests. Or at least what she could guess. "Have a great day."

He took the bookmark and tucked it into the bag, then left the shop. Killer had gotten up from his nap by the fireplace, probably when Archer had come in. He now stood by the walkway, watching the door close after Josh.

"Hey, buddy, do you need to go out?" When he barked, she grabbed his leash, and putting a sign on the counter saying she'd be right back, she grabbed the register key, and they went out the back door to the alley where the sun hadn't heated up the asphalt. Killer had a fake grass pad out there too, and he quickly smelled the area and did his business. After cleaning up, they went back inside, and Rarity locked the back door again. She washed her hands, then got out one of Annie's peanut butter treats from the fridge. As she was giving it to Killer, she heard the bell go off on the front door. "I'll be right out."

Killer got there first and headed straight for his bed to enjoy his treat. Rarity looked around the area, but no one was standing in the entryway or by the register. Nothing looked out of place. She hurried and scanned the bookshelf aisles, but there was no one there. Then she went to the front door and stepped out, the bell ringing behind her. People were walking on the sidewalk past the businesses. Some stopped at the walkway to Madam Zelda's fortune-telling shop, pointing and talking. But no one seemed to be focusing on the bookstore.

She turned toward Sam's crystal shop, but she didn't see her friend in the windows or out front. Finally, still confused, she went back into the bookstore and looked up at the bell as she shut the door. It rang again.

She had heard the bell ring out front. She knew it. So why wasn't anyone there?

Chapter 5

Killer was doing his host rounds just before the Tuesday night club was to start. He went to greet the regulars, getting loves and pets from each of them, then he would go and sit in front of anyone new. Rarity was amazed at how the dog always knew just the right pose to make the newcomer notice him, and she was sure he was assessing their dog affection as he watched. Then, if they returned the next week, they went into the rotation. If anyone missed a week, Killer didn't greet them with the others.

Her dog was brutal on attendance.

He always stopped at Shirley last, and as soon as she gave him a treat, he'd go back to his bed to watch the meeting. Rarity sent up a thought to Martha, Killer's first owner, about how much Rarity loved this little guy. She thought if Martha was listening, she'd be proud of her dog and his ability to make people feel welcome. Or maybe not. Martha hadn't been much of a people person the one time Rarity had met her.

By the time the meeting was to start, only four members had shown up. Holly, Malia, Shirley, and Sam. The sleuthers' club subsection. The other four women who loved the club, but not sleuthing, had stopped by earlier that day to pick up the book they'd be reading for the next two weeks and had told her how sorry they were about Janey, even though they'd only met her the one time.

Rarity knew they didn't like being part of the mystery solving, so they'd probably assumed that unless Janey's death was ruled an accident or suicide, the Tuesday night group was going to be trying to solve it. Rarity didn't hold it against the four. They all were women with families still at home. The book club outings were just a way for them to talk to people besides their kids.

The door opened, and Rarity glanced up, expecting to see a customer. Instead, Jonathon Anderson, Drew's father and a retired NYC police officer, strolled into the store. He waved at the club members as he walked by and then met Rarity at the counter. He gave her a hug. "I bet you didn't expect me tonight."

"Actually, no, this is a surprise. Drew didn't say anything about you and Edith coming to visit." She really liked Drew's parents. She patted his arms. "You're just in time for book club."

"I know. I figure you could use some of my specific skills this week. Let me buy the last book and the next one so I'll have some reading material when I head back to Drew's. Edith stayed home this trip." He walked over and picked up the books from a display Rarity had set up by the register. "These are great. I haven't read either one."

Rarity took the books and rang them up. "They're a little out of your typical reading genres. One's a women's fiction, and one's a domestic suspense. Edith will probably steal them from you when you get back home. How's that grandbaby?"

"She's growing like a weed. Edith's always out buying her new clothes. Someday, Drew should have a kid. That way he'll get some of the inheritance money that Edith's bound and determined to spend on onesies and fancy strollers." He gave her his credit card. "I was sorry to hear about your employee. Drew's been busy since I arrived, and we haven't really talked, but I hear she was a very nice young woman."

"Janey was special. I didn't know her well, but I liked her. And I thought she was going to be great with the new book clubs for kids. Shirley's taking them over for a while until she decides if she wants to continue." Rarity blinked back tears. It didn't seem like she'd known Janey well enough to cry at the thought of her death, but it was the loss of all that potential amazing life she'd had cut short that made Rarity sad. She finished the transaction and handed Jonathon's credit card back to him. He had a backpack on his shoulder. "Do you want a bag?"

"Nope, they can fit in here. I'll go over and get some coffee so we can get started." Jonathon squeezed Rarity's hand. "Let's do coffee this week. I'm not sure how long I'll be here, so whenever you can fit an old man into your busy schedule, I'll make it work."

"Tomorrow, seven thirty at Annie's?"

He grinned. "I'll be there with bells on. I'll have to get up early anyway if I want to see Drew before he heads to the station. You know how he gets during an investigation."

As she moved the book club sign into the walkway for any random customers, Jonathon made his way into the group for hugs and hellos, coffee, and a plate full of Shirley's cookies. Killer came up to greet Jonathon after he'd sat down, and Rarity got out the list that Shirley, Holly, and Malia had helped make on Sunday after they'd found out about Janey's death.

"I guess we're ready to start. The rest of the book club members came in today to get the new book and to wish the sleuthers good luck in our new investigation. I'm afraid our secret mission for the club isn't much of a secret anymore. But before Drew can shut us down, he'll have to deal with his father, Jonathon, who is our true secret weapon." Rarity smiled at Jonathon. "Thanks for coming up from Tucson to help out."

"If you talk to Drew, I'm just here to see some old friends. Of course, he'll call it meddling, but let's just try to keep our activities out of the official range of interfering-with-an-investigation area, and we should be fine." He smiled at everyone. "I'm very glad to see you all again."

Rarity caught up Sam and Jonathon on the facts of the case as they knew them.

When Marcus's name came into the discussion, Sam held up her hand. "The rest of you know, but I'm saying this for Jonathon's benefit. Marcus is my brother. I know he and Janey dated just before her death, but there's no way he could have killed her. I've talked to him, and he's crushed about what happened."

"That must be hard on you as well." Jonathon smiled at Sam. "Did he tell you about when he last saw the victim? When they met?"

Sam blew out a breath. "Let's get it out there. Then I don't have to keep saying he didn't do it. You guys will see the same thing."

"I'll take notes," Shirley said as she handed Jonathon the new pages for his murder notebook that he'd pulled out of his backpack.

"Okay, so we saw their first meeting here at the bookstore. And then again when we were at Darby's going-away party, they talked and just clicked," Sam started.

Rarity stepped in. "Janey came with me so I asked her if she was okay staying, because Sam, Drew, Archer, and I were going to leave and go grab an early dinner. The party was still going strong when we left. Anyway, she said she had her car at my house, and she'd walk over and get it when she left. Then Marcus said he'd walk her there and for me not to worry."

Sam nodded. "That's what Marcus told me too. They stayed for another hour or so, but then they decided to leave since the party was a little wild for them to talk. He walked her to her car. Then they went to Annie's for some coffee before she drove home. She dropped him off at the hotel about ten. Then she came back into town Friday morning, and they went hiking for the day and out to dinner."

Rarity nodded. "She said that on Saturday when she worked with me. She was meeting Marcus again for dinner that night. Janey was so happy, and she really liked him. I didn't see her again after that. Drew called me Sunday afternoon to tell me about her death."

Sam continued the story from her brother's viewpoint. "Marcus said they went to dinner. The next morning, Sunday, they met at the quarry to swim. He said he had to go back into town for a virtual meeting with his boss. She wanted to stay at the quarry and write. She'd driven her own car, and the hike to the quarry isn't far, so he felt comfortable leaving her. He told her to stop by the hotel on her way out of town if she wanted to have dinner. When she didn't show, he figured she just needed some time alone. He says she was fine when he left the quarry."

"What time did he leave her there?" asked Holly, who was setting up a timeline on the flip chart.

"His meeting was at one thirty. They were doing some restructuring for him to be full-time remote rather than in the office," Sam explained. "He said he wasn't sure of the exact time, but before noon. He had time to shower, and it's only about thirty minutes from the quarry to his hotel."

They looked at Holly's timeline. "Well, as long as the time of death was after one thirty, he's in the clear."

Rarity shook her head. She grabbed her phone and scrolled down the recent calls until she found what she was looking for. "It can't be after one thirty. I got the call from Drew at two. We need to know when the hiker found Janey."

Holly flipped over the timeline and put a question mark on the page. "Okay, so that's a few questions. When did the hiker find Janey? What is the time of death? How was she killed? Anything else?"

"Where is her journal? If she was writing when Marcus left, how much writing did she get done? That would tell us how long she was alone," Rarity pointed out.

"That's good." Holly glanced at the list. Then she turned to Jonathon. "Any way you can ask Drew for some of these? I'm not scheduled to work on the computers at the station for two weeks, so me showing up to do an IT update might be a little suspicious."

Jonathon made notes. "I'll see what I can find out. So if we're able to rule out Sam's brother, and I hope we are, who else could have done this? Any ideas?"

Everyone looked at Rarity.

She shook her head. "I don't know. Maybe we should talk to some of her classmates. If she had issues with the last guy she dated, maybe she told someone."

Malia held up her hand. "I'm the only one on campus, so I'll handle this. I have class Thursday on campus, so I'll go over to her department. What was she studying again?"

Rarity had Janey's employment file and looked at her resume. She listed it off, and Malia wrote down the department. Rarity glanced at the emergency contact number Janey had on the sheet. It didn't show a relationship. "I'll call Drew and see who he notified as next of kin. If it's this same name, I'll call them with my condolences and find out when funeral arrangements are being made and where."

"Some clubs have fun field trips. We go to funerals." Holly shook her head. "I don't even want to think what that says about us."

"Dear, you're just getting ready for when you're my age. I swear, I attend a funeral a month as my old friends leave this world." Shirley closed her notebook. "I'll take on the task of treats for the next three weeks. We can go back on our rotation when this is done. I think better when I'm baking."

The group disbanded a few minutes later. Sam stayed behind to help clean up. Rarity watched Sam put the flip charts away as she put all the coffee and lemonade containers on the cart to take into the back room and clean. "Are you okay with this? If you want to sit out this investigation, no one would hold it against you."

"I would. I would hold it against me." Sam closed the closet door and picked up a paper plate that had been left on the coffee table. "I know Marcus didn't kill Janey. At least that's what my heart says. My head I still have to convince."

"Is there something you're not telling us?" Rarity had never seen her friend as quiet as she'd been during the discussion this evening. She'd told Marcus's story, then sat and listened. She'd taken notes all during the meeting.

Sam ran a wet rag over the treat table and moved it closer to the wall. Then she followed Rarity toward the kitchen after turning the closed sign on the door and locking it. Sam pushed the event sign into the corner where it sat when not in use. They'd closed up the shop together just like this for years. But tonight, Rarity thought Sam's attention was somewhere else.

When they finished cleaning up the drink station and checked the lock on the back door, they went back into the darkened bookstore. Archer would be here soon to walk her home. Drew typically came to get Sam.

Rarity wondered if he would tonight. If he wasn't coming, she and Archer would walk Sam home, then go on to her house.

"Rarity, I need to tell you something. But until Drew finds it, I need you to keep it between us." Sam sank into a chair by the fireplace. "Okay?"

"Okay." Rarity wondered what she was agreeing to, but she trusted Sam. Sam had been there throughout the year of cancer, unlike Rarity's ex-boyfriend, Kevin. Even living so far away, Rarity knew she could call Sam for anything, and it would be okay. She needed to give her friend the same courtesy now.

"When we were kids, a girl went missing. A girl Marcus had been dating." Sam shook her head when Rarity's eyes widened. "See, that's why I haven't told Drew about this. He'd have the same reaction. But Marcus didn't kill this girl. They found her body at a local quarry where all the kids swam. He was questioned, but they found evidence that she'd committed suicide. There was a note left in her bedroom. Marcus was just at the wrong place at the wrong time. He'd been swimming with some friends, she showed up, and they stayed to talk. Then he went home, and I guess she overdosed. He was devastated."

"The situation is eerily similar," Rarity commented.

Sam sighed as she closed her eyes. "I know. And that's why I'm still trying to find out who killed Janey. If it was Marcus, I need to know that too. But my heart says he wouldn't do this. Especially after what happened to Connie so many years ago."

"You need to tell Drew," Rarity said.

Sam shook her head. "No. That's the last thing I need to do. Marcus would know I betrayed him."

"But, Sam—" Rarity didn't get the rest of her sentence out before she heard a knock on the door.

"Rarity, you promised," Sam hissed as they walked to the door.

Archer was standing there and, Rarity saw, Drew behind him. That was a good sign. At least for Sam and Drew's relationship. "Hey, guys, let me get Killer, and I'll be ready. Good to see you, Drew."

"I take it my father arrived in time for book club?" Drew asked, his eyebrows raised to let her know he knew why Jonathon had come to town.

"Yes, Jonathon was here. So good to see him. You know I love your parents. I'll be right back." Rarity hurried back inside to get her tote and Killer's leash since he'd followed them to the door and was now in Archer's arms. When she got back to lock the door, Drew and Sam had already left.

"Man, I'd hate to be Drew tonight. I bet Sam's furious at him for looking at Marcus as a suspect." Archer took Killer's leash and snapped it onto his collar. Then he held out a hand for Rarity's tote. "I'll take that."

"Okay, but if someone gives you crap about your man purse, I'm not standing up for you," Rarity teased, hoping to get the subject off of Drew and Sam. And Marcus. But then she slipped. "I'm glad he came to walk her home."

Archer put his arm around her as they walked down the sidewalk. "So am I."

When they got home, he opened the fridge and pulled out some chicken. "Stir-fry okay?"

"Sounds wonderful, but you could just warm up soup. Or I could," she amended.

"I like cooking you dinner after a long day at work. It makes me feel domestic. Do you want a beer to sip on while I cook, or are you swimming?"

She needed a swim, but she hated leaving Archer alone to cook. Apparently, she hesitated just a little too long, and he guessed the answer.

"Go have a swim. I'll start up some rice and turn on the baseball game. I know how to entertain myself." He leaned over and kissed her. "Besides, you look like someone stole your kitten. Are you sure you're up to the club investigating Janey's death? Maybe this one's just too close."

"It's because it's close that we need to investigate. I know Drew doesn't believe in our meddling, as he calls it, but the hive mind is better at putting together clues than just one person. Besides, Jonathon will keep us out of legal trouble. He's an asset to the group."

"He's a pain in Drew's backside." He waved a green pepper at her. "Go swim. I don't want this epic stir-fry to have to wait while you finish up."

She hurried to her bedroom to change. Maybe after she did her laps, she could stop thinking about the girl who died when Marcus was a teenager. And wondering if he had killed Janey too.

Chapter 6

Wednesday morning, Rarity tried to keep busy at the store. She was losing the battle. Janey had been a big part of a lot of the changes Rarity had planned on implementing, including today's Mommy and Me class. Now, she had the class covered with Shirley stepping in, but she was still missing Janey's excitement about the project. She pulled out her laptop and searched the web for Janey Ford. The first articles were, of course, about her death. The funeral was being held on Friday at Flagstaff Lutheran at eleven. She wrote the time and place on her calendar and emailed the Tuesday night group about attending. Then she ordered flowers and sent a contribution to a scholarship fund at the college.

With that done, she focused on the obituary. Janey's parents were deceased, but she had a sister who also lived in Flagstaff. She opened Janey's employee folder that she'd kept in her tote, hoping she'd find something that might explain what happened. The sister's name according to the obit was Trish Ford. The emergency contact was Cara Mantle. Definitely not her sister.

The store was still empty. Shirley would be here at two to prep for the three o'clock reading, but it looked like Rarity had some time. She picked up her phone and dialed Cara's number.

A sleepy voice answered, "Hello?"

"Hi, is this Cara Mantle?" Rarity asked.

"Yes. Who is this?" Now the woman on the other end seemed a little more alert. "If this is a reporter, I don't know anything about Janey's death. So please stop calling."

"Cara, this is Rarity Cole. Janey worked for me at The Next Chapter. I'm just calling to see if there is anything I can do. Anything you need." Rarity prayed the woman wouldn't just hang up.

"Oh, Ms. Cole. Thank you for calling. I'm Janey's roommate. She was so excited to work at your store." A sniff interrupted her words. "I can't believe she's gone. We've been friends since high school. We both hated the dorms, so we moved into this apartment. Now, I'm working for Flagstaff Memorial, and Janey, she was finishing her master's. But you know that. I'm sorry, I'm rambling. I did that with the first reporter who called, then I just kept getting more calls."

"I'm sorry you're being bothered. Are you working with her sister on the funeral arrangements? I'm coming with a few of my patrons." Rarity hoped she'd have at least one person with her. She hadn't heard back, but at least Shirley would come with her. She hoped.

"Miss Perfect? No, Trish will be at the funeral, all dressed in black and weeping for the cameras, but she can't be bothered with dealing with the planning or anything. Janey's parents left her some money, and since I'm her heir according to the lawyer who called yesterday, I'll pay for the funeral out of that." A dog barked in the background. "And I guess I'm taking over mom duties for Whiskey."

"I didn't know she had a dog. She spent a lot of time with my fur kid here at the shop. I should have asked." *But,* Rarity thought as she paused, *I thought we'd have more time.*

"Whiskey's a rescue mutt. Part lab, part chow, part something else. He's missing her something awful. They used to run every day. I guess I'm going to have to take up the hobby. I work nights, so Whiskey's used to me being here sleeping most of the day." Cara sniffed again. "I'm sorry, I'm not sure what else to say. Again, I'm rambling. Thank you for making her so happy in her last days. You would have thought she won the lottery, what with the job and then that new guy."

Rarity held her breath, then asked, "Marcus?"

"Yeah, that was his name." Cara laughed softly. "She was head over heels for that guy as soon as she met him. She thought he was her soulmate. Now they're looking at him for her killing? I don't believe it. How can you get someone to trust you that deeply and have those kind of intentions? Janey was smart. She would have known. She wouldn't even let Caleb take her for coffee, and she'd known him for years."

"Caleb Thompson?" Rarity had seen Caleb watching Janey, but she thought they'd met after she'd hired them. Not before.

"Yeah, the guy was always following us around campus. Janey called him her shadow. He kept asking her on dates, but she told him they were better as just friends." A loud barking sounded in the background. "Sorry, I've got to go and take Whiskey out. I'll see you at the funeral. Thanks for calling. It was nice to talk about Janey to someone who knew her."

Rarity hung up and wrote down what Cara had said. She felt bad that Cara had thought she'd called just to talk, but on the other hand, Cara would want Janey's killer to be found. Rarity finished her notes and looked at the words. What was she doing? Did this all come down to some need to get justice? Or was there a hidden need for Rarity to go looking for the monsters in the world?

Maybe after surviving her own death sentence when she got cancer, she'd developed this vigilante need to save others. Maybe that was why the Tuesday night survivors' group had turned so fast into a sleuthing group. Whatever it was, this need to right the wrongs in the world wasn't in just her blood. The others from the club felt the same way. Or had it just been that they'd been thrown into situations where they cared about the others who had been killed? Martha had been a reluctant member of the book club. Darby was a member, and it was her grandmother who'd been killed. And now, a bookstore employee.

Rarity glanced around the wood, steel, and brick interior of her building. There was one link to all of this, besides a cancer diagnosis for someone. The bookstore. She pushed the idea away as Sam walked into the store, a bag of food in one hand and a drink carrier in the other.

"What are you doing here?"

"Lunch is delivered. I need a friendly face, and we both need food. So my treat. Shall we sit by the fireplace?" Sam nodded to the open area where the book clubs were held.

"Sounds amazing. Just what I needed as well." Rarity closed her murder notebook and her laptop and hurried over to meet Sam. Killer, having smelled the food, was already there.

Sam pulled out sandwiches. "Sedona French dips. They have pepper jack cheese and a ton of onions and peppers."

"Sounds amazing." Rarity sat on the couch and pulled the coffee table closer. Killer whined at her feet. "If the French fries are cool enough, I'll give you one."

"And if she doesn't remember, I will," Sam promised. She took a bite of the sandwich, then sighed. "Best food I've eaten for days."

"Have you even eaten anything lately?" Rarity asked. Sam didn't look like herself. She looked worn out and tired. "You've been so worried about Marcus, I'm guessing you haven't taken good care of yourself."

"Nailed it on the head. Drew said the same thing last night when he walked me home. He brought me a bag of cookies, and we sat and talked for a while before he went home." Sam wiped her mouth with a napkin. "He's a good guy. Too bad he's trying to send my brother away for twenty to life."

"He's not. He's just trying to find out who killed Janey. If Marcus didn't do it—"

Sam interjected, "And he didn't."

"Okay, *since* Marcus didn't do it, Drew will rule him out and find who did. You know Drew. He won't stop at an easy but wrong answer." Rarity gave Killer a French fry after testing the temperature by eating one first. "He gets his sense of honesty from Jonathon. Speaking of, I can't believe he came here to help us with the investigation."

"I think he's a spy for Drew. I think Drew called his father and told him to watch us so Drew could work on the case without worrying about what we were doing." Sam shrugged at Rarity's shocked expression. "Don't tell me the thought hadn't crossed your mind."

"A lot of things have been going through my mind today, but no, I didn't see that one coming." She nodded, thinking out Jonathon's suspiciously fast arrival. "I have to admit, you may be right. We'll see what clues he brings us, and if it looks like he's playing double agent, I'll talk to him. I don't think he'd lie if we confronted him and it was true."

Sam took another bite of her sandwich. "I have to agree; he wouldn't lie to us. Or I don't think he would. It's hard to tell sometimes."

Rarity wondered if Sam was thinking about her brother and his declarations about not killing Janey, but she'd let her friend deal with the truth once they found it. "So can you get away for a long lunch on Friday? Janey's funeral is in Flagstaff at eleven, and I'm going. I'd like to have a few of our book club regulars there too."

"You want people to watch the mourners for something off?" Sam asked.

Rarity thought about her question. "Actually, yes, but no. I just think Janey deserves to have some people from her life here in Sedona at the funeral. I guess her sister is a pill. And I want to talk to her best friend again."

"Wait, you talked to her best friend? What did she say?" Sam set the sandwich down on the wrapper. Killer moved closer to the table. She gave him another French fry. "Go on, spill."

Rarity told Sam about the conversation and what Cara had said about Janey's feelings for Marcus. And about the dog.

Sam narrowed her eyes. "You're not thinking about adopting him, are you?"

Rarity laughed. "I'll admit I thought about it when I found out Janey had a dog. But Cara said she was keeping him. I just didn't want him going back to a shelter because his person had died. He's older, from what I could surmise from my conversation. Senior dogs aren't the first to be adopted. Besides, Killer wouldn't like it."

"True. Your guy here is pretty spoiled. I'm not sure how he'd take another dog in his realm." Sam gave Killer a third fry. This time, he took it to his bed. "I think he's done."

"He saves treats for later." Rarity watched as Killer circled, then lay down. "He's full, and it's time to sleep."

"If only our lives were as simple. Eat, sleep, poop, then repeat." Sam rolled her shoulders. "No worries. Your food arrives when you want it. And you have a dedicated servant who will rub your tummy anytime you want."

"Drew would rub your tummy. I'm already committed to Killer." Rarity liked seeing Sam smile. During the last few minutes, her friend had seemed more like herself. She decided to ask Sam about the building. "Do you know what this space was before I bought the building?"

"A café. It didn't last long. I don't think the owner realized what he was getting himself into. Running a restaurant is hard work. This guy wasn't even a chef. He was out of the navy and decided he wanted a barbeque spot here. The problem was that the food wasn't great." Sam held up the sandwich. "Not like the Garnet, or even Carole's. So the restaurant went out just as fast as it came into town. Before that, the building held some sort of gift shop. Cheap stuff. T-shirts and stuff. And before that, there were offices here. A lawyer, if I remember right. Maybe an accountant. Why are you asking?"

Rarity wondered what Sam would think of her bookstore link between all the latest murder victims. Probably that she was reaching for a connection. Besides, it couldn't be the building's fault. She was also a common denominator between the three murders, and she knew she didn't do it. "Just curious."

Later, Shirley arrived fifteen minutes early, and she'd brought cute cookies made into flowers. "Should I set up coffee and lemonade?"

"And ice water. We'll see what they like and adjust next week." Rarity had pulled out the boxes holding the weekly book order, which would give her something to do while Shirley was running the book club. That way, if Shirley needed help, Rarity would be close by. They got set up with copies of this week's book at the counter as well as next week's. Janey had done a great job setting up the orders and the process. Rarity felt a twinge of sadness as Shirley added a few chairs to the club area along with napkins and wipes nearby.

Women started coming in at two thirty. Most bought both books before the reading as well as a couple from the shelves for "mommy." Shirley held court over by the fireplace, cooing at the children, talking about her own grandchildren and showing pictures.

The last woman in line to purchase books smiled at Rarity. "Shirley goes to my church. You should have heard her talking about today's event. She even got up to the front during announcements and called out for new moms to come by today. She's an amazing marketer."

Rarity watched as Shirley called out a three-minute countdown to start the program. She handed the woman her credit card. She glanced at the name. "Thanks, Vivian. I know I couldn't have pulled this off without her. It's been a little disjointed around here."

"Viv, please. I heard about the young woman who was killed by the quarry. My husband's an EMT. He said she'd been in the water, but someone pulled her out and posed her at the shore. I know the rumors are she committed suicide, but from what Matt said, I don't believe it." Viv took the books and tucked them into her stroller, which she parked by the others in the entryway.

Rarity watched as the group got started and thought about what she'd said. Then when Shirley started reading, she pulled out her murder book and added Vivian's account. The note didn't clear Marcus at all, but it did point to the killer being someone who knew Janey. Not just a random killing. And it totally ruled out suicide.

Rarity wondered if Jonathon had any luck in finding out how Janey was killed. But before she could go down that rabbit hole again, she closed the notebook and tucked it under the counter. Then she grabbed Killer's leash and snapped it onto his collar. He'd moved to behind the counter as soon as the first stroller appeared. "Ready to go outside?"

He pulled toward the back door in a *Yes, please, and now* gesture. Rarity might not be able to speak dog language, but she tried really hard to keep up on what Killer needed. And right now, that was a short walk. She held the leash up to Shirley, and she saw her nod.

"Let's go before we're needed," she told her dog.

When they got back, the group was talking about the book and what it meant. The good news about a Mommy and Me class was that it wasn't scheduled for long. Maybe they could find someone to do a kid-friendly exercise class or age-appropriate crafts to add to the fun, but for now, it was about the book.

Shirley went around to each parent and child to say goodbye as the group disbanded. When the last mommy had left, Shirley poured herself a cup of coffee and sank into one of the chairs.

Rarity joined her with a cup as well. Killer reclaimed his dog bed by the fireplace and went straight to sleep.

"That was brutal, but fun. I can't believe how many people showed up. I thought most of our residents in Sedona were older." Shirley sipped her coffee. "The babies were so cute. Not a one cried the entire time."

"Crying babies, I hadn't even thought about that." Rarity shuddered a bit. "Maybe we should make this club every other week."

"It's only an hour at most. You can deal with babies for that long." Shirley smiled at her. "Besides, it's only a matter of time before you and Archer start making some of your own. You can use this as preparation."

"I'm not sure about that." Rarity hadn't thought about kids. Especially after Kevin dumped her. And then the cancer. She needed to do the genetic testing that the breast health center offered. And talk to Archer. Maybe he didn't want kids. He was her age without any commitments. Maybe he liked it that way. Did she?

"You'll know when you know," Shirley said.

Rarity turned toward her. "What on earth does that mean?"

Shirley stood and went over to the table. "I'm not sure. It's what my mom always said when I'd ask her about anything."

Rarity laughed as she took a tulip cookie that Shirley offered her. "I've been falling down rabbit holes all day. I guess that saying is as good as any other one I could wind up with."

Shirley sat back down and glanced around the club area. "I think today went really well. Thank you for letting me do this. I needed the distraction."

"Well, you know when you know, I guess." Rarity threw Shirley's quote back at her, and they both laughed. Then she updated Shirley on what she'd learned from her chat with Cara, and now what Viv had said.

"Viv and Matt are good people. Matt is a long-term member of the EMT department. He started doing rescue as a volunteer before the city made the department official. He's a straight shooter, and he's seen his share of deaths. If he says it's not a suicide, you can bet Drew's listening to his opinion." Shirley mused as they put away the leftover cookies and cleaned up the drinks station. "I'm afraid the facts aren't pointing Drew away from Sam's brother."

Rarity thought the same thing, but she didn't say it. Shirley didn't even know the bombshell that Sam had told Rarity on Tuesday night.

All in all, Marcus Aarons was looking more and more like a murder suspect, no matter what his sister thought.

Chapter 7

Wednesday evening, Drew showed up at the bookstore at closing time. He took his hat off and picked up Killer, who'd run to greet him as soon as he'd come inside. "Hey, buddy, it's nice that someone's happy to see me."

"Killer loves you. You know that. And you're always welcome here." Rarity glanced out the front window, where she could see the entrance in front of Sam's crystal shop. "I take it there's trouble in paradise."

He shrugged as he walked toward the counter, where she was finishing up her closing activities. "I'm not sure. Sam's having dinner with Marcus tonight, and I'm sure my name will be mud in that conversation."

"Sam knows you're just doing your job." Rarity tucked her murder notebook into her tote. "So what are you doing here?"

He rubbed Killer under the chin. "Archer's has an early evening hiking tour, so I said I'd walk the two of you home. Are you ready?"

"You and Archer realize I know where my house is located, right? It's not dark. And I have a protector, anyway." She reached up and rubbed Killer's head. "Who's a big boy?"

"Killer would yip at an attacker. And you'd be dead." He put his hand over the dog's ears. "Don't tell him I said that."

"Whatever. But I *can* get home on my own." She moved to the back and checked the lock on the door, then moved through the rooms, turning off lights.

"I know, but I wanted to ask you some questions about Janey. This way, I get my investigative work done, and you get home safely. Which means Archer doesn't mess up my face for not protecting you." He opened the door and held it for her. "Okay with you?"

"Not really, but I get it. Besides, Archer wouldn't hit you. You might never see Killer again, but he wouldn't hit you." Rarity locked the door and dropped the keys into her purse. "If you get to ask me questions, do I get to ask some of you?"

"Of course. I may not answer the questions, but you can ask away. And it might give me a feel for what your group of Agatha Christie wannabes are thinking on the case." He put Killer on the ground after clicking his leash onto his collar. "Who wants to go first?"

"You can." Rarity enjoyed spending time with Drew. Not in a relationship kind of way but as friends. He was smart, and they had a lot of the same interests. She wondered if their sameness was why she didn't have chemistry with the tall, handsome lawman. Instead, she was head over heels in love with the hiker guide who also made her dinner several nights a week.

"You're thinking about Archer, aren't you?" Drew raised his eyebrows as she looked shocked. "Fine, don't tell me. I get it. You're not in love with me. Besides, I've moved on. So Janey—when did you first meet her?"

Rarity told him the story of how she'd put an advertisement for help in the student center employment board. It had been Darby's idea, and Rarity thought it was a good one. She only needed part-time help, so reaching out to college students who were interested in books and retail marketing seemed the best way to hire. "I called Campus Employment in mid-August, and I interviewed five candidates. At first, I was just going to hire one, but then we got to talking about opportunities for different clubs, and I hired the best two out of the bunch. Both Janey and Caleb were well read, and both had the energy and experience working with youth."

"When did you interview and hire?" Drew turned them down the road that led to her house.

Rarity tapped her finger on her lips, trying to remember. "It was the week before Labor Day. I finally called Caleb's reference, so I made offers on that Wednesday. Then Janey and Caleb came in the next week, and we did an orientation. The following week, I had them sit in on the Tuesday night club. And that Saturday, we hammered out the details for the four new book clubs. After she left that last day, I didn't see her again."

"Stupid question, but did she seem down, depressed, suicidal?"

Rarity shook her head. "No to all of that. She was excited. She really liked the job and was looking forward to her first Mommy and Me class today. And she was excited about seeing Marcus again. They'd had several fun dates."

"Yeah, I thought you'd say that." He nodded to her house on the left. "Can I come in for a bit? Maybe a soda?"

"Sure. If you're done asking me questions, it's my turn anyway. But hold on a second, I need to grab Terrance's paper and put it on his porch." Rarity took her keys out of her pocket and turned to her neighbor's walkway. "I'll get it." Drew handed her Killer's leash. He grabbed the paper and ran up the stairs to put it with the others. "Hey, there's a box here. Do you want to hold on to it so it doesn't get ripped off?"

"Sure, bring it over. I'm surprised they delivered it. Terrance put a hold on his mail with the post office."

Drew studied the box as he brought it over to where she now stood on her driveway. "It's not from the post office. It looks like a local carrier dropped it off at the house. There's no stamping at all."

Rarity glanced at the box Drew held. "That's strange. Maybe it's from one of the clubs he's in."

He sniffed it, and Rarity laughed. "Is that an official investigation technique?"

"I just don't want it to be rotting on your kitchen table while we wait for Terrance to retrieve it." He held it with one hand. "It's not real heavy. Maybe it's a hat or something."

"I bet you knew exactly what you were getting for Christmas." Rarity opened the door and walked into her house. "Set it on the table there so I don't forget to hand it over when he gets back from his cruise."

He followed her direction and shut the door. "Mind if I make some coffee?"

"Not at all. I take it you're on the evening shift tonight." Rarity unclipped Killer, and he ran to his water bowl for a drink. "I'm going to change out of my work clothes, if you don't mind."

"I'll be here playing with my favorite dog." He moved to the kitchen, and Killer followed him.

Rarity thought Drew really needed his own dog, but she understood. He was gone a lot for work, so the dog would be stuck at home alone. If Sam moved in, at least the dog could go with her to work. Although Rarity could see Drew's objection there too. If the dog spent the majority of his or her time with Sam, it might like Sam better. She quickly changed into sweats and a loose T-shirt and headed back out to the kitchen, where the boys were talking about the best kind of treats, at least in Drew's mind. Killer sat on the floor, focusing his complete attention on Drew. The dog loved Drew, Archer, Sam, Shirley, Darby, and most of the Tuesday night club members. He was a people dog. Maybe spending his first few years with only Martha made him appreciate having more people around now that he lived with Rarity.

She poured a cup of coffee, adding whipped cream and some salted caramel flavoring. When Drew raised his eyebrows in question, she shrugged. "When I have coffee at night, it's a treat, so I want it creamy and sweet. Don't be so judgy. Are you done asking me questions about Janey?" "I think so. I was hoping there would be some guy who didn't get the job that threw bricks through your window saying they were going to kill everyone you hired since you didn't choose him. But no, you disappointed me." He got up and added some of the salted caramel flavoring to his own cup and warmed it up. He took a taste. "It's good."

"I know. That's why I do it. Anyway, since I didn't solve your case for you, I've got some questions from the Tuesday group. We know it wasn't suicide, so are you saying she was drowned?"

He took another sip of his coffee. "What if I don't answer you, but if you're close, I don't say anything. If you're wrong, or I'm confused, I'll ask a question back."

"Does that go against your police training?"

"Most definitely." Drew laughed and picked Killer up from the floor.

Rarity made a note in her notebook saying Janey drowned. Then she looked up at Drew. "Wait, was that a question, which means no, she didn't drown, or just a setting of the ground rules? I'm confused."

"It was a setting of the ground rules. And one more rule. No one in your group will go looking for this murderer. If you have someone in mind, you'll come to me with your reasoning, and I'll go talk to that person. You aren't getting killed just because I let you play detective." He leaned forward. "Do I have your promise?"

"Yes. None of us want to be out confronting a killer. Well, maybe Malia. She's pretty focused when she gets her mind set, but I think Holly can keep her from going off and doing her own thing." Rarity looked at the paper. "We know a hiker found the body. Any chance it's him?"

"Not unless he did the deed while his wife waited a few miles away getting coffee. And he'd have to have been speeding there and back, because he went to the restroom for maybe three minutes, five at most. The waitress who gave me this information was bored that day so she was watching pretty closely. And he's kind of cute, her words, not mine. Besides, he's married." Drew held up his hand. "I swear all of that is almost word for word what I got from her and totally true."

"People are weird." Rarity put a check and crossed off "hiker who found Janey" from the list of possible suspects. "She had some issues with her sister according to Cara, her roommate. Have you ruled her sister out?"

Drew's eyes narrowed. "Her sister? You talked to her roommate? When?"

"Okay, I see we hit an area where either you know more, or you haven't talked to Cara yet. I was wondering if you'd met Whiskey." Rarity circled Trish Ford's name. "Are you going to the funeral on Friday?"

He shook his head. "Apparently, I've been talking to the wrong people. What's her sister's name? Who is Whiskey? And do you have this Cara's phone number? I left a card on Janey's door, but no one's called me back. Someone from Flagstaff's department was supposed to go over today and talk to the landlord."

"I called Janey's emergency contact from her job application." Rarity handed him the paper and pointed to the bottom of the form.

"This is her sister's number?" He took the form.

Rarity sipped her coffee. "No, that's Cara's number. She's her roommate and a friend. I told you she wasn't on good terms with her sister."

He took out his phone and took a picture of the job application. "Thanks for the coffee. I need to go."

"I have a few more questions." She stood and followed him to the door.

"Sorry. I need to drive to Flagstaff. Apparently, if you want something done right, you should hire a bookseller." He waved and then took out his phone.

Rarity smiled and watched him hurry off, his phone to his ear. Whoever had dropped the ball on calling Cara was probably getting an earful right now. Killer stood by her side, watching him leave, a small whine coming from him. She scooped him up before he decided to take off after Drew and gave him a kiss on the head. "Your buddy is busy finding the bad guy right now. He'll come back and play later."

From the look he gave her, she wasn't sure he believed her. She locked the door, then went to the bedroom to change into her swimsuit. Now, she had more to think about with Janey's death. Maybe this sister would be a good lead, and she'd have a reason to kill Janey. Or have her killed. Sometimes people didn't like others to be happy. And Janey was really happy on Saturday when Rarity last saw her.

* * * *

Thursday afternoon, Caleb showed up for his work shift. He looked like he'd gotten at least some sleep. The deep circles were gone from under his eyes, and the red had turned to pink. He smiled sadly as he came into the store. "I made it. I wasn't sure I could do it yesterday, but I made myself get up and shower today. Janey wouldn't want anyone wasting away because she's gone."

"Probably true. Anyway, I'm glad you're here. I know losing Janey was a shock, but life does go on, and we honor those who don't by living a good life while we're here." Rarity didn't want to sound like a commercial, but since she'd survived cancer, she knew the value of life. And not to leave with any regrets. "So let's get busy. I'm closing the shop midday tomorrow for Janey's funeral. I probably won't reopen until Saturday morning, so we need to be on point for Saturday's book club today. And I hired someone to do the Mommy and Me club. Do you want me to transfer Janey's elementary school club to someone else? Or do you want the extra hours? It's up to you."

"So I'd work every Saturday? I could do that. I need the money until I graduate. Then I'll be hopefully working full-time at some college." He twisted his lips into a sneer. "If someone hires me."

"I'm sure you'll get placed. And until you do, you're welcome to run all three Saturday book clubs. But if you need a break, just let me know, and I'll either step in or Shirley will." She thought about the book club breakdown. "Honestly, Shirley's probably going to be better at the younger club, not the teenager one. Anyway, we'll handle any time off you need."

"Sounds good." He nodded to the back. "Did our books come in for Saturday?"

"They're in the boxes by the back door. I've checked them into our system, so let's figure out a way to display them here by the register." Rarity followed him into the back room, and they both brought out a box. Then they got busy setting up the room and the store for Saturday's event. Working felt good. She might have been pontificating about the value of purpose to Caleb earlier, but she believed in it. Working didn't make the sadness disappear, but it did allow room for the happy memories to float up when you weren't paying attention. Those memories eased the pain of losing someone at least a little. And that and time was all you could count on while your heart healed.

When it was time to close up the shop, she sent Caleb home first, then she worked on closing the till. They were as ready as they could be for an inaugural book club. Now, all they needed was for kids to show up. This was the middle school group, and the group that Rarity had gotten the most RSVPs from both kids and parents. The book had pre-sold well, and she had hope that the club would start out strong. Next week, they'd open the elementary school club. And then the high school one. Then they'd have an event empty Saturday and start all over again the next week.

If the clubs took off, she'd need to replace Janey. Or ask Shirley to take the elementary group. Shirley had done well with the Mommy and Me group, but Rarity wasn't sure if she wanted more hours. The woman did a lot with the community and still saw George every night after dinner for a few hours. He had good days and bad days as far as remembering her and their life together, but his health was good, and he'd be around a long time. Rarity didn't want Shirley to wear herself out or not spend the time she wanted to with her husband. But on the other hand, it really wasn't Rarity's decision to make. She put a pin in it, as her mom used to say.

The door opened, and Archer came in. Again, Killer hurried over to greet him. Her dog loved a lot of people. If he didn't do the same when Rarity entered a room, she'd worry that he loved other people more than her. But he just had a lot of love to share.

"Hey, are you here to walk me home? I'm beginning to feel like I'm a kid who stayed too long at the library." She smiled as he picked Killer up and walked toward her.

"I know you can find your way home. Drew just wanted a friendly face to talk to yesterday, I think. He'd called me to see if I could have dinner, but I had that group. So I offered you up as a replacement." He leaned on the counter and gave Rarity a kiss.

"Now I really feel wanted." She closed the register and got her tote. "I heard that Sam had dinner with her brother."

"Have you talked to her today?" Archer put his arm around her as they walked out of the store.

"No. And it's not unusual, but we typically talk on the phone when we don't see each other. I'm beginning to think she's isolating herself." Rarity locked the shop door and looked over at Sam's already dark crystal shop. "I know he's family, but she can't shut the rest of us out of her life."

"Maybe she's afraid we'll think he's guilty."

Rarity looked at Archer in the gathering twilight. "I'm not sure he's not. Maybe it was an accident, but the hiker who found her didn't kill her. Drew told me that much last night. And it wasn't a suicide. I don't want to be on the other side from Sam, but she has to be questioning Marcus's innocence."

"I don't think she does or is. I think Sam's just supporting her brother. Good or bad, she's going to be there for him. He's family." Archer pulled her closer. "I know you don't like to go out on Thursday night, but I'm thinking we order in. You can swim while I finish up some work. Then we get dinner and watch something that meets both of our entertainment needs."

"So no zombies." Rarity squeezed his hand.

"Yep. And no made-for-television romances." He countered with his own Do Not Watch list item.

"Sounds like a plan."

Chapter 8

Rarity kept watching the clock, afraid she'd get busy with something and miss her closing time. She'd left Killer at home and driven her Mini Cooper to work. She'd had a sign up for the last few days, warning customers that she'd be open for just a few hours today and would return to normal hours Saturday. Which was probably why her shop was dead this morning. She probably should have just closed the shop for the day. She went back to reviewing the list of romance books Janey had made for her to order. She'd forgotten to order them this week, with everything going on. She was getting them into the system now, before she forgot again.

She smiled as she came across one of the books Janey had suggested. She'd read it a few years ago with the rest of the series. *A Discovery of Witches* was one of those books you weren't quite sure where to shelve as a bookstore. Romance, time travel, paranormal, historical. The series covered several genres. Rarity flipped through the pages until she found Janey's notes on how to set up the romance section. She'd done a lot of work there. She'd listed a ton of subgenres. Rarity wasn't sure if she'd divide the section into all these different subsections, but maybe she'd combine a few. She turned to the last page and found a to-do list Janey must have left with the work notes by accident.

Rarity read it, smiling at parts like "do dishes" and "schedule Whiskey's annual vet check." We all had normal life seep into our must-dos. But then there was "dinner with Marcus" with two little hearts. And "show him the quarry." Rarity started to put away the page, wondering if she should give it to Drew or not, when she realized she recognized another name on it. "Coffee with Caleb. Let him down easy."

Had Caleb and Janey been dating? Cara had said Janey hadn't wanted to do coffee with Caleb. Yet Rarity had seen the way he'd looked at Janey when he thought no one was looking. And he'd taken her death hard. She tucked the paper into her purse to give to Drew at the funeral. She was pretty sure he'd attend, if only to see who else showed up.

Rarity finished ordering the missing romance books and then ordered the books for next week's book club. She didn't want to over-order, but on the other hand, she didn't want to make a kid wait a week for the book either. She checked the sign-up list and ordered twenty more than that. Fingers crossed, it would be enough but not too many. Maybe after running this for a few months, she'd figure out what they needed. Rarity pulled out Shirley's list of upcoming books for the Mommy and Me class and ordered two weeks' worth of those as well. Her book bill this month would be crazy, but hopefully the books would sell, and she'd have a great month.

Hope, guess, maybe. She used those words a lot. The only time she knew how many of a book she'd sell was when a customer came in and ordered it. She guessed a lot in her job. Even just replacing the books that had sold wasn't a guarantee that the replacement book would sell anytime soon.

Working in marketing, she made up campaigns. She set up open houses and parties. Sometimes those were estimates of who would show up, but mostly, she produced a product. It worked or didn't. She went on. The bookstore business was more fluid than that. If two tour buses hit town in the same week, she might have a great week. Or with the same number of buses, she might not sell anything. It was all a crap shoot.

The bell rang over the doorway, and Shirley walked inside. She wore a black linen skirted suit. No hose and black flats. She had on a black hat with a small flat brim to finish the look. "Good morning. I didn't know if you wanted a ride to the funeral."

"I brought my car, but if you're wanting company, I'd love to ride with you." Rarity closed the laptop, put it into her tote, and stuffed it under the counter. "I'll just need to be dropped off here when we get back."

"That would be nice. The girls met up in Flagstaff earlier this morning and are doing some shopping. I didn't want to go through the outlet mall looking for more clothes. I have too many in my closet now that I never wear." Shirley glanced over at the fireplace and Killer's empty bed. "I take it you left the pup at home?"

"Yeah, and I'll pay for it tonight. I think I'm keeping the shop closed for the day and just going home after this." Rarity turned off the lights to the back room. "I wanted to talk to you anyway about next Saturday's book club. I didn't know if you wanted to help out with the elementary group or even just take it. I hate to overload Caleb right now."

"One Saturday a month?" Shirley asked as we moved outside. "I could do that. I really loved working with the group on Wednesday."

Rarity locked the door. "You did a great job."

As they moved toward Shirley's black Yukon, she saw Sam pull up at her shop. She waved, but her friend didn't see her as she unlocked the door and hurried inside. Rarity got into Shirley's car. "I wonder if Sam's going to the funeral."

Shirley peered over the hood. "There's a man in the passenger seat. Is that her brother?"

Rarity turned from watching the shop and stared into the car. It looked like Marcus. And if she wasn't wrong, it looked like there were two large suitcases in the back. Was Marcus moving out of the hotel and in with Sam? Or was he running away from Sedona?

Rarity picked up her phone and called Sam.

She saw her stop at the register and glance at the display. She picked it up. "Hi, Rarity. Sorry, this isn't a good time. Can I call you later?"

"Sure. I was just wondering if you were going to Flagstaff."

"Why would I be going to Flagstaff?"

Rarity could hear the tension in her friend's voice. "For Janey's funeral. I know things are weird right now, with Marcus and all. But Shirley's offered to drive."

"Oh, that, no, I'm home. I'm not feeling well," Sam lied as Rarity saw her taking money out of the till. "I'll call you later."

"Sam, don't do anything stupid," Rarity said, staring at her friend through the shop window, willing her to look over at Shirley's SUV.

"I don't know what you mean. Look, I've got to go." Sam hung up the phone and tucked it into her back pocket. Then she tucked the cash into her jeans and grabbed the shop keys. She left the shop and got into her car, driving off without looking back and seeing Shirley's car or the occupants.

"So she's driving herself?" Shirley put her seat belt on. "Shall we go?"

Rarity put her phone on her lap. What should she do? If she called Drew, Sam would be mad, and maybe it wasn't what it looked like, even though Sam lied to her. "You better know what you're doing, Sam."

"I'm sorry, do we follow her to the house?" Shirley turned toward Rarity.

Rarity shook her head. "Sorry, I was just talking to myself. Sam's not feeling well. Let's go to Flagstaff. We don't want to be late."

When they got to the church, they were able to park in the lot next door. Shirley glanced around when they got out of the car. "Maybe we're early."

"From what Janey said, she didn't have much family. Maybe this is it." Rarity pointed to a car she recognized. "Looks like Holly and Malia beat us here."

"We should get lunch at that tearoom across town before we go back. I'm sure Holly and Malia would enjoy it." Shirley chattered as they walked to the front door of the church. It had a small overhang in front, where a mortuary van was parked. "When George or I pass on to the heavenly gates, we're having our service in Sedona at our church. It's not huge, but it's just enough for what's left of our friends. Flagstaff's churches are all so big. It's like they're a corporation, not a gathering for parishioners. The more people who attend, the more money they raise, and the bigger church they build. It's a vicious cycle."

Rarity must have kept nodding at the right places, because Shirley kept talking. When they came into the vestibule, Holly and Malia hurried over to greet them.

"Hi, guys. Sorry if we're a little late." Rarity gave the women a quick smile.

"You're fine. We haven't been waiting long. There's a lot of people from the college here. Guys keep coming up and asking if we're in their English or History class. I think they're looking for dates." Holly shuddered. "I did my time in the college dating scene. You either meet your Prince Charming or you kiss a lot of toads. I'm done kissing toads."

Malia giggled. "I don't know. That last guy, Todd, he wasn't bad."

"He wanted to go get beer and chicken wings after the funeral." Holly lightly punched her friend in the arm. "You need to up your standards to wine and dinner, at least."

"College guys are all broke," Malia countered. "You have to find one with potential."

Holly looked over at Rarity. "Exactly my point."

"Well, if you aren't swept away by Mr. Right during the service, Shirley thought we could go over to the new tearoom for lunch after this. I've got some new information on the case," Rarity offered.

Malia nodded. "Me too. I guess I have been hanging out at the college a little too much this week, but I've learned a few things."

Drew stepped into their circle. "Now what would the four of you be talking about in this quiet corner?"

"How hard it is to get a date nowadays," Rarity quickly answered, smiling up at him.

"Do I need to tell Archer to up his game?" Drew said.

Jonathon stepped around his son. "I'm sure Rarity was just summarizing the discussion, not commenting on her own relationship. So good to see you all."

"Can you give my dad a ride back to Sedona after this? I need to make a few stops while I'm in Flagstaff."

Rarity turned to Shirley. "I rode with her."

"As long as you don't mind getting lunch with a bunch of women." Shirley gave Jonathon a quick hug. "Or should I say as long as Edith doesn't mind you getting lunch with a bunch of women."

"Edith won't mind a bit. Besides, how do I get the gossip she wants if I just hang out at Drew's house? My son is a little tight-lipped." Jonathon nodded a greeting to Holly and Malia.

"Only around an open investigation," Drew responded. Then he nodded to the chapel doors, where everyone seemed to be gathering. "I think it's time to start."

Rarity walked with the group to the ushers, who were handing out the memorial flyers. She glanced at the picture of Janey with what must have been Whiskey on the front. The big dog grinned at the camera almost as widely as Janey. She looked happy. The picture almost broke Rarity's heart.

As they sat, Rarity scanned the room. Caleb was there, sitting near the back. And, surprisingly, her new customer, Josh, who had said he was in town for business was in the front, in the second row. Or at least she thought it was him. She wished Archer was here to double-check her memory. Looking around, she didn't recognize anyone else. A woman in all black sat at the front, staring straight ahead. When she turned, Rarity swallowed a gasp. She had to be Trish Ford. She was Janey's double. Could they be twins? She leaned over to Drew, who had sat next to her. "Is Janey's sister a twin?"

He followed the direction of her gaze. "Wow. She looks like it. I only met Janey the one time, but even comparing her with the photo here, I would lay money on it."

Rarity sank back into the pew, lost in thoughts. Maybe whoever killed Janey had just gotten the wrong Ford sister. Drew met her gaze and nodded. He was thinking the same thing.

After the service, Rarity went up to Trish Ford and introduced herself. "I was Janey's boss in Sedona. At the bookstore."

"I didn't know she had started a job. With our trusts, we really don't need to work. I assumed Janey would be a perpetual student for the rest of her life. I didn't like the college scene, so I left as soon as I got my bachelor's." Trish glanced around the room at the younger crowd who'd attended. "College just isn't real life, you know?"

"Yes, I felt the same way. I couldn't wait to be done and get a real job. Janey never mentioned where you worked."

"I'm surprised Janey mentioned me at all. We didn't really get along. I decided to do charity work rather than toil for a dollar I didn't need. She said I just liked to go to parties." She glanced over to where the casket still sat. "I wish she'd gone to more parties in her life. Now, she can't."

"I think she liked her life," Rarity said, but then a man stepped in between them.

"Trish, it's time to go to the cemetery. You'll ride with me in the front car." The man put a hand on Trish's elbow, and Rarity saw a look of pain flash on the woman's face.

"Are you all right?" Rarity took a step forward, but Trish shook her head.

Trish looked over at the man, and disgust flashed on her face. But she hid it well, and a mask went back on before Rarity could make sense of the emotions she was watching.

"I'm sorry, I need to leave. Thank you for coming." Trish nodded at Rarity, then fell in step with the man, shrugging off his grasp.

Drew stood next to Rarity as they watched the two walk away. "So that's the sister. Did you ask if they were twins?"

Rarity shook her head. "No, but I found out something interesting. Janey had a trust. Trish is living and giving to charity from it, so it must be substantial."

"It looks like my investigator didn't go deep enough into Janey's family history. Anyway, Dad and the others are waiting for you outside by the cars. I guess Malia's starving." Drew walked with Rarity to the main entrance. "I've decided to go to the cemetery. Maybe I can talk with Trish there."

"Do you know who the man was who came to get her? I got the feeling she didn't like him much." Rarity turned her head to see if they were still in the chapel, but they'd gone out through a side door.

"Him I know. Allen Holbart. He's a local Flagstaff attorney. High-end. All of his clients have money. I think we need to look more closely at the Ford family and see where this trust came from. I'm learning there's a lot more going on here than we thought before."

As they reached the chapel doors, Rarity grabbed Drew's arm. "Do you think Marcus did this?"

"His past doesn't make it look good." Drew's face hardened. "But I haven't issued any charges yet."

"So you know about what happened when he was a kid." Rarity let out a sigh of relief. "I'm so glad Sam told you."

"He was a teenager, almost an adult, and no, Sam didn't tell me. Those things don't just drop off your record. Sam's not talking to me right now." Drew nodded to the group that was watching them talk. "Your friends are waiting."

Rarity thought about Sam grabbing the cash from her crystal shop. And the bags in the car. Sam was her friend. And she was driving off a cliff. "I think Sam's helping Marcus leave the area."

"I wondered if you knew." Drew shook his head. "Anyway, she's not now. I had someone watching him, and when they got to the airport, Marcus was taken into custody. I only have seventy-two hours to charge him but tell your friend she's lucky she's not in a jail cell next to her brother."

Drew walked away, leaving Rarity standing there, staring at him.

Holly came over and put an arm around her. "Are you okay?"

Rarity blinked tears away and nodded. "I'm fine. Sam's in big trouble, though. And I think Drew just broke up with her."

Chapter 9

Rarity didn't say much as they drove to the restaurant. Since Jonathon had joined them, they changed their destination and went to a local steak house that was on the highway on the way back to Sedona. Rarity let Jonathon ride shotgun, and as they traveled, she could feel Shirley's and Jonathon's attention on her. She didn't know what to say. Drew and Sam were perfect for each other. Or they had been, until Marcus got in the way. How could Sam let her love for her brother destroy her relationship with Drew?

Rarity didn't have any close family. Maybe some cousins in other states, but her parents had died young, after Rarity was on her own, and she was an only child. So the relationships she built were as tight as family, at least to her. And she couldn't see sacrificing one for the other. Drew had been Sam's first real relationship where they'd even started talking about marriage. She'd lived with people, or losers, as she liked to call them, before. But no one had talked about how to make a future together. Drew had. His family loved her, and they'd gone on a family vacation to Disneyland together a few months ago.

Then Marcus came back to Arizona, and Sam had lost all perspective. Rarity needed to talk to her, but she wasn't sure what she could say to make her see Drew's side.

"Ready for some lunch?" Jonathon asked as he opened the back door for her.

Rarity blinked and realized they were parked in front of the restaurant.

He took her hand and pulled her into a hug. "Look, I know you're worried about Drew and Sam, but sometimes things have to run their course."

She looked at Jonathon. "You don't think that this will kill their relationship?"

He put an arm around her as they walked to the restaurant entrance. "Sometimes couples need to learn what they mean to each other. If they let this break them up, they weren't meant to be. You have to be able to weather the storms as a couple. This is nothing compared to what could happen between them. Edith and I are praying for them and hopefully giving good counsel when they ask for advice. Besides that, we're keeping our opinions to ourselves."

"That's probably a good suggestion. I've been sitting here wondering how to get through to Sam. You're saying ignore the fact that Sam's ruining her future and just chat about other things." She went inside the restaurant and moved around a saddle that was on the side of the entry with a stand holding VIP sign-up forms. In all the time she'd lived here, this was the first time she'd been in this restaurant, so she didn't think she was their target customer. But maybe she should think about having some sort of program for the bookstore. She grabbed a flyer to review it.

"I didn't take you as a steak-and-potato girl," Jonathon said as Shirley went to the hostess stand to get them a table. "And yes, just stay out of the relationship issue. You can't win when you take one side or the other."

"This is research for the bookstore." Rarity tucked the flyer into her purse. "Drew's a good friend and a good man. I'd never jeopardize my friendship there. But I don't see many double dates in our immediate future."

"Probably not. But let's put that worry away. We've got a murder to solve. So what did you think of Janey's sister? She's pretty high-class. I never met Miss Janey, but I got the impression she was more down to earth."

"Exactly. I was shocked when she told me they both had a trust fund. I wonder if Janey had a will. I'd suspect so if the money was significant, and Trish implied that it was." Rarity followed the hostess and the group as they moved toward a large booth near the back. The restaurant was busy. "We can talk more after we order. I'd hate to be overheard."

Shirley settled in the booth and glanced around at the other tables. "Every time I come to Flagstaff lately, I'm shocked at how many people I don't know. George and I used to come into town at least once a week for an event or dinner. We had friends here. But so many people have moved to be closer to their adult children, I guess we're becoming isolated."

Malia, who was sitting next to Shirley, gave her a nudge with her shoulder. "You are not isolated. You have us. And we're not going to let you feel a bit lonely. You'll probably be trying to get us to leave you alone soon."

Shirley laughed and opened the menu. "I think you girls keep me around because of the treats I make."

"It's one of the positive benefits of being friends with you, but no, that's not the only reason," Holly said, then she pointed to the menu. "Does anyone want to share an appetizer? Or get two and split?"

"I might just get one for my dinner. They always give you so much food here," Shirley mused. "I wonder if they have a senior menu."

Malia turned Shirley's menu over for her. "It's on the back."

As they settled in for lunch, Rarity realized that Jonathon was right. Things happened between people. But if they were truly friends, or family, or even in love, they got through the mess and became stronger. This group had meshed because one of their members had been murdered. Something like that could have ended the book club before it got started. Instead, the group had banded together and solved not only one murder but a second one. It was beginning to be their thing.

Rarity wished people would stop killing other people so the group could go back to being just a book club.

"So what are you having?" Shirley asked, bringing her back to the conversation. The waitress was there, taking orders.

Rarity went with her standard order when she was out and it was available: salmon, salad, and a vegetable. She tried to eat healthy eighty percent of the time, and with the book club always tempting her with sweets, she had to eat clean at meals to counteract the cookies.

After the waitress had delivered their drinks and finished taking their orders, Shirley pulled out her notebook. "Any notes we need to make? I know Rarity talked to the sister, but anyone else pop out to the rest of us? I saw a man who has been hanging around Sedona for the last few weeks. I saw him at the Garnet last night when I met a friend for a late dinner."

"I think you mean Josh. He was there last night when I was waitressing," Malia added. "He's on a job here. He comes into the Garnet a lot for dinner. He's pretty chatty. He asked me out the other day, but I turned him down. I hate dating tourists. They always say they're going to call or write when they get home, but they don't."

Rarity smiled at her friend's assessment of Josh and the other tourists. She probably got hit on a lot, but Josh didn't seem to have a type, since he had flirted with her as well at the bookstore. "He came into the bookstore and bought several thrillers. Same story, in town for a couple of weeks, needed reading material. And a dinner date."

Malia turned her head fast toward Rarity. "He asked you out too?"

"Well, kind of. Archer was there, and he had just confirmed our standing Monday dinner. So then Josh, after Archer left, mentioned that he'd been thinking about asking me to dinner." Rarity shrugged. "Maybe he's just lonely."

Jonathon shook his head. "A man who's supposed to be working shouldn't have time to date while he's out of town. I'd worry that he had a wife and family back at home."

"And leave it to our token male to bring the conversation back to reality." Holly laughed. "I didn't like the guy who was sitting by the sister. He seemed creepy."

"He's her attorney." Rarity added what she knew. "And yeah, I got a creepy vibe too. But I only saw him for less than a minute."

"Well, at least the sister is another lead. Especially since they looked so much alike. I can't believe she didn't say anything about having a sister. Although we didn't talk much that Tuesday night when she visited." Holly cut into her steak. "Caleb seemed quiet today. He sat alone in the back. Do you think he's handling this okay? I guess if they just met, he'd be like us."

Rarity thought about the note that Janey had written with the romance novels. "According to her roommate, they hadn't just met. Janey was constantly shutting down any romance between the two of them." She remembered she hadn't given Drew the paper. She took it out of her purse and gave it to Jonathon. "Would you give this to Drew? I forgot when I saw him earlier."

Jonathon nodded and tucked the paper into his suit jacket without looking at it. Rarity admired his self-control. She would have at least asked what it was that she'd given him. Instead, the ex-cop just assumed it was important and none of his business.

"Okay, so we need to get together and talk about all this new information and see if it leads us somewhere. Do we want to wait for Tuesday? Or do you want to meet at my house Sunday afternoon?" Rarity pushed her salmon around with her fork.

"I can be there after church." Shirley raised her hand. "Shall I bring something to eat?"

"Let's do a potluck," Holly said. "That way I can stop at the Garnet and get a chicken bucket."

"I'll bring a side and a dessert," Shirley volunteered.

"I make a mean salad," Jonathon offered. "And I'll bring a variety of dressings."

"Okay, the rest of us can just fill in things," Rarity said. She'd talk to Archer and see what they could make on Saturday after work. "So for now, let's just enjoy this lunch and the company. I'm feeling very grateful for this group today, especially after that service."

The group held up their cups, and Jonathon toasted. "To The Next Chapter's Tuesday night sleuthers' club. I'm so glad you let me crash your party."

When she got home, it wasn't long before Archer knocked on her door. "Hey, I know we didn't have plans, but I've been thinking about you. Can we do something tonight?"

"As long as dinner's here at home and I don't have to get out of my yoga pants, I'm up for it. The funeral was nice, but going to those things always makes me a little emotional."

"I'll cook. We can talk and just relax. I had a crazy week, and tomorrow's hike is going to be early and long. So I could use a little break." Archer came in and saw Killer still on his bed with his back turned to the humans. "I take it he's still mad he was left behind today?"

"He's been there since I got home, except for the quick visit out to the potty pad." Rarity went over to the couch and sank into it. "Maybe he'll talk to you."

"Just give him some time. He needs to express his outrage for being left behind." Archer leaned over and kissed her. "Anything special you want, or can I rummage through your kitchen?"

"Rummage away. And while you're there, think of something we can make for a Tuesday night potluck on Sunday." She grabbed the remote and turned on a favorite movie to watch while Archer cooked.

"Wait, for Tuesday or for Sunday?" Archer held open the refrigerator door and looked back at her. "I'm confused."

"We're having a sleuthing meeting Sunday afternoon with a potluck. Not sure that's the way Sherlock Holmes would have done it, but we're a unique group." Rarity curled her feet under her. "Let me know if you want me to chop or anything."

"You chop things into too big of pieces. I can do this." He started pulling out ingredients. "What about a white chicken chili for Sunday? That way we can make it on Saturday, and all you have to do is put it in a Crock-Pot early on Sunday. I'd come and set it up, but I've got a private group hike for a bunch of lawyers. They're doing a retreat, so I have three different private hikes set up for next week starting on Sunday."

"Sounds like a busy and profitable week." She had a book club tomorrow that Caleb was running. Shirley wanted to at least help with the one next week. And now she had a weekly Mommy and Me group as well as the normal Tuesday night book club meeting. "I only have Monday, Thursday, and Friday free next week. I think I overbooked this week."

"You're just getting into the feel of the book clubs. And you think you have to be there for everything. You can use that time that others are there running your clubs to do other work tasks. Me, I lock up the office if I'm out on a tour." Archer had had an assistant, but she'd moved away a few months ago. And he hadn't replaced her.

"I didn't expect to lose someone I just hired. Then Darby goes off to another country, so I can't even call her in for a few hours a week. Caleb's nice, but I haven't seen him in action yet. I'll loosen the reins soon, but for now, yes, I have to be there. It's my shop." Rarity closed her eyes and felt the weight of Killer, who'd just jumped up on the couch and into her lap. She opened them, and he was staring at her. He licked her cheek, then cuddled up to go back to sleep. "Okay, fine, my dog says I'm overreacting too. Is there a beer in the fridge? I'd get up to get it, but Killer just cuddled in."

"Can't disturb the dog." Archer put down the knife and got Rarity a bottle. "You'll be fine. Are you going to hire someone else? Or just see how Shirley does? I think she'll surprise you."

"She was wonderful. That's not a surprise at all. I just don't want to barge in on her retirement." Rarity took a sip of the beer and set the bottle down. "And then there's the George factor."

"I think Shirley having something to do besides the George factor is a good thing. She needs to be around people. To be needed." He returned to the kitchen. "We're having a potato, cabbage, and Italian sausage hash. Any issues?"

"Not a one." She leaned back. "I met Janey's sister today. I think they were twins."

"Is she nice?" Archer continued chopping the vegetables.

"I wouldn't say nice. Classy. Put together. Not warm and friendly like Janey was. But again, I did meet her at a funeral. Maybe she was just sad." Rarity stroked Killer's back. "I don't have any siblings. What about you?"

"I have a brother. He lives in New York and works on Wall Street. Sometimes it's hard to keep up with what he's doing since I don't understand finance, but he's my parents' pride and joy." He met her gaze. "I'm the disappointment."

"Why? You run your own business. You almost own the building. You're very well known in hiking circles. You're such an amazing cook that you probably could be a chef. How on earth can you be a disappointment?"

He shrugged, going back to the chopping. "I'm not a doctor, lawyer, or banker. My folks see a profession as the important part of working. I take people on hikes. That's a hobby, not a job. At least that's what my dad said last year at Thanksgiving."

"That's horrible. You should be able to be who you want to be, not what your parents expect you to be. You're not in jail or living on the streets. That should count for something." She gave Killer a kiss, then stood, setting him down on the floor. She moved into the kitchen to sit at the island, where Archer was making dinner. "Next time he says something like that, you have him call me."

"Or you could just go home with me for Thanksgiving," Archer suggested. "I know we weren't there relationship-wise last year, but I think we're at that place this year."

"I hate to leave the gang here alone." Rarity had assumed she'd host Thanksgiving this year. "Shirley doesn't like to leave George to go visit her kids that long."

"If you don't want to meet the folks, that's fine." Archer put a hand up on his forehead. "I'll just say you're too busy."

Rarity laughed and took a piece of raw cabbage from the pile. She popped it in her mouth. "Let's just think about it. I'll put out some feelers to see where the others are going to be for the holidays, and if I think I can get away, I'll let you know."

"You're a good friend." He turned on the heat and started frying the potatoes, seasoning as he went.

"I want to be a good girlfriend as well, but I just don't want to leave anyone hanging for the holidays." Rarity came around the island and gave him a hug. "But thanks for asking me."

"I'm asking you to be my protector in front of my family. I think I'm the one who should be thanking you for even considering the job." He used a wooden spoon to stir the potatoes as he held her with the other arm. "Of course, Killer would be welcome as well."

"Where I go, he goes. It's a house rule." Rarity looked down at the little Yorkie, who was watching them to make sure they didn't drop anything. "Isn't it, buddy?"

Killer barked his agreement and politely didn't point out the fact that he'd been left home earlier that day.

Chapter 10

Saturday afternoon, the bookstore was a madhouse. Caleb was trying to wrangle the kids over to the club area so they could start the discussion of the book, but several were still in line with their parents, reading as they waited for their turn to check out.

Finally, Rarity made an announcement. "Kids who are still in line, take your book and go over to the fireplace and find a place to sit. Parents, stay here in line, and I'll use a store copy to check you out. And you might want to pick up the next club read while you're here."

The kids all made a dash to the fireplace, except one girl who was still in line, clutching the book.

Rarity met her gaze. "Your folks can stand in line for you."

The girl's face turned red, and she mumbled, "My mom's working. I've got the money for the book."

Rarity glanced at the woman who was next in line, silently asking her for permission to move the child forward. She nodded.

"Come on up here, and we'll get you over to the club before you miss anything."

The girl slowly moved through the space the other parents had made for her. She put the book and a stack of ones on the counter. Rarity rang up the book and counted out the money. The girl was a dollar and forty-two cents short.

Rarity keyed in the full amount and made a note to add the rest later, when the girl wasn't around. She shut the register and handed the girl a bag, where she'd put the book and the receipt. She met the child's eyes. "Next week, come by when you can, and we'll get you set up with the next book."

She blushed. "I'm not sure I'll be able to make enough money babysitting to buy a book a month."

"Then we'll figure something out. Maybe you could help me with Killer in exchange for your book costs." She handed the girl one of her cards. "Just drop by next week, and we'll make a plan. What's your name?"

"Amy." The girl took the card and stared at it. "Thank you."

"No, thank *you*. I've been looking for some help around here. Now go get settled for the book club. I think Caleb's about to start." Rarity smiled as the girl hurried to sit on the floor and watch Caleb.

The woman who'd been next bought the current book and the next for her son. Then she put a third book on her stack. It was a second copy of the next club pick. "I'll get next week's book for Amy. That was nice what you did. I'd like to keep her reading too."

"Thank you. I'll pull her aside and give it to her before she leaves." Rarity rang up the charges and put Amy's book under the counter.

"Just don't tell her who bought it. I'd rather stay anonymous. She's a smart girl and works hard. Her mom works at the diner, and she's single. I'm sure it's tough." She nodded toward the book club area, where Caleb had started talking about the book. "I'm so glad you opened up something for the kids. I've been trying to get Jake here to pick something out to read with little success. But then his best friend mentioned he was coming today, and he's all 'let's go.' It's all about the peers at this age, right?"

Rarity handed her back the credit card. "Thanks again for getting Amy's book."

"I saw you shortchanged your register. It's the least I could do." The woman nodded toward the other side of the building. "Is your romance section over there? I need a few books for Mommy time."

Rarity pointed her toward the right section and turned to the next person. This woman had a twenty-dollar bill out as well as her credit card. "Sunny needs both books, and put this away for when someone else needs a book. I'll do my part too."

By the time she'd finished ringing up all the kids' books, Rarity had an envelope with over a hundred dollars and a few business cards promising to buy a book when she needed more money. She was shocked at the community's support of one little girl's reading habit. And after they'd gotten their kids' books taken care of, many of the parents bought something else to keep busy while they waited. Several moms went out to the front to sit on benches near the shop to read. Others found little nooks and crannies to sit on the floor and read.

Rarity felt blessed for the community support. And her week was going to be amazing with the books she'd sold. She'd originally assumed she was mostly going to be serving the tourist crowd that came to Sedona. Today's club and Wednesday's class had taught her different. She had a strong community here that was willing to support the store. She just needed to give them a reason to do it.

As the book club was going, another woman came inside the bookstore. Looking around, she spied Rarity sneaking in some ordering while everyone was busy. She hurried over. "Sorry to bother you, but do you know when the crystal shop is reopening? I've been trying to get a necklace I saw last week, and we're leaving next Friday."

"She's not open today?" Rarity craned her neck to try to see Sam's lights, but as the woman had said, the shop looked dark. Rarity realized she hadn't seen or spoken to Sam since she'd seen her trying to sneak Marcus out of town on Friday. "Well, I guess not. She had a family emergency. Let me call and see if she's going to open later today."

Rarity used her cell to call Sam, but no one picked up. She left a brief message about a customer needing to buy something and that she'd have their contact information here at the store. "Can I get your contact information so I can give it to her?"

The woman smiled and gave Rarity a business card. "That's my cell, so she can reach me anytime. I really need that necklace. It's for my mother-in-law's birthday next weekend. She's really picky, and this will be perfect. I knew I should have grabbed it when I saw it."

"I'm sure I'll talk to her soon." Rarity wasn't really sure, but she didn't want to give this woman the idea that Sam was flighty, either.

The store cleared out quickly once the book club was over. A few kids brought their parents over to buy the next in the series, but after that rush was over, she helped Caleb clean up after the event. "So what did you think? Did you like running the club?"

Caleb nodded, his grin as big as some of the participants' had been as they left with several books in their arms. "I can't believe how much fun it was to talk about the book with the kids. They were even able to give me examples of when they felt the same way as the main character. I only wish Janey had been here to see it. She would have loved talking with them."

Rarity put a hand on his shoulder. "I bet she would have. But you did an amazing job. I have someone coming in next week for the elementary-aged club, but if you want to come and help, that would be awesome."

"Several of the kids said their little brother or sister were planning on coming and asked if I'd be here. I'd love to come if it doesn't mess with your staff hours."

"If next Saturday is even close to being this big, we'll need you." Rarity bit into one of the few cookies left over. "I think I need to order more treats too. Annie's is going to love us."

After Caleb left, she took Killer out front for a potty break. Sam's shop was still dark, and she hadn't returned Rarity's call. She took her cell from her pocket and dialed Sam's number again. "Hey, it's just me. I'm wondering what's going on. Are you okay? Do you need anything? The group is getting together tomorrow to talk about what we learned this week on Janey's murder. Come by early, and we can talk. And don't forget to get that woman's number. She really wants a necklace. Anyway, I'll get you..." The message had been too long, and she'd been cut off. She tucked her phone away and looked down at Killer. "Ready to go inside?"

He barked and went to the door to wait for her to open it. Dogs were so much easier to understand than humans. She hoped Sam was all right. She knew Drew and Sam had fought, but that shouldn't mean that she'd stop calling Rarity.

Archer showed up right at five and helped her close the bookstore. "I wanted to come by during the book club, but I got slammed with customers right then. I must have handed out fifty or more of your bookmarks."

Rarity had seen the hikers show up after the book club ended, and she'd sold a lot of the suggested hiking books as well as several popular fiction books due to Archer's referrals. "You probably need some more, then. I definitely need to reorder your hiking books. Anything new I should add to the list?"

They chatted for a while, then he clicked Killer's lead onto his collar. "Do you think Killer would mind if we headed over to the Garnet for dinner? I know I need to make white chili for your thing tomorrow, but I thought we'd eat out tonight. I have a reservation out on the deck, and it's cool enough that we shouldn't roast."

"I'd love to." Rarity tucked a bottle of water and a plastic dish into her tote. "Killer should be fine. And after Friday, I think he'd appreciate going rather than staying home by himself."

"He runs your social calendar, you know." Archer held his hand out for her bag, and she gave it to him as she turned off the lights and locked the doors.

"I know, but he's so cute. I hate to have him mad at me."

"There are these places called pet spas, and they have doggie day care as well as overnight boarding," Archer said as they walked toward the restaurant.

"I want to be the one who Killer relies on for his care. He's sensitive about me leaving because of what happened to Martha. I'm sure he's still waiting for her to show up and take him home." Rarity wondered what her dog thought about the loss of his first owner. Did he still mourn? Did he wonder if living with Rarity was temporary too? And did he worry about her not coming back when Rarity left him alone? "He's probably been traumatized."

Archer glanced down at Killer, who was prancing in front of them, checking each smell as it came to him. "Yeah, he looks upset."

"Stop teasing. I know he's fine now, but how do I know he's fine when I leave?" Rarity took Archer's arm in hers and leaned closer. "He could cry the whole time."

"You could get a nanny cam to watch him while you're gone. Or a trail cam that snaps pictures when it sees movement. We'd have to install it at floor level since he's so tiny."

"Height challenged," Rarity clarified. "He's sensitive about his size."

"Now you're just messing with me." Archer checked in with the hostess and pointed to a table near the edge of the outdoor section. "We're over there."

As they settled in and ordered, he sipped his beer. "Tell me about your new book club. This was the middle schoolers, right?"

She told him about the day, how well Caleb did with the kids, and the random act of kindness for Amy, the little girl whose mother had been working.

"I think that's Joni's kid. She usually has her at a table in Carole's after school unless it's busy. Then I suspect the kid hangs out in the office in the back. Joni's a hard worker. Her husband died when she was pregnant with Amy, so it's always been just the two of them. The town helps when she lets us. Two years ago, we did a fundraiser for a new roof on her house."

"So the parents who donated probably knew the story about the family."

Archer nodded. "More than likely. And Amy's a smart kid. Keeping her involved in school means that she'll probably go to college and invent something huge."

"I should let her mom know that Amy can hang out at the bookstore while she works if she'd like." Rarity bit into a French fry as she thought. "I wanted to be more active in the community. And the bookstore is closer than the town library out on the highway."

"I bet she'd take you up on it. Let's go to Carole's soon for dinner, and I'll introduce you to Joni." He cut his steak and took a bite. "So work was good. Why are you down in the dumps? It can't be Amy."

"No, it's Sam. She didn't open her shop, and she's not returning my calls. I haven't talked to her since, what, Thursday? This isn't like her." She bit into a piece of the trout she'd ordered.

"She hasn't been going through a time where her brother's being accused of murder before." Archer met her gaze, then set his fork down. "Wait, what aren't you saying? Did Marcus kill someone before?"

She shook her head. "I don't know. All I know is he was accused, and the woman was found at a quarry, just like Janey. I guess they'd been going out. He wasn't charged, or wasn't found guilty anyway. I don't know all the facts. And Sam's going to kill me because I told you."

Archer took another bite and thought about the information. "I bet that's why Sam's so involved in trying to prove Marcus didn't do it. She feels like if he was charged once, he could be again and not be as lucky."

"What are we going to do?" Rarity set her fork down and took a sip of her beer.

"Did you tell her that the sleuthers' club is getting together tomorrow?" Archer asked.

Rarity nodded. "I left her a message. I'm sure Shirley tried to call too. Maybe she got through."

"Call Shirley, Malia, and Holly tonight and ask them all to call her. If nothing else, she'll know that they're calling about the club. Maybe one of you will get through to her." Archer pointed to her dinner. "Eat. That cost me one hiker sign-up, and you're not letting it go to waste. Starving children in China and all."

"Are you sure there really are starving children in China? Maybe you should do some research before you make broad statements like that." She picked the fork back up. No matter where kids were actually starving, she did owe it to Archer to eat the food she'd ordered. Otherwise, she could have refused the invitation. "Anyway, I just miss my friend."

"Sam will come around, you know that. Sometimes it takes a bit for people to see the whole picture and not just their little corner."

Rarity hoped Archer was right. Maybe she was just being too sensitive of Sam not calling her back or picking up her calls. Maybe it had nothing to do with her. She put her worry about Sam aside and tried to enjoy dinner out with Archer. "So how was your day?"

After dinner, when they got to the house, Archer started pulling out the ingredients for the chili. "Go swim. I'll get this started. Mind if I turn on the television?"

"I'll get the remote, and you can choose what you want. I need to clear my head." She leaned down and gave Killer a head pat. "You make sure Archer doesn't steal the family jewels."

"You have family jewels? I was going to go after the silverware." He took the remote from her and turned on a sports channel. "I'm behind on college football scores since I was swamped today."

"You make my choice to swim so easy." She gave him a kiss, then went to change. The pool was chilly, but she loved the feel of the water against her skin. She did her laps, then realized Archer was at the front door, talking to someone. She leaned back in the water, not wanting to deal with reality or anyone who needed something. Besides, it was probably a local kid looking to sell popcorn or cookies. She did one last cooldown lap, then grabbed her towel, climbed out of the pool, and dried off.

By the time she got in the house, Archer was back in the kitchen.

"That smells amazing."

"I know. It's an easy recipe too. I'll show you sometime. I think your group will love it." He nodded to the door. "Terrance is home. He came by to thank you for gathering his papers, so I gave him the box. He thinks it's a new hat for one of his local clubs."

"Well, I hope so. I guess if it was a bomb, it would have gone off in my house days ago." She moved to the bedroom. "I'm going to change."

The doorbell rang when she was in the bedroom. When she came out, Terrance was in her living room, looking shaken.

She looked between him and Archer, who had just hung up the phone. "What's going on?"

"It wasn't a hat. It was a finger. A human finger. And there was a note." Archer held up the phone. "I've called Drew, and he's on his way."

"Oh no. Terrance, I'm so sorry. Do you know anyone who's missing?"

Terrance looked up at her and took her hand, pulling her down to sit on the couch with him. "Darling girl, the note was addressed to you. They dropped the box off at the wrong house."

Chapter 11

Drew showed up and opened the box. He read the note, put it into a plastic bag, and wrote something on the front. Then he pulled a kitchen chair over to where Rarity still sat with Terrance. Killer was curled on her lap.

Drew leaned toward her. "Hey, how are you?"

"I was all relaxed and ready for a movie. Now, I'm just confused. What's going on, Drew?" She scooted closer to the edge of the couch. "Why would someone send me a finger? And whose finger is it?"

"Nobody's. At least that's my guess. I think it's made of rubber. The *why* is pretty clear from the note. They think you're too involved in the investigation. I've warned you before, this sleuthing club was going to get you in trouble. Now, it's possible the person is from out of town, since they left it on Terrance's doorstep rather than yours. I guess I should have looked at it closer when we found it. Did Killer show any interest in the package when you had it here at the house?"

"Nothing. If it was a real finger, he would have smelled the decay, right? Heck, I should have smelled the decay." She took a sip of the coffee Archer had made after he'd called Drew.

"Yeah, that's another reason I'm pretty sure it's fake." He rubbed a hand over his crew cut. "But if they were from out of town, how would they have known about the sleuthing club?"

"I don't know." Rarity leaned back into the couch.

"And with that, I'm heading back home. If you want to question me more, I'll be up for a few more hours. I haven't unpacked or started laundry yet." Terrance patted Rarity on the shoulder. "Hang in there. We'll find out who sent this to you and why. They can't be all that smart since they left it at my door instead of yours."

After Terrance left, Drew refilled his coffee cup. "I'm sure it's someone who doesn't live here. Anyone in town knows where you live. It's not a secret."

"What did the note say?" Rarity asked.

Drew and Archer exchanged a look.

"Oh, no. We're not playing the 'take care of Rarity' game. Not tonight. What did it say?" she pushed.

Drew got up, took the bag off the table, and handed it to her. "The note says that you should stay out of Janey's murder case, or you'll be the one missing a finger. They don't want you dead. Just something to warn you off."

"Well, that's comforting." She read the note, then handed it back to Drew. Then she glanced over at Archer. "Do I need to finish the chili?"

"Nope, it's done. I'm just letting it cool. Then it needs to go into a plastic container, and it's ready for tomorrow. Just put it in the Crock-Pot two hours before you want to serve, and you're done." Archer explained the process.

"Are you having a party without me?" Drew asked.

"I'm sure you know that the sleuthers' club is coming over here for a meeting. And a potluck, since your dad is bringing a salad," she added. "Hey, have you heard from Sam? She's not returning my calls."

"She's home with her brother. The DA allowed me to put a tail on him, so I get reports every time they leave the house. I wish she'd call you. I know she's not likely to talk to me until this is all finished. And who even knows about then." He stood and put the chair back at the table. "I'm heading home with your package. I don't think you need to worry, but maybe Archer should stay over for a few nights."

"And what if I don't want him to stay over?" Rarity stood and followed Drew to the table. "He can't be here tomorrow. He has a hike. I'm not letting him turn down work to babysit me."

"My dad will come early and stay with you. He might as well be useful if he wants to be involved in this. So, Archer at night, my dad during the day, until we catch this guy." He juggled the box. "Rarity, this threat changes things. I don't want you to be alone. I couldn't live with myself if someone hurt you because I didn't take this threat seriously. Even though it seems silly."

"Okay." She took her cup to the sink.

Drew and Archer exchanged looks, and Rarity almost laughed. They'd been expecting more of an argument from her. Drew nodded and headed to the door. "Okay, then. I'll talk to you as soon as we know something about this box or who might have sent it."

"Sounds great. Thanks for coming over, Drew." She waited for him to leave and then shut the door and locked it. She turned to Archer. "Good thing you brought over an extra set of clothes last month."

"I really wasn't counting on using the clothes due to homicidal maniac alerts." He put his arms around her. "Are you sure you're okay? That had to be quite a shock."

"Just a little odd. Someone knows the area enough to know that the book club is looking into Janey's death but doesn't know what house I live in?" She rinsed some dishes that Archer had used to make the chili and put them into the dishwasher.

"I can clean up after myself." Archer took a spoon out and tasted the chili. "I think it's cool enough to put away. Do you have a large plastic container?"

They dug through her leftover containers and found one big enough. Then she looked at Archer. "I'm going to bed."

"My morning starts a little later tomorrow, so I'm staying up and watching the rest of a game. Mind if I sleep on the couch?"

"You know where the linens are." She gave him a hug and leaned into him a little longer, trying to calm her racing heart. "I don't care what his motivations are, this is just mean."

"He's trying to scare you." Archer rubbed her back.

She didn't lift her head off his chest when she answered, "He's doing a good job."

* * * *

The next morning, she woke to the smell of bacon. She hurried and got dressed and went out to the kitchen, where Archer was making omelets.

He poured a cup of coffee and set it on the island for her. "We're going to have to go to the store. You don't have any cookies or other necessities."

"Sorry, I didn't realize I was having a houseguest until last night. Do you want to run to Flagstaff tonight? After your hike and my club?"

"Sure. I'll pack a bag at the apartment, too, so I'm ready for a few days." He smiled at her. "It's going to be okay. Drew's going to find the guy."

"So you don't think it's Marcus?"

He frowned as he turned back to check on the eggs. "What do you mean?"

"You said 'find the guy.' He knows who and where Marcus is, so you think someone else killed Janey?" She sipped her coffee. "Why? What do you know?"

"The hiker who found the body. I talked to him last week at the shop. He said he ran into Marcus on the way out. Marcus told him that his girlfriend was at the quarry and asked if he would look out for her." Archer shrugged. "I know it doesn't mean he didn't kill Janey, but if he had, why would he send someone directly to the quarry to look for her?"

"Yeah, that's not logical." She pointed to the stove. "Anything I can do to help?"

"I've got this. You get ready for your group. I take it they're showing up around twelve thirty?"

"Yeah, Shirley wanted to go to service, so we just set it later. I can hang out here by myself if you have to leave before Jonathon arrives."

"Not going to happen. Besides, he called a few minutes ago. He'll be here by seven thirty so I can meet my group at eight." He slid the finished omelet onto a plate. "Here you go. Eat it while it's hot."

"You know, I might just keep you after this is all over. I like being served breakfast at home." She smiled as she took the plate from him.

"It's Sunday. Monday mornings are much more hectic." He poured more eggs into the pan and got the other ingredients ready. "By the way, Killer went out with me about thirty minutes ago. And I put the bedding away in the linen closet, so there won't be questions from your group about me staying over."

"Protecting my honor?" She took a bite of the omelet.

He laughed and shook his head. "Protecting me from all the 'when are you going to marry the girl' questions."

"Self-preservation. I like that in a man."

He turned back to the stove. "Whatever. Just get busy eating. I don't want you sitting here eating when your group arrives."

The phone rang, and she picked it up. "Hey, Drew, how are things?"

"Busy. I'm sending some information from Janey's sister over with my dad. Do you think one of your group members could verify her alibi? I haven't been able to reach the guy she says she was with during the time Janey was killed."

"Sure. But why?"

Drew sighed. "It's a day spa, and he's her hairdresser. His name is Roger Kamp. I was wondering if you could go visit the spa to make sure she was there. I know the last time I sent you into a spa, you were nearly killed, but I'm sure this one's on the up and up. Mom used to go to the same place, and I think so did Sam."

"So you'd call Sam, but she doesn't want to talk to you right now. And now that the killer seems to be after me, I might have some vested interest?"

He paused. "Something like that. Is Archer still there, or did you run him off?"

"Hey now, he actually likes me. Did you want to talk to him?" I looked over, and Archer was putting his omelet on a plate.

"No, I just wanted to make sure you weren't alone. I mean, that you and Killer weren't alone. You know I love that dog," Drew teased her. "Dad's on his way over now. I know you feel like this is overkill, but I don't want anything to happen to you, okay?"

"Drew knows best." But Rarity smiled when she said it. "Look, I've got to get busy. If you talk to Sam, tell her to call me. I'm getting worried."

"I know, Rarity. So am I." Drew sighed. "Tell Archer thanks."

"I will." Rarity hung up the phone and relayed Drew's message. "He's asking me to get involved. That's when I know he's conflicted on a case. And I know Marcus isn't getting out of his focus anytime soon."

"If you were to guess right now who killed Janey, do you have an answer?" Archer took his omelet over to the table with a full cup of coffee.

She thought about his question. "No. And that worries me. I have plenty of people I think might have. Marcus, Janey's sister, that creepy lawyer. But if I was under oath, I couldn't say yes or no to any of them."

Maybe talking with the sleuthers' club would help narrow down at least one suspect that might also be the one sending her a fake finger with a warning she was busy ignoring.

* * * *

Sunday's meeting went off without a hitch, but no one had added an additional suspect to the list. Everyone gave their report and updated their books. Then they got ready to eat. Sam didn't come to the meeting.

Shirley came into the kitchen to help pull out plates and bowls. "We could have used paper. That way you wouldn't have to do dishes."

"I like doing dishes. It helps me think." Rarity pulled out silverware and napkins. "Okay, guys, everything's out. Come grab some food."

The line started, but Rarity stayed on the edge, watching her friends. She dug her phone out of her pocket and called Sam, again. When she got her voice mail, again, she left a message. "Hey, just letting you know we're eating now if you're hungry. I'm worried about you."

She put her phone on the foyer table by her purse, just in case Sam actually called. Then Shirley handed her a plate. "I was waiting for everyone to get through the line."

"And they have. So come on, fill your plate. I know you're worried about Sam, but not eating doesn't solve anything. Of course, I've never tried the technique, but you know what I mean." Shirley put an arm around Rarity, and they walked together back to the kitchen. "Oh, I heard your Saturday book club went amazing. All the parents at my church loved Caleb, by the way. I think he's going to be a keeper."

"Me too." Rarity started to fill her plate, and her stomach growled at the smells. Okay, so she was hungry. She sat down at the table next to Jonathon. "Hey, I hope you're being paid market rate to be my babysitter."

"Not a babysitter. Drew's just concerned about the special delivery you got earlier. Someone knows we're looking into this murder, and they think if they scare you, we'll stop looking." Jonathon took a bite of the chicken. "It's just the game. This killer has to be someone who wants to stay around in the area and not be caught. So it rules out any random tourists or drive-through suspects."

"Does it?" Rarity liked hearing Jonathon's logic, since he'd been with the police for years. He was their logical, systematic voice to the group. "But if it was a local, wouldn't they know my house versus Terrance's?"

Jonathon ate some of Shirley's scalloped potatoes, then went back for a second bite before answering. "Honestly, you're right. There is that little hiccup in my analysis. But it could have been a local who wanted to delay you finding the box. So they put it on Terrance's porch, knowing he was out of town and he'd get it to you."

"Okay, I'm following your logic. But why did they want to delay the package? What were they waiting for? The funeral?"

Jonathon set down his fork. "Sometimes killers don't make sense. They get something in their heads, and they just do it. You're assuming we're working with a logical or even rational mind."

"The world's crazy, and this is just one more bizarre act?" Rarity shook her head. "I can't leave it at that. I need to know who killed Janey. She was on my watch. I brought her to Sedona to work. I invited her to the party where she met Marcus. If this is him, or about him, I started that chain reaction in motion."

"So if it was about Janey and Marcus, without us thinking Marcus did it, who else would care?"

Rarity sipped her water. "Someone who wanted Janey to his or herself. If Marcus was seen as the disruptor, maybe someone followed her to the quarry, and when Marcus left, they fought, and Janey was killed."

"It's a short window. Marcus left and ran into the hiker on the trail. Then the hiker found her body, what, thirty minutes later?" Jonathon stood and grabbed another piece of chicken and put it on his plate. "I know Sam's not going to like this, but my money's still on Marcus. And I think Drew's thinking the same thing."

"He asked me to check out Janey's sister's alibi. Do you want to drive into Flagstaff with me tomorrow? I'd ask Archer, but he's working with that corporate group for the next few days." Rarity took another bite of her dinner, trying to not think of death and Marcus and Sam. She should be focusing on Janey. Why had she been killed? If she found the why, she'd find the killer.

"I'm here to serve. At least until sometime next week. Edith and I were invited to a party in a couple of weeks, and she hates to go to those things alone." He nodded to her plate. "Eat. We'll figure this out. I'll buy milkshakes for the drive back to Sedona. Just don't tell Edith. She thinks I'm not going to fit into my suit soon."

"I don't know. I don't want Edith to be mad at me." Rarity finished eating as she watched her friends, minus a few, enjoy their meal and conversation. Thank goodness she'd moved to Sedona. Otherwise, she'd be spending this afternoon doing laundry, watching movies, and working on her latest project. Even when Kevin had been in her life, she'd spent most of her free time alone. He'd been too busy with his work, golf, and friends to spend time with her, except of course, at night. She'd felt lonely a lot then. Now, all she had to do was step outside and chat with her neighbor if she needed adult, non-canine companionship.

After everyone finished eating, Rarity boxed up four plates of food. When Jonathon looked at her, she shrugged. "Archer will be here soon. And I've got a visit to make."

Holly and Malia left first, after the rest of the food had been repackaged and divided between the people who wanted leftovers. Shirley wanted to make sure everyone had food before they left. Jonathon put his food into the fridge so he could take it home to Drew for their dinner. Shirley was the only one who didn't take any leftovers.

When Rarity asked, she shrugged. "I like cooking. And I've got to go spend some time with George. He's not fond of cold fried chicken. Can you imagine? So we never went on a picnic, even with the kids. He had us eat at home either before or after. Or on rare occasions, we'd stop at a drive-in. The kids would be in heaven."

Soon, it was just Rarity and Jonathon. He grabbed Killer's leash. "Do you have a bag for those dinners?"

"You want to come with me?" Rarity tucked enough food for two into a canvas bag and grabbed her phone and house keys.

"I'm not letting you go alone." Jonathon stood at the door with Killer, waiting.

Chapter 12

Rarity and Jonathon didn't talk much as they walked the few blocks over to Sam's house. Her car was in the driveway, and there were lights on in the living room. Rarity glanced over at Jonathon, who was standing behind her on the steps. "Here goes nothing."

"Rarity, Sam loves you. You two are more like sisters than friends. So just play it cool. Don't ask about Marcus, just offer the food. Maybe she'll invite us in." Jonathon smiled. "It's just a Sunday afternoon visit. That's all."

Of course, it wasn't just a Sunday afternoon visit. Sam had been ignoring all of them, trying to protect her brother. But if he didn't do it, Drew wasn't going to charge him. Sam had to know that. Rarity realized she kept saying that, yet Marcus was still on the suspect list. She shook off her doubts and knocked on the door.

Sam opened the door, dressed in gray sweats. Her hair wasn't brushed, and she looked like she'd been sleeping. "Oh, hey. Sorry I didn't get over to your house for the meeting. I didn't get much sleep last night. Marcus is a night owl."

Rarity held up the bag. "I brought sustenance."

"Tell me Shirley made some sort of dessert." Sam reached out for the bag and looked inside. "Cherry pie?"

"Yep. And fried chicken from the Garnet, a salad, and a quart of Archer's white chicken chili." Rarity relaxed a little. Her friend seemed fine, if a bit frazzled.

Jonathon asked, "Can we come in?"

"Oh, Jonathon, I didn't see you there. Of course, come in. Marcus is in the guest room sleeping. He has a totally different schedule than me, and I've been trying to spend as much time with him as possible, before..."

Sam let the sentence drop off as she held open the door and waved them inside. "Let me put this in the kitchen, and I'll be right out. Have a seat."

Rarity looked around and moved a quilt off the sofa, folding it as she did. There was a man's jacket on the wing chair next to the sofa, and she moved it as well. Empty soda cans and coffee cups filled the small table. Killer found a piece of pizza crust under the sofa, and Rarity took it from him and put it next to the soda cans.

Sam came back into the room with an empty trash bag. "Sorry about the mess."

Rarity watched her friend gather the clutter, and she picked up coffee cups and took them into the kitchen. Sam wasn't a great housekeeper, but her place had never looked like this. She set the cups on the counter and opened the dishwasher. It was filled with dishes. She called out to Sam, "Are the dishes in the dishwasher clean?"

"No, sorry, I haven't run it yet today," Sam called back.

Rarity opened the cabinet under the sink and filled the detergent pouch. Then she started the dishwasher, leaving the cups on the counter since the sink was filled with dirty dishes as well. Sam hadn't started the dishwasher for a few days.

Rarity got a dishcloth and ran hot water over it. Then she added some liquid dish soap. She went out to the living room and washed off the coffee table Sam had just finished cleaning off. "There. Now you can sit with us and talk for a bit."

"I was waiting for Marcus to wake up before I cleaned. I didn't want to wake him. He's been through a lot," Sam explained as she sat on the couch. Killer jumped into her lap and licked her face.

Neither Rarity nor Jonathon said anything.

Sam began to cry. She stroked Killer's fur as tears fell down her face. "I can't believe my life has turned into this. Drew stopped Marcus from flying out of here last week. Now he has a car parked outside all the time. I've been trying to get Marcus to realize he's just doing his job, but he thinks Drew is out to get him."

"Sam, this isn't sane. You need to stop protecting Marcus and go back to your life. He's a big boy. He can take care of himself." Rarity rubbed her friend's shoulder. "Did you get my message? You've got customers who want to buy things. You need to get back to work."

"I know. I'll be there on Monday, I promise." She glanced over toward the hallway that led to the bedrooms. "I just wanted to let Marcus settle a little before I went back to work."

"I'm worried about you." Rarity got up and found a tissue box. She handed it to Sam.

Jonathon leaned forward. "You know Edith and I think the world of you, Sam. If there's anything you need."

"I need Drew to find out who killed Janey and stop harassing my brother about it." Sam glared at Jonathon, her eyes bright with tears and anger. "Just because Connie was found the same way doesn't mean Marcus killed either one of them. He's being set up."

"No, Sam." Marcus stood in the hallway, watching them. "I'm not being set up. I'm just having to deal with my history. Your boyfriend didn't kill Connie or tell me to go down to the quarry with her. We were doing drugs. She overdosed. It was that simple. I could have said no. I should have, but I knew she'd just find another ride. I thought Janey was my new start. She was so full of life. And now she's dead because I let her talk me into leaving the quarry without her. I didn't kill either one of those women, but I didn't save them either. Maybe I should go to jail."

Jonathon stood. "I was a police officer all of my working life. I've seen people racked with guilt for things they didn't do. It does no one a favor to have a killer run free because someone felt like they should be punished for a crime they didn't commit. Now, I think you need to get an attorney and fight for your life. Because if you're being honest, that's what Janey would want you to do. And we need to find out who killed that girl so they can go to jail where they belong."

Marcus walked over and sat on a chair. Then he started crying too. Sam handed him the tissue box. Finally, he looked up at Jonathon. "Thank you. I don't care if you believed me or not, but you gave me hope. Hope that this isn't going to ruin my life."

"Son, you are the only one who can make sure that doesn't happen." Jonathon glanced over at Rarity.

"We probably should be going. Archer will be at the house soon." Rarity hugged Sam. "I'll see you tomorrow at the shop? And hopefully Tuesday night?"

Sam nodded, her eyes bright. "I'm not hiding anymore. I'll be there. And thanks for dinner."

"Thank the club on Tuesday." Rarity stood and snapped her fingers for Killer. "Ready to go home, big guy?"

Killer barked and jumped off Sam's lap. His tail wagged the rest of his body.

Marcus chuckled. "He has a lot of swagger for such a little guy."

"He knows who he is and who he can trust. It gives him confidence." Rarity met Marcus's gaze, and he nodded. He'd gotten the message.

They walked to the door and waved goodbye.

The conversation on the walk home was as nonexistent as on the way over, until Rarity looked up at Jonathon. "Do you think he killed either girl? Did his story ring true?"

Jonathon didn't answer at first. "It's hard to say. I've had people lie to my face, and I never suspected. But my gut says he's being honest. And he's tired of hurting his sister. So I think he would have told us if he'd killed Janey. Unless..."

Rarity looked up at Jonathon. "Unless?"

"Unless he's a sociopath and enjoys the game. Then he'd be getting off on convincing us that he was the victim in both cases. But something about his words rang true. I'll ask Drew if I can look at the case file on what happened with this girl. Maybe they closed the case. Giving Marcus that comfort at least, would help." Jonathon pointed to Archer's truck in the driveway. "I bet your boyfriend's wondering where we are."

"More likely, he's catching up on paperwork while he waits. He's a one-man shop now that Calliope left." Rarity saw that Killer had noticed the truck as well and was pulling on the leash, trying to get home faster.

"Her leaving was probably for the best. The girl was in love with Archer," Jonathon said.

Rarity met his gaze. "I thought I was just seeing things."

"No, I saw it too. He didn't. He thought they were friends. She wanted more. It's the oldest story in the book. And I'd lay money on the fact that it was why Cain killed Abel in the Bible. Over a woman." Jonathon nodded to the house. "Let's go hand you off. I'll pick you up at eight tomorrow? Is that early enough?"

"Should be. I looked up the salon, and it opens at nine. Hopefully it's not the hairdresser's day off. Although we might just be able to get answers from whoever does the scheduling."

"I'm looking forward to being your Watson tomorrow, then." Jonathon handed over Killer's leash to Archer when he opened the front door. He must have been watching for them. "She's back in your care. I've done my shift."

"And you are relieved." Archer took Killer's leash and held the door open for Rarity. "Thanks. I'll be leaving tomorrow at eight. Will that work?"

"Perfectly. We've already discussed my arrival time." Jonathon shook Archer's hand. "See you both in the morning."

As Rarity walked into the living room and shut the door, she gave Archer a kiss. "Thanks for caring, but why do I feel like I'm a piece of china being passed from one guard to another."

"I don't know. Jonathon's a great guy. Not sure why you're feeling that way. Maybe you need to talk to a counselor?"

"Funny." She went to the living room and sank into the couch, pulling off her shoes. "There's food in the fridge."

"I saw that. I'm warming up some chili. Do you want anything?" He took Killer off the leash and put it down on the table near the door.

"No, we just finished eating. Then Jonathon and I went to Sam's to drop off food." Rarity closed her eyes.

"How is she?" Archer asked from the kitchen. She could hear how far away he was, and he probably had his face turned to the wall. His voice was muddy, distant.

"She's good. Or I think she will be. She was being so strong for Marcus, she forgot to take care of herself. I'm hoping she'll be at the shop tomorrow." Rarity realized she still had that woman's card in her tote. She started to stand, then sank back into the sofa. This could wait until tomorrow. "Jonathon's going with me to talk to the hairdresser tomorrow. Maybe we'll get some information that will contradict Janey's sister's statement. I just don't want it to be Marcus. He gave an impassioned speech telling us he didn't do it. I'd hate for Sam to find out he's a killer and a liar."

* * * *

Archer left as soon as Jonathon pulled in the driveway. Rarity knew she shouldn't feel like she was being babysat, but the feeling was there, nonetheless. She wished Drew would figure out who sent her the finger so she could go back to her normal, boring life.

Jonathon came inside. "Do we have time for a cup of coffee?"

Rarity poured him a cup and moved to the kitchen table. "So what's going on? What do you need to tell me?"

"Why would you think there's something going on? Maybe I just like coffee." He sat at the table, then took a sip of his coffee. "Fine, you got me. I needed to ask you about Janey's sister, Trish. Should we look into her while we're in Flagstaff?"

"We are. We're verifying her alibi." Rarity wasn't sure what Jonathon was thinking, but he was the ex-cop, not her.

"I'm thinking a bit more. I'd like to at least drive past her house. Maybe go in and introduce ourselves as Janey's friends from Sedona. Seeing where a suspect lives sometimes gives you more information." He stirred some sugar into his coffee. "Thoughts?"

"Does Drew know what you want to do?" Rarity studied Jonathon's face, and from the blush she saw developing, she figured the answer was no. "You're the cop. What will we learn from going to her house? I'm thinking we might jeopardize the case more than help Drew."

"No, he's all but removed her from the suspect list. I'm thinking there may be people that both Janey and Trish knew. That could be a link to the killer." Jonathon sipped his coffee. "And I'm feeling a little useless since I don't have my badge anymore. Being a civilian limits my reach so much. It's frustrating."

Now Rarity understood Jonathon's motivation for coming up from Tucson. He wanted to be useful again. And having a murder case to work on had given him a purpose again. "I get that it's hard not to be in control. But we appreciate your insight with the club."

"So you don't think we should drop in on Trish?" Jonathon finished his coffee.

"I don't know. I talked to her at the funeral, so it might be a little weird to just stop at her house. However, I think Cara Mantle, Janey's roommate, might talk to us. She seemed willing to chat about Janey and what was going on." Rarity held up her cup. "More coffee, or are you ready to go?"

"Let's go. If I drink more coffee, I won't sleep tonight." He took his cup to the sink and rinsed it out. "Drew said this Cara said she was Janey's heir?"

"That's what she told me." Rarity turned off the coffeemaker and started turning off lights. She checked Killer's dry food and water levels as she grabbed her purse. "Are you driving?"

He nodded and stood at the door. "Do you want me to bring you back here? Or straight to the shop?"

"I'll need to come back here for my tote and Killer." Rarity gave the little dog a kiss on the head and set him down in his bed. "Be good, sir."

"Does that work?" Jonathon asked as they left the house. "Telling Killer to be good?"

Rarity shrugged. "Sometimes."

When they got to Flagstaff, the salon wasn't open yet, so they drove to Janey's former home. A car was in the driveway, which was a good sign. Rarity climbed out of Jonathon's car, and they headed to the front door. When she knocked, she heard a deep bark. She turned to Jonathon. "That's probably Whiskey, Janey's dog. Cara said she was keeping him."

"It's good when pets have a place to go. I'm surprised Drew hasn't pulled the trigger on a dog yet. He talks about Killer all the time." Rarity grinned as they waited. "Well, he's not getting my boy."

"Whiskey, hush," a female voice said, and then the door opened. "Can I help you?"

"Hi, Cara? I'm Rarity Cole. We spoke a few days ago. This is my friend, Jonathon. Can we ask you a few questions about Janey?"

"Sure, let me come outside. Whiskey doesn't like new people very much, especially men. We think, I mean, Janey thought he might have been abused at his last home. He's a rescue." Cara came outside and pulled the door closed behind her. She wrapped a big cardigan sweater around her and then leaned on the doorway. "What can I help with?"

"We were just wondering if we could ask you about Janey's last few days. Did she tell you anything about an old boyfriend or anyone bothering her?" Jonathon pulled out his notebook and pen.

"Are you with the cops?" Cara's eyes narrowed.

Rarity stepped in. "We've been asked to do some background work on Janey's life. Jonathon's a retired police officer who does work for the Sedona department at times. I told him we'd talked a few days ago, and he thought we might just review some things. I know you want to help in finding Janey's killer, right?"

"Oh, okay. I've just had so many reporters trying to make up a story. Like Janey was some coed that played with men. Janey was the most down-to-earth person I knew. She rarely dated. She was waiting for Mr. Right. We had a joke when she'd come home from a first date. I'd ask, frog or prince? Most of the time, the answer was frog. This last guy she met in Sedona, though, she said she was hoping he was a prince."

"Marcus?" Rarity asked.

Cara nodded. "He fit the mold for her. Hit all the right bells. He was employed, not in a relationship, and just a really nice guy. She said she was hoping for a prince there."

"Did she say anything about Caleb?"

Now Cara frowned. "Caleb was in the frog category. He's the guy she was working with, right?"

Rarity nodded. She'd seen the way Caleb had looked at Janey. He was smitten with her, at the least. She just wondered if he'd ever acted on his feelings.

"No, she mentioned him. Said he was nice. They'd met before in a class, and he'd tried to continue the connection, but Janey definitely wasn't interested." A car pulled up at the curb, and a man got out. He checked the address on the house and then on his paper. "Uh-oh, I think another reporter is here."

The man smiled at them, then approached. He looked between Rarity and Cara. "Cara Mantle?"

Cara held up her hand. "What can I help you with?"

He held out a folded paper. When Cara took it, he nodded. "You've been served."

Chapter 13

Rarity watched as the guy turned and sprinted toward his car. Then the process server drove away. She turned back to Cara and nodded to the paper still unopened in her hand. "What's the issue?"

Cara opened the paper and read the first page. "I'm being sued for Janey's estate. Her sister wants the money to revert to her."

"Has the will even been probated yet?" Jonathon reached out for the summons and read it. When he finished, he looked up at Cara. "Do you have an attorney?"

"No, the will is still in court. Janey's estate attorney said there might be a challenge, and if there was, to call her." Cara sighed. "Janey owned the house. If I lose this case, Whiskey and I will have to find somewhere else to live."

"Call your attorney. If the will is valid, you shouldn't lose. Just don't give up." Rarity wanted to give the woman a hug. She looked worn out with grief.

Jonathon handed the summons back to Cara. "Look, I know this is a lot, but don't worry until you have something to worry about. Just call your attorney."

They walked back to Jonathon's car and didn't say anything until they were heading back to the salon. Rarity turned to Jonathon. "Why would someone who already has money want to stop Cara from getting Janey's money?"

"Maybe Trish doesn't have as much money as she wants, or she already spent her part of the trust. There are a lot of reasons people sue. But it sure shines a different light on Janey's sister." Jonathon glanced in the rearview mirror as they left Cara's street. "I think maybe Drew should have a closer look at Trish and her motivation."

"So let's go poke a hole into her alibi." Rarity set the GPS back on the path to the salon. "It should be open by now."

"Do me a favor. Call Drew while we're driving. I think he needs to know about the suit. If Trish assumed Janey would leave her fortune to her, she could have killed her, not knowing that Janey had changed the will." He turned onto the freeway. "Money is a big motivator. Especially when you need it to keep up your lifestyle."

"Which doesn't rule out Cara as a possible murderer. She could have known about her inheritance and needed access to the money now." Rarity glanced back at the way they'd come. "Although I don't see her as a killer."

"You have good instincts. No wonder Drew trusts you." Jonathon pointed to her phone. "Call Drew. Tell him what we found out and about the challenge to the will. This just opened up Trish for him to examine her more closely."

She found his name and hit Call. Then she waited for him to answer.

"Hello? Rarity? Don't tell me you and Dad got in trouble already." Drew didn't sound happy.

"No, we just have a bit of information to tell you." She went through the meeting with Cara, then told him about the server and the court case. "Jonathon thinks you might want to look at Trish a little closer."

"Have you two talked to her hairdresser, yet?" Drew asked.

"We're on our way there now. We had some time before the salon opened." Now Rarity felt guilty for going to talk to Cara.

"Okay, but can you do me a favor and limit your involvement to this one question? We just need to know if Trish's alibi holds up. I really don't want you to go around Flagstaff trying to find Janey's murderer. You two are scary together."

Rarity rolled her eyes, and Jonathon laughed.

"Yeah, that's your dad and me. Private investigators on patrol."

"One, legally you're not a private investigator. They have a license with the state. And two, Dad's not a cop anymore. So you're just private citizens getting a little information for me. Don't make me regret this idea any more than I already do."

Rarity had Drew on speaker so Jonathon could hear too, but after that comment about him not being a cop, she wondered about the wisdom of letting him listen in. That had to hurt. "Look, Drew, you sent us here to check on a few things. If we have access to talk to the roommate, that's not your business if we do. I've told you what she said, so you can't say I'm holding back evidence. I think you should be nicer to people who are just doing you a favor."

Rarity hung up the phone before Drew could answer. She tucked it in her purse.

Jonathon looked over at her. "Are you okay?"

She nodded and stared straight ahead. "Let's go talk to this hairdresser so we can go get those milkshakes. I'm getting a little worked up here, and sugar will help."

"Sugar always helps." Jonathon turned the car onto the street where the salon was located and found a parking spot. He looked over at the place. "It looks fancy. Maybe I should stay in the car."

"Are you afraid they'll force cucumber water on you?"

He chuckled. "Edith has already done that. Actually, I'm thinking they might talk a little freely without a big guy who looks like an ex-cop hanging around."

"Whatever you want." Rarity focused on what she needed from the conversation. "So we just need to know if Trish really had a hair appointment the Saturday morning that Janey was killed."

"And the times she arrived and left. Sometimes you can't overlook the obvious." He pointed to a bench. "I'll wait here. Scream if they try to do the Stepford Wife treatment."

She shook her head. "You really need to watch some new movies."

"I read the book, I'll have you know." He settled on the bench and pulled out a paperback novel. "Now I look like a long-suffering husband just waiting for his wife to finish."

"And apparently, I'm the trophy wife. Not one of my ambitions in life." Rarity patted his shoulder. "I should be back in a few minutes. If I go past fifteen, come and rescue me. Unless I'm getting a massage."

"Got it." He grabbed her arm. "Just be careful."

"It's a beauty salon."

"And you're asking about a murder," he reminded her. "Just don't take anything for granted."

Armed with that advice, she squared her shoulders and headed to the door. She had been referred by Trish Ford. She couldn't remember who she saw, but she'd been in for an appointment on Saturday. Could the receptionist look up who she saw that day? And, how long it took? She wanted the same cut and style but had to fit it in between real estate showings. That should be enough of a story to get what she needed. If she needed to prime the pump any more, the guy's name had been Roger Kamp. Maybe she could ask for an appointment with Mr. Camper? She shook her head. She'd leave that in case the woman couldn't find Trish's appointment. Trish had looked like she had a regular cut and at least highlights put in her hair.

Rarity glanced at her clothes. Maybe she should have upgraded a bit. But at least she had her high-end purse. That got a lot of attention from women wanting an upscale look. She was always being asked if it was real or not. She'd bought it as a birthday present for herself just before she'd left St. Louis. And, yes, it was real and had a real price tag. She'd had sticker shock for a while after she'd bought it, but she had to admit, she loved the look and the feel of the purse.

She moved the purse closer to the front of her body and pushed the door open. The spa smelled like she'd walked into a secret garden of flowers. She moved toward the Queen Anne–style table where a woman sat with a laptop. She wore a name tag. Fay looked up from her work and smiled. "Are you here for an appointment?"

Rarity took a breath. "Actually, no. I'm here to try to get an appointment. One of my friends had her hair cut and highlighted here. I'm ashamed to say I don't remember who she said did it, but I met her and a few others for lunch two Saturdays ago, and she'd just had it done. I really want something like her cut done to my hair."

"Oh, what's your friend's name?" The woman didn't look up, but Rarity could see that Fay was looking at a calendar on her computer.

"Trish Ford. I'd call her, but she just lost her sister, and I don't want to intrude on her at this time." Rarity leaned over to watch the woman search appointments.

"Here it is. Trish Ford saw Roger Kamp at eight that morning. He's one of our most popular stylists. I'm not sure I can get you in this week." She looked up at Rarity. "When did you want your appointment?"

Rarity pulled out her phone and pretended to be scanning her calendar. "Not this week, darn. How long of a session do I need to have something like Trish's hair? Not that I want to copy her, you understand."

"Your hair is a different texture from Miss Ford's, so it will look different, even if Mr. Kamp does exactly the same process." She smiled. "Don't worry, we won't tell her."

"That's a huge relief. Anyway, how big of a block am I looking at?" She held a finger on her phone, pretending to be waiting.

"Let's see." Fay scrolled back and leaned in to look at the appointment. "Miss Ford was here from eight to eleven thirty. She must have had a nail treatment or facial as well. I would block off at least two hours."

"Okay, what's your first appointment with Roger?"

"Saturday at seven." The woman wrote down the time and date on a card. "Now, what is your name?"

"Rarity Cole." She took the card. She needed to get her hair done anyway. And with her luck, if she'd said her name was something else, she'd run into someone she knew who would rat her out. She might not be done asking questions anyway.

She left the spa and went to sit next to Jonathon. "She was here from eight to eleven thirty that day. At least that's what the receptionist said. I have an appointment next Saturday with this Roger guy, so if we still need more information, I can ask him then."

"If not, are you still keeping the appointment?" He linked her arm in his, and they walked back to the car.

"Maybe. Probably. Hairdressers love to talk. Especially when there's drama involved. If I throw Trish's dead sister into the conversation, you know he's going to blab about something or someone." Rarity climbed into the car. "I'll let Drew know what we found, and you drive us to the milkshake place. Maybe they have fish burgers too. I'm starving."

* * * *

When Jonathon dropped her off at the house, he offered to wait and drive her to the shop.

"No, go on about your day. Killer will need the walk after being cooped up this morning without me." Rarity shut the door and waved as he drove away. Drew had been quiet when she gave him the details about Trish's appointment. If what she'd found out was true, her hair appointment gave Trish an alibi that cleared her from being charged with killing her sister. At least with her doing the deed. She still could have hired someone. Then Drew had told her to cancel the hair appointment. But she hadn't.

And as she gathered her things for a half day at work and clicked a leash onto Killer's collar, she didn't think she would. She might not find out anything new about Janey's death, but people talked when they were getting their hair done. Maybe she could find out how Trish felt about her sister. And if Trish was involved with anyone. That could be the person who actually killed Janey. Rarity wasn't ready to give up on Trish being responsible for Janey's death. Even if she'd been getting her hair done an hour away at the time.

Killer was ready to go, and Rarity realized they'd been standing at the door for several minutes as she thought out her plan to keep researching Trish. She leaned down and gave him a pat on the head. "Sorry, boy. I'm a little distracted today. Let's go to work."

He pulled at the leash until he found a spot of grass he liked. Then he was ready to go. Luckily, this time she didn't need a bag, but she always had one on hand, just in case. They walked into town, Rarity's head in the clouds thinking about this morning's field trip, and Killer sniffing at every street sign and light pole on their way.

She was about to walk over and unlock her bookstore when she saw lights on at Sam's crystal shop. Rarity still had the card from the woman who wanted a necklace, so she kept walking past the bookstore and over to Sam's. Killer, confused, kept trying to turn around to go to the store. Finally, she picked him up and carried him the rest of the way to Sam's shop.

She opened the door, and bells went off. Sam was nowhere to be seen. Rarity called out, "Sam? Are you here?"

No answer.

Rarity went around the counter and into the back room, where Sam worked on her jewelry. "Sam?"

A sound came from her left, and all of a sudden, Rarity found herself falling to the floor. A blinding light flashed in front of her eyes, and a sharp pain seared the back of her head. Killer started barking, and then everything went black.

A bright light shone in her eyes. A man asked, "Miss? Hey, can you hear me?"

Killer was still barking but farther away. She reached for the leash but couldn't find it. Why wasn't he on the leash? She blinked again. Then she croaked out, "Killer? Where are you, boy?"

"Killer's your dog, right?" the male voice asked her. He was calm, which made her even more scared. She tried to focus now that the light was gone. A man's face swam in front of her.

"Yes. Is he all right?" She tried to sit up, but something held her down, and her head hurt. Bad. "Killer?"

"He's fine. My buddy's got him a few feet away from you. I need to know how you're doing before I can let him over here. What's your name?"

Now Rarity could see the voice was coming from the man she saw above her. "What happened?"

"Answer my question, and I'll try to answer yours. What's your name?" The man smiled, and for some reason, she smiled back.

The action made her head hurt even more. She groaned, then answered him. "Rarity Cole."

"Hi, Rarity. And your dog's name is Killer? It's a little optimistic for his size, isn't it?"

Rarity almost laughed, but the action made the pain worse. "He came to me with that name. He's okay?"

"He's fine. What happened? Why are you on the floor in the back of the crystal shop? Do you remember?"

"I was looking for Sam. Her lights were on, and I needed to give her a card." Rarity closed her eyes again. The lights were too bright when she had them open. But with them closed, she felt like she was falling. Although she felt the floor on her back. So where could she fall to? She opened her eyes again. "Is Sam okay?"

"I'm here, Rarity. I'd gone out back for a smoke, and when I came inside, Killer was barking. Who hit you?" Sam's face came over to the other side.

"Ma'am, you need to stay back until I stabilize her." The man's voice sounded closer. He put a neck brace around her neck. "We need to take you to the hospital to be checked out."

"Is that necessary?" Rarity was starting to wake up. She lifted her head, and a blast of pain made her close her eyes. "Okay, fine, I'll go. Sam, can you take care of Killer? And put a sign up at the store. Just say I'm closed for the day."

"Sure. But I'm following you to the hospital. I'll drop Killer off with Shirley," Sam said. She was somewhere to Rarity's right. "I'm sorry this happened."

"Me too. Why would someone hit me in your shop?" Rarity asked, but no one heard her since the EMTs were wheeling her out of the shop and into a waiting ambulance. Drew's voice stopped her movement.

"Where are you taking her?" Drew grabbed her hand and leaned close. "Rarity, are you all right?"

"Someone hit me in Sam's shop." Rarity relayed the obvious. "Killer, he's still there."

"We'll take care of your dog." Drew squeezed her hand. "I'll check in with Sam. What hospital?"

"Flagstaff South. She needs scans, and the Sedona hospital isn't equipped for that," the EMT said.

Rarity felt herself wanting to go to sleep.

"None of that. I want to hear the story of how that cute little dog got such a big name," the EMT said. "We need to get going."

Rarity thought she really should figure out what his name was. She felt Drew let her hand go.

"I'll see you soon, Rarity." His words were tight. "I'll call Archer."

"Okay." Rarity saw the EMT's shirt and a nametag, or at least one of them, near her head. She squinted to read it. "Mark, do you have a dog?"

Chapter 14

By the time she'd arrived in a hospital room for the nurses to watch her and finally give her some pain meds, she decided she might have seen all sections of the hospital besides maternity and the cancer section. She'd come to the hospital for a scan a few months ago, but she'd been in and out before she could evaluate the place. That was the one thing about being a cancer survivor—you got to know hospitals and cancer centers well. Each one was a little different. Each had its own feel. But they were all positive, hopeful, and the white walls had upbeat posters both for staff and patients. Or at least the ones Rarity had been in.

She'd heard horror stories about other places, but she'd been lucky. Sam believed in the power of being positive, or at least she had before this Marcus thing. And Sam's words had transferred over to Rarity. There was no need to add worry to the discussion until you had something to worry about. "One step at a time" had to be her motto. Breast cancer or a bump on the head, it didn't matter. You didn't cry wolf until you saw the drool dripping out of the jaws.

Sam hurried into the room as soon as the nurse had settled Rarity into bed. She'd given her a pain killer in her IV, and for the first time since she'd gone down in Sam's shop, her head wasn't throbbing. She smiled at Sam. "Hey, you didn't have to come."

"Of course I did. No matter how horrible I've been acting lately, I'm still your best friend. At least if you haven't given up on me." She pulled a chair closer and sat down, dropping her tote on the floor. "Shirley has Killer. He didn't want to leave the shop with me. He kept barking at the door the EMTs took you out of, but Drew picked him up, and then I got him to Shirley's. He's not happy, but she had pumpkin dog treats, so that helped."

"I wonder how much he remembers about Martha disappearing. Poor little guy." Rarity felt the medicine pulling her toward sleep. "So who hit me?"

"We don't know." Drew thinks they might have been waiting for me to come back from my smoke." Sam blushed. "Sorry, I picked the habit up again when Marcus moved into the house. He smokes, and things were just so crazy."

"You'd been smoke-free for years." Rarity shook her head, but then the pain hit. "I guess the pain's telling me not to be judgmental. Just be careful. I don't want you to get cancer."

"I promise, I'm quitting again." Sam sank into the chair. "Anyway, I heard Killer barking and ran back inside, but the guy that hit you was gone. Drew's talking to the neighbors and pulling street camera footage to see if he can find him."

"I'm sorry I'm such a bother," Rarity said, the sleep pulling her down.

"You're kidding, right? You didn't ask to be attacked."

Rarity squeezed her friend's hand. Sam was nice. She had always been there for her. But there was something she needed to tell her. The meds were making her eyes close. "You have a customer who wants something. I have her card in my tote. I think..."

"I'll find it. One sale isn't going to wreck me." Sam shushed Rarity. "The nurse says you need to sleep so you can heal. I'll be here when you wake up."

"Archer..." Rarity said, then she closed her eyes.

When she woke up, it was night. The room was dim, but she could see someone sitting in the shadows. A man. Fear gripped her, and she reached for her call button, but it had fallen out of her hand, where the nurse had put it when she settled her into the bed.

"Rarity, what do you need?" the man asked, and as she watched, he stood and moved closer to the bed. It was Jonathon. "I sent Sam and Archer to get some food and told them I'd be here in case you woke up."

"I—" She swallowed hard. "I'd like a sip of water."

He smiled at her, and she felt safe. A feeling that she hadn't had before she moved to Sedona. Now, she had family. Sam, Archer, Drew, Jonathon, Shirley, the list went on and on. If she'd had a dog in St. Louis, she would have had to put him in a kennel if she needed an overnight stay in the hospital. Which was why she didn't get a pet after Kevin moved out. Well, that was one of the reasons.

Jonathon moved a glass of water toward her, and she moved the straw to her lips. The water felt cool going down, but then she started coughing, and the pain came back to her head. It wasn't as strong this time, though.

He wiped the water from her face. "Maybe that's enough."

"You don't have to take care of me." Rarity licked her dry lips. The water had felt good. She wondered if it was the hospital air or the pain meds that had made her lips dry. Or maybe she'd been asleep longer than she'd thought. "It's still Monday, right?"

Jonathon chuckled. "Barely. It's eleven. I sent Archer and Sam away at ten. I'm sure they'll be back soon. Edith wanted to come up, but I told her that you had enough people taking care of you. She sends her love."

"Tell her thanks." Rarity moved the glass closer and took another small sip. "I can't believe this happened. I went to Sam's shop to give her a card from a customer, and the next thing I know, I'm here."

"Did you see the guy?" Jonathon asked, his voice now all cop.

"No, he hit me from behind. I walked into the back because I'd heard a noise and thought Sam was grabbing stock or working on a piece. She has a bell that rings in the back when someone comes in, but sometimes she has music going. When I walked into the back, it was quiet and Sam wasn't there. I could see where she'd been working, and I walked toward the bench, but then my head exploded." She pushed the cup away. "Killer's all right, isn't he?"

"Shirley called me about thirty minutes ago to check on you. Killer's curled up on her couch watching *Harry Potter* with her."

Rarity smiled and leaned back on her pillow. "He does love those movies."

"Don't we all." Jonathon chuckled. Then the door flew open, and Sam, Drew, and Archer came into the room. Jonathon stepped away from the bed. "She's awake."

Sam ran over to one side, Archer to the other. Drew followed Sam.

Rarity looked up at the three. "Sorry I messed up your day."

"You need to stop saying you're sorry." Archer squeezed her hand. "I'm sorry it took me so long to get here. I was out on the last hike with my corporate client, so I didn't get the call until I dropped them off at the hotel and turned on my phone."

"You had work. What would you have done, left those guys out on the trail?" Rarity turned toward Sam and Drew. "Any luck finding out who likes cracking my skull?"

"No, but I've got Holly going through street cams to see what we can find." Drew squeezed her foot that was under the covers. "You don't worry about that. Just get better."

A voice came from the back of the room. "I'm sorry, but visiting hours are long over. And you're over the two person per room max anyway. Decide who's staying, and the rest of you say good night."

Jonathon smiled at Rarity. "I'm out. I'll see you tomorrow."

"I'll stay with her." Archer looked at Drew and Sam. "I know you guys have some things to talk about anyway."

Drew glanced at Sam. "Can I get a ride back to Sedona with you? I rode in with one of the guys from the station, and he's already back in town."

"Sure." Sam bit her lip. She gave Rarity a hug. "I'll see you tomorrow."

"From what the doctor told me, you might be released sometime tomorrow." The nurse pushed a cart close and started hooking up Rarity to a machine to check her vitals. She met Rarity's gaze. "You're a lucky girl. The blow didn't hit square. You must have surprised your attacker, because he didn't try a second time."

"I don't know. I'm feeling like he hit me pretty hard." Rarity shrugged. "Now you're telling me it could have been worse."

"That's always good news, right?" The nurse turned on the machine, and it took her blood pressure. She wrote something down and then took off the finger monitor as well. "You're looking good. I'd like for you to get some more sleep."

"We get the hint." Drew stepped toward the door. "We'll talk soon. Hopefully Holly has found something."

"See you soon." Jonathon squeezed her hand again and stepped out of the room.

Sam stayed behind.

Archer nodded toward the doorway. "Drew's waiting."

Sam sighed and gave Rarity a kiss on the forehead. "That's what I'm worried about. Call me if you need a ride home or if I need to sub in for Archer."

Rarity waved at her friend, who moved toward the door and Drew like she was going to a firing squad. She turned to Archer. "Sure, it takes me being in the hospital for those two to finally talk."

"They're both stubborn. Not like us. We're very pliable. A feature that might have saved your life." He moved a chair closer to the bed. "The only place we could find to eat was a Burger King down the street. So I don't have any food-related stories to tell you."

"Right now, that sounds amazing. I haven't had food since my protein shake this morning." She studied his face. He looked tired. "Why don't you go home too? I'll be fine."

"No, someone is targeting you. First the plastic finger, now this. I'm not leaving you alone until Drew figures out who killed Janey. I have a feeling this is connected. Not sure how or why, but connected." He glanced at the food menu that was on the bedside table. "This says you can get a sandwich or ice cream at any time. Are you hungry?"

"I'm starving." Rarity yawned. "I'm also beat. Can you order me a turkey sandwich if they have one? Maybe we should find a movie to keep me awake for a bit until it gets here."

"Dinner and a movie. I say this counts as a date night," Archer teased as he picked up the phone to call for her food.

"You take me to the nicest places." She found the television remote and started scanning for movies. At least she wasn't alone. The last time she'd been in the hospital, it had been just her. Kevin hadn't even tried to visit. He didn't like hospitals. And apparently, he hadn't loved her enough to get past his own discomfort to ease hers. Here, the nurse had to kick people out of the room. It was weird, feeling at home in a hospital bed. But her friends, no, the family she'd built, had made it feel like home. She just missed her dog.

* * * *

When Archer drove her back to Sedona the next day, she pointed toward the store. "I'm opening for a few hours."

"You don't want to head home and rest? Maybe shower?" He glanced over at her. "See Killer?"

"Killer's going to be at the shop with the rest of the Tuesday night crowd. Shirley called me earlier when you were out of the room, and the sleuthing club asked if I wanted to meet them to go over what we've found out." She leaned against the back of the seat. "I said yes, but I don't think I can go for very long. I'm still feeling tired. I haven't done anything for two days, and I'm tired."

"One full day. And you're healing. It takes a lot out of you." He pressed his lips together but didn't turn on her street when they passed it by. "If I think you need to go home, I'm taking you there. No arguments."

"Yes, mother." She smiled as she watched through the window. There were cones in front of the store, and as they pulled up, Malia ran out of the shop and moved them out of the way. "Apparently they set up front row parking for us."

"It's good to know someone in the police department." Archer turned off the engine. "Remember our deal. If you feel like you're getting tired, just give me the sign."

"You mean like this?" She put her hand on her forehead, mimicking a fainting woman.

"You're such a drama queen." He chuckled as he got out of the truck.

She took off her seat belt and took a breath. She'd overestimated her energy level for Archer, but she wasn't going to let him see her wilt. She opened the door, and he was there, waiting for her. She slid out of the truck and onto the sidewalk, taking his arm for balance. "You're a worrywart."

He pulled her close into a gentle hug. "I care about you. So get over it."

She smiled as she made her way into the store. There, she turned toward the fireplace and found a chair. Killer was at her feet, trying to get her attention, so as soon as she sat, he was on her lap, sniffing and licking and welcoming her home. "Sorry, buddy. I hope I didn't scare you."

He stared at her, then curled up in a ball on her lap. She was forgiven.

Shirley beamed at her and brought over a plate of cookies. "You probably need some nourishment. Coffee or lemonade or water?"

"Coffee please. I swear they were giving me decaf at the hospital." Rarity put the cookie plate on a table next to her chair where Killer wouldn't be tempted. Then she took one and ate it while she waited for her coffee. She noticed everyone was watching her. "Oh, did you want me to lead the meeting?"

"No, we're all just glad you're back home." Jonathon stood. "So we think Rarity was hit by the killer, but because she was in the wrong place."

"Great, so I was just target practice?" Rarity glared at him as Shirley gave her a cup. "That makes me feel so much better."

"It's not an insult, but we think the true target was Sam." Jonathon pointed to the paper. "We think Sam was targeted because they wanted Marcus to be the scapegoat for the murder, and Sam was trying to debunk that story with Drew. With Sam out of the way, Marcus might be charged."

"Marcus wouldn't have Sam to stick up for him," Holly added to the story. Then she looked at Rarity. "So that's when you walked into Sam's shop and ruined the killer's frame of Marcus. And we know Marcus didn't hit you since he was at the police station talking to Drew at the exact time you were attacked."

"So the killer just admitted that there had to be someone besides Marcus involved," Shirley commented. "That was a mistake, at least on the killer's part."

"Yeah, he thought Marcus would be home alone with no alibi when Sam was alone in the shop."

"I still don't get why he'd attack Sam. Either Marcus or someone who wanted it to look like Marcus. Sam was his main supporter. And his sister." Rarity watched as Shirley picked up a second notebook and started writing in it. "Shirley, what are you doing?"

"Updating your notebook as we talk. That way, next week, you'll be all caught up." She glanced at the list of assignments for last week. "Rarity, did you get over to the salon?"

Rarity took a sip of her coffee and set it down by the cookies. Then she proceeded to tell them all about her visit to the salon. "So Trish does have an alibi. She was getting her hair done."

"Darn. She was on the top of my suspects list. It would have been the husband, but Janey wasn't married, and we're trying not to focus on Marcus," Malia mumbled, then looked up and noticed everyone was staring at her. "What? It's true. These things are usually due to a relationship with the wrong person. If Marcus wasn't related to Sam, we wouldn't even think twice about having him as our primary suspect."

Rarity was about to say something, but Sam spoke instead. "She's right. And I know this is a leap of faith for all of you, but I know Marcus didn't kill Janey. So I appreciate you helping me prove it."

Chapter 15

After the meeting ended, Archer insisted that Rarity stay seated while he and Sam put everything away.

"You realize tomorrow I'm going to be up and doing everything myself again."

"Actually, Shirley's coming in early to help open with you, and she'll be here all day," Archer corrected her. "It's Mommy and Me day, remember?"

"Yes, but Shirley doesn't work a full day on Wednesday."

Archer grinned at her. "She does tomorrow. Be mad at me, not her. I adjusted your schedule. Caleb will be here Thursday afternoon, but Jonathon will be here in the morning. He'll just be working on a project, but if you need anything, he'll be here."

"So you got all the babysitters in place? You're still staying at the house?" Rarity felt a little guilty that everyone was uprooting their lives for her. "What about all that discussion we just had where the group decided I was just collateral damage and the guy was going after Sam?"

"That's a great theory, but I'm not risking your life on a theory. Anyway, you love being around people all the time, right?" Archer laughed at the look she gave him. "Don't worry, I'll give you space at the house. Tell yourself I need to make sure you're safe because I'm clingy and all that."

"Sure, you're horribly clingy." Rarity rubbed Killer's ears. He wasn't letting her out of his sight either. "I guess I'm just going to have to get used to it."

She glanced at the notes Shirley had added to her notebook. Something was ringing a bell, and she couldn't quite place it. Mostly because she was tired and confused and, yes, had a head injury. She closed the notebook. She'd go back tomorrow and look through the discussion. Sam was right on one thing. Marcus would be a perfect suspect if she wasn't there to declare his innocence. But Janey's sister. Rarity would have bet money on the sister being involved. Yet she had an alibi. Maybe she didn't kill her, but Rarity wasn't willing to give up totally on blaming Trish. She could have paid someone or had an accomplice do it for her.

"You look deep in thought." Archer had returned and had Killer's leash. He clipped it onto his collar and lowered the dog to the floor. Then he held out his hand. "Ready to head home? I'm warming up soup, and I brought home fresh rolls for dinner earlier."

She took his hand and stood. "When did you have time?"

He kissed her forehead. "I have my ways."

* * * *

The next morning, Rarity felt better. She still ached all over, but the pain was gone. She got up and swam, which eased out more aches. She was just getting out of the pool when Archer came out to the backyard with coffee. She wrapped her oversized towel around her and took the cup. "Thanks, I needed this."

"Are you going into work?" He sat at the table on the deck.

"Yes. I've been closed long enough. I'd say my month was going to be down, but we've been having such good response to the book clubs, I think I'm good for now, but I don't want to push it. I'd rather put the extra money into the capital outlay fund. I know that air conditioner is older than dirt."

"True." He glanced at his watch. "I need to get in as well. I've got some follow-up on the group from last weekend, and I've got a hike scheduled for tomorrow morning. I'm sure you don't want to get up and be at the store by five tomorrow, do you?" He actually looked hopeful.

"You and Drew really think I need someone watching me all the time?" She unconsciously reached back to touch the bump on her head. "Didn't we decide it was Sam the guy was after? Maybe we should be focused on keeping someone with her."

"She has someone with her. Marcus. And Drew's been checking in." Archer chuckled. "It makes Marcus uncomfortable to have Drew in the house, so he's been stopping by a few times a day."

"Men and their games." She took another sip of her coffee. "If you think I still need someone around tomorrow morning, I'll get up early and let you walk me to the bookstore. Then Jonathon can meet me there whenever he wants. I'll keep the doors locked until nine, which should give him enough time to get over there."

"You won't take Killer out for a walk?" Archer knew she would, especially if Killer needed it.

"I'll keep the food up until the store opens. And with walking him to the store, he should sleep for a good four hours." She could see Archer frown at the word *should.* "And I'll take a potty pad just in case. I promise I won't go outside."

"Okay, then. Tomorrow's set. I'll walk you to work this morning, Jonathon will be there at nine until Shirley arrives, then I'll pick you up on the way back to the house. Any thoughts for dinner?"

After they chatted for a bit, she got ready for work, and when she got back out to the living room, Archer was sitting on the couch, talking to Killer.

"Now you be a good guard dog and watch out for your mommy this week. If you feel like someone's a bad guy, you make sure to tell her," Archer told Killer as the little dog stared at him, trying to understand the words.

"Killer's on the case. He's a great guard dog." Rarity went over and got his leash off the hook by the door. "Ready to go?"

"Whenever you are." He stood and followed Killer to the door, turning off lights as he passed them. When he reached the doorway, he met her gaze. "I'm only here for safety reasons, but it's been nice spending a lot of time together this week."

"Every couple should have a possible stalker issue. That way they could find out if they like to be together in stressful situations."

"I know you're kidding, but it does have a certain logic. Maybe that's why weddings are so stressful. If you can get through that together, you can do anything." He shut the door and checked the lock. Then he waved at Terrance, who was sitting on his porch. "Was it a good night?"

"Quiet night. That's all anyone can ask for. I'm on watch this week because the guys were mad I went on a cruise without them." Terrance chuckled. "The joke's on them, though, I was ready to get back to doing something. Sitting around for a week drinking fruity drinks really isn't my style."

They were up the road and out of Terrance's earshot when Archer glanced down at Rarity. "So why did he go on the cruise?"

"He's not telling anyone, but he's seeing a woman in Flagstaff. She talked him into the cruise. His navy buddies go every year with their wives. I haven't caught up with him since he's been back to see if the relationship survived the forced relaxation and proximity." Rarity smiled at him. "It's not just stressful times that fracture a relationship. Good times can as well."

"You're just the little relationship guru, aren't you?" Archer teased. "You been reading some of your books on the subject?"

Rarity felt the flush on her cheeks before she could stop it. She turned toward Killer and loosened the leash from around his leg. He'd totally called her out without knowing it. "Maybe."

When they got to the bookstore, Jonathon was sitting outside, three coffee cups and a bag of donuts next to him. And he had a briefcase sitting on the ground next to him. She grinned at him as she dug out her keys. "If you were in a suit, I'd say you were going for the friendly FBI look."

He stood and handed Archer one of the cups. "Nothing friendly about the FBI. At least the ones I worked with. I just have a project I'm working on. Might as well work here rather than Drew's house. At least here I don't get yelled at for not using a coaster. That son of mine needs something else to focus on besides work and keeping his house clean. Sam was good for him. She loosened him up a bit."

"Well, we'll just have to get this case settled, and we can all go back to our normal lives." Rarity shot a look at Archer, who nodded, getting the hint.

"I'm heading to my shop. Have a good day, everyone." And then he handed Killer's leash over to Rarity. Killer took the time to go water his favorite spot on his artificial grass. Then he hurried into the shop after Jonathon.

"So what's the project?" Rarity locked the door behind them. She still wasn't opening until nine, even if her babysitter had already arrived. She had inventory today.

"Oh, just some record keeping." He blushed and went over to a table where he set the briefcase and his coffee. "Do you want a donut?"

"I won't say no to a blueberry cake." She unclicked Killer's leash, then walked over and waited while Jonathon found the donut and handed it and coffee to her. "Thanks, this was nice."

"I think better with caffeine and sugar." He opened his briefcase and took out a laptop and a notebook.

"For your record keeping project."

He blushed, hard. He glanced around the empty bookstore. "Fine, I'll tell you, but you can't tell anyone else. Not Archer, not Drew, not even Sam."

She held up her hand, her fingers in a scout salute. Or what she thought a scout salute looked like. "I promise."

"I'm trying to write a book."

"That's amazing." She grinned at him. "Why would you keep that a secret?"

He sank into the chair and opened his laptop. "Because I'm *trying* to write. I don't know if I can, and I don't want people asking for years what happened to that book. There's no way I'm going to be that guy."

"So you're going to write it and then tell people?" Rarity thought about her nonfiction section. "I've got a ton of writing books over there if you want one."

"Thanks. I might take you up on that. I'm attending the writers' group in Flagstaff while I'm here. I've been in their online group for months now. Tonight, I'm reading my first chapter and getting feedback."

"That should be fun." Rarity hadn't ever considered writing a book. Who would want to read about her? The most interesting thing in her life had been the cancer journey, and she'd rather not think about that time again.

"It's horrible. I've hunted down serial killers and put cuffs on them. But walking into that meeting last week was gut-wrenching. Maybe I'm not meant to do this." He straightened the pen on the table to line up with his notebook.

"Jonathon Anderson. You can do anything you want to do. If this is what you want, push past the fear and go to those meetings. Get whatever tools and information you need to write this book. Then write the best book you can. If you don't, you'll always wonder what if." She sank into a chair so she could meet his gaze. "I quit my high-paying job and moved states to open this bookstore after I beat cancer. I was more scared about that than going to treatments or surgery. Taking a chance is always scary, but it's so worth it."

He smiled at her. "You're right. I should have known you'd knock some sense into me. I should have talked to you months ago when I first started thinking about this. Thanks, Rarity."

"You're welcome. And get to work. That book isn't going to write itself. And I have just the space for it on one of my shelves when it gets published." She stood and walked over to the counter.

"I've got a long way to go before that happens, but if I want it bad enough, I'll get there." He focused on his computer.

Rarity smiled as she went about her day. The one thing she'd learned after having cancer was that tomorrow wasn't promised to anyone. And if you had a dream, you needed to fight for it. She was living her dream. Good or bad, she'd jumped. And her life was better for taking the chance. A lot better. Not just in her career, but in her life. She had a community here. And no one was going to rip that apart.

Shirley came in about ten to get ready for the Mommy and Me class. As customers wandered in, she started greeting them like she'd known them for years, not just from last week's class. Shirley was a natural at this. Besides, it gave her something besides George to focus on. Rarity thought at least one good thing had come from Janey's death. Shirley had bloomed as she took over the Mommy and Me class.

Rarity frowned. Maybe they were looking at this wrong. They were looking at trying to prove Marcus didn't do it. Maybe they should focus instead on why someone would? Shirley's new energy was a motivation, even though it was unintended, and there was no way Shirley would have killed Janey to get her out of the way. But what about others?

As Shirley worked with the moms and kids, and Jonathon worked at a table on the other side of the shop, Rarity sat in the middle, writing down people who might have benefited from Janey's death. On top of that list was Cara, her roommate who'd inherited Janey's money, house, and dog. And her sister. Trish might have thought she'd be Janey's heir. And maybe one of them was wrong.

Rarity wrote the word *Trust* in the middle of her page. Then she grabbed her cell and called Drew. She left the register and caught Jonathon's gaze. She pointed to the back room, and he nodded that he understood where she was going. When Drew answered, he didn't wait for her greeting.

"What's wrong? Are you okay?"

"I'm fine. I just had a question. You might not be able to tell me, or maybe you can. Either way, I think it has something to do with Janey's death." Rarity waited for a signal to go ahead. Drew was conflicted on giving her information because he thought it put her in harm's way. In a way, she was already there. Whether she wanted to be or not.

Drew must have thought the same thing, because he didn't disagree. "What do you need to know?"

"Who gets the trust money when Janey dies? Is it her sister or Cara?"

He didn't answer at first. Then he sighed. "You know, I don't know. I've got an appointment with the family lawyer today at ten. Maybe he'll be able to tell me. I know Cara thinks Janey transferred the house and the trust to her so she could take care of Whiskey, but maybe the trust was set up so her share just went back into it for Trish if she died."

"That was what I was thinking today," Rarity agreed. "I was doing a 'who benefited' brainstorm, and the idea just hit me."

"Where are you?" Drew's voice sounded wary.

"At the shop."

"Alone?"

Rarity laughed. "Drew, I haven't been alone since I was hit the other day. Your dad is here. Archer transferred me over to him as soon as we got here. Shirley's teaching the Mommy and Me class."

"Just don't do anything stupid and go out back or take Killer for a walk, okay?"

"I've been informed that both of those items are off my list. At least if I'm alone." She glanced through the back door into the bookstore and met Jonathon's gaze. He'd been watching for her to come back. "Look, I've got to go. Let me know if you can. I think Trish isn't off the hook until we know about the money. And maybe not even then."

"I agree. And surprisingly enough, as a trained investigator, the idea was already on my list to explore."

"Fine, I'm an amateur, and I'm putting my nose where it doesn't belong. I get it." She leaned on the doorway. She could see the back door, front door, Jonathon, and even Shirley when she stood still from this vantage point.

"I wasn't saying that, but sometimes I think you don't trust me." He said something she couldn't hear. He must have had his hand over the receiver. "Sorry, I've got to go. Stay safe, okay? I've got enough on my worry list. I don't need you on there too."

Chapter 16

Nothing happened to Rarity on Wednesday. She finished her day, talked to an overly excited Shirley about the next book on the list, and congratulated Jonathon on his word count for the day. Tomorrow, she'd do it all again. But Caleb would be here instead of Shirley. She smiled as Archer came into the shop. "Today was a good day," she announced as he walked back to the counter.

"Who's here with you?" He looked around, and then Shirley popped out of the back and headed out to the club meeting area.

"Jonathon just went home. He left during Shirley's class and got us lunch. Then we ate, and Shirley told us all about the new moms in her group. She's really loving this. Then she took on shelving the new books, and Jonathon went back to his project. Then he packed up and left. He had a meeting in Flagstaff."

"Oh, I didn't know that." Archer didn't push.

Rarity wouldn't have told him about Jonathon's project or what meeting he was going to anyway. But he didn't even ask.

Shirley packed up her tote bag. "I can't believe it's so late already. I've got to run and see George and tell him all about today. He's going to be amazed at all the stuff I'm learning."

Rarity and Archer watched as she headed to the door. "I'll see you Saturday morning."

"If not before," Shirley called back, and then she was gone.

The bookstore was quiet, and Rarity let out a breath. "That woman is a ball of energy. She sucks all the energy from the room, then shoots it back out at people, covered in pink and red donut sprinkles. She lights up the entire store when she's here. The moms love her. She holds court for at least an hour after the session is done. And several of the moms tell me how much they're learning about raising a baby when they buy the next book." "The job has been good for her and the community." Archer reached down to rub Killer's head.

Rarity was closing up the register as she talked. "This energy wouldn't be happening if Janey was running the group. She didn't have the experience that Shirley has. One woman told me it was like having her mom around to ask questions. I guess her parents had died a few years ago. Everyone loves Shirley."

"As it should be. The woman's amazing. And this is with her worrying about George all the time. I think this job is helping her as much as she is helping others. She needed this, Rarity. Thank you."

"I should have thought of it sooner," Rarity admitted. She clicked Killer's leash on and handed it to Archer. "Hold him while I check the back door. I didn't go out, but you never know. Jonathon or Shirley might have taken Killer out."

He reached down and picked up the little dog. "Just hurry. I'm starving, and I want to make fresh French fries to go with the grilled burgers tonight."

"I'm hurrying because that sounds awesome." She went to the back room, then hurried over to the door. She checked the lock, then tried the door. All solid. As she was leaving, she saw something out of the corner of her eye. A face plastered itself against her window, and she screamed. She took two steps backward and ran into a table.

Archer ran in, with Killer now on the floor and on his heels. "What's wrong?"

"There was a face there." She pointed to the window.

"Hold Killer and stay here. I'm locking the front door just in case this is a trap." He took off from the back, and she could hear his footsteps as he ran to the front. When he got back, he had her baseball bat. She kept it behind the counter. She didn't think she'd scare anyone away by waving it, but it felt good to have it nearby. Especially if Archer was swinging it.

No one tried to open the door while Archer was gone, but Rarity didn't step closer to look out the window either. She'd seen too many horror movies where the arm broke through the glass or the door and pulled the victim through to the other side. Probably made up, but she wasn't taking any chances. She had no desire to be a final girl in someone else's story.

Archer came through the door. "Everything still all right?"

"Not sure, I didn't play Scooby Doo." She pointed to the outside window. "Can you see anyone in the alley?"

He leaned over and took a quick look into the alley. Then a second one. Finally, he opened the door and leaned out. "No one's out here. They must have run when you saw them."

Rarity went over and checked out the alley herself. She repeated, "I saw a face."

"I believe you. I think they just ran when they saw you. Maybe it was a kid just checking out the place." He closed the door and rechecked the lock. "Anyway, it's clear now. Let's go home. I'm starving."

"Me too." She stood from the table where she'd been leaning more than sitting. Just to be safe, she checked the lock and looked out the window to the alley before turning off the lights. She saw Archer watching her. "Sorry, I'm a little OCD on my closing process. I need to know the locks are set."

"Okay, I'll remember that." He took her in for a short hug. "I know things are crazy right now, so whatever you need to do to make yourself comfortable is fine by me."

She nodded as they left the room. "Worst-case scenario, they were looking for Sam's back door and just got the wrong window. Which means I need to call Sam and let her know that someone might be looking for her."

"I'll call Drew. Call Sam and see if she's still at the shop. If so, we'll go over there and wait." They stayed inside the bookstore while they made their calls.

"Sam's already home," she said when Archer hung up.

He nodded. "Drew's on his way over. He said he'd call Sam as soon as he checked it out. I guess we can go home."

Rarity snuck a peek out the window by the door. The outside didn't seem menacing, but she had seen someone in the alley. She took a deep breath, and Archer put his arm around her.

"It's going to be okay." He opened the front door. "This too shall pass."

"You sound like my cancer group. Always look at the bright side. And if things are bad, just push through." She locked the door and tucked her keys into her jacket pocket.

"Does it work?" Archer waited for her to turn around before walking toward the sidewalk.

"Sometimes," she admitted. "Other times, the darkness just needs to be pushed away, and you have to feel your feelings."

They walked in silence toward home. Rarity felt comfortable just being with Archer, not having to chat all the time, but she didn't know if he felt the same way. This was not the time to have a heart-to-heart since Archer was at her house until this murder was solved. But still, Rarity worried.

"Penny for your thoughts," Archer finally said.

"I was just thinking about Janey. Drew was supposed to find out who got her trust money. I wonder if he did?"

"You think someone thought they were inheriting, so they killed her for the money?" Archer nodded. "The thought had crossed my mind too."

"Everyone loved her. I can't see any other reason besides her money. And it had to be someone close. I didn't even know she had a trust. She didn't seem like the type."

"Marcus knew," Archer said.

Rarity turned her head. She could barely see his face in the darkening light. "What do you mean?"

"I talked to him at the Garnet that Saturday night. He was waiting for Janey to get off work. He said Janey kept surprising him. She appeared to be one thing, then she'd blurt out something, and he'd learn something new. Like her trust. He thought she was a poor college student. He joked that maybe he'd found himself a sugar mama." Archer shook his head. "Sorry, I know we're trying to get Marcus out of the suspect pool."

"Well, that helps. If he wanted her money, he'd have to marry her to get it, right? Just killing her wouldn't get him anything." Rarity walked up the steps to her porch. "Did we have a date that Saturday?"

"Actually, I met with Calliope. She wanted to talk to me." He followed her into the house after she unlocked the door. "She wanted a reference letter for a new job. Or at least that's what she said. I told her I'd write her one whenever. She didn't have to ask, just call me."

"You think she was checking in?"

He nodded. "She was friendly until I mentioned you. Then she clammed up and said she needed to leave. She gave me a piece of paper with the new employer name and fax number and then left."

"She still likes you." Rarity didn't want to say the word *love,* but she knew Archer's ex-assistant had it bad for her former boss.

He held up his hand. "We were just friends. At least on my part. I feel bad for her, but there isn't anything I can do to change my feelings. I love someone else."

Rarity smiled at him. "I hope so."

They spent the rest of the night not talking about Calliope or Marcus or the murder. Instead, they focused on dinner and what movie to watch. They even looked at calendars to see if they could fit in a short vacation soon. When she went to bed, she gave Archer a hug. "Thanks for being you."

"I think you're delirious." Archer laughed but hugged her back. "And thanks for being you."

* * * *

Thursday morning, Jonathon was waiting at the bookstore again when she showed up. He had his briefcase sitting beside him along with two coffees and a bakery bag. "Good morning. I heard Sam's shop had some excitement last night."

"What did Drew say?" Rarity unlocked the door and waved at Archer, who was already heading to his shop.

"He found traces of someone hanging out in the alley. He thinks it might be someone who's sleeping there at night. He's going to go back tonight and see if he can find the culprit." Jonathon followed her into the shop.

"He doesn't think it's tied to Janey's case, then?" Rarity unclipped Killer, and they moved into their daily chores.

"Not so much. I know it's possible, and it feels like someone's out there to get you, but sometimes, the right answer is the simplest." He held up his hand. "Occam's razor at its finest."

"Until he's wrong." Rarity held up her hand. "Don't worry, I'm not challenging Drew's conclusion. I'm just tired."

"You need a vacation." He settled back at the table he'd used yesterday. "I think I'm coming here to write more often. I got more words done yesterday than the last week at home."

"It's a bookstore. The books are supporting your endeavor." She opened the computer and started going through the inventory, finishing her order for the next week. Before she could finish, the phone rang. "The Next Chapter. This is Rarity."

"Hi, Rarity, it's Caleb. Sorry, I can't come in today. I'm under the weather."

"Oh no. I hope you didn't catch something from the kids on Saturday. They say that being around a lot of kids at first has you catching all kinds of things. You probably haven't talked to that many middle schoolers since you were attending one."

He laughed. "Probably not even then. I was a bit of a loner. Anyway, if I feel better, I'll be there Saturday, but don't count on me."

"Shirley's looking forward to running it, so I think we'll be fine. Of course, you're always welcome since I'm not sure how crazy it will be. Get better soon."

She hung up the phone and made a note on the calendar so she wouldn't forget and pay him for the day. She looked over at Jonathon. "Caleb's a no-show. Do you need to be somewhere else?"

He shook his head. "That's the joy of retirement. I get to make my own schedule. I'll run out at lunch and get us something to eat, but other than that, I'm at your beck and call."

"If you do that, you won't finish your words. You focus on what you need to do. I'll do the same. At the end of the day, we'll compare notes and see who was more productive."

"I do love a challenge. Game on." He focused on his laptop.

Rarity did the same. She didn't mind someone being around, like Jonathon, as long as they could entertain themselves while she worked.

After she got her Thursday tasks done, she looked at the plan for Saturday. The items were mostly done, just not treats ordered or the letters sent out. She sent out emails to the ones who'd signed up, using a picture that Caleb had sent her last week showing the book and the details about the club meeting. It was cute, and using emails kept the cost of announcing the club down. She'd continue to use the template, or Caleb would for the duration of the book club. She'd planned on running it for eight months, but if it was as successful as last week's meeting, she could see it going indefinitely. She needed to rethink what to do in summer and if they needed some advanced clubs or if you could move up a club level based on your reading level.

She was playing with some ideas when her first customer arrived. A young woman walked in with a black lab. Rarity glanced over at Killer, who was sleeping in his bed. She'd leave him there until she knew how the dog was with other dogs. As it was, she didn't have to worry. Jonathon had stood, stretched, then walked over and plucked Killer out of his bed and was walking around the store with him. Away from the other dog.

Bless you, Rarity thought.

"How can I help you today? Are you looking for something special?" Rarity smiled at the newcomer, finally looking at her face. "Oh, Cara, I'm sorry, I was focused on the dog. This must be Whiskey."

"Say hi to Rarity, Whiskey." Then Cara pulled a piece of paper out of her pocket. "I found this on the windshield of Janey's car. I think someone was stalking her."

Rarity took the paper and laid it on the counter. She grabbed a ziplock bag from Killer's tote and slipped the page into it before even looking at it.

"What are you doing?" Cara looked at Rarity like she was crazy.

"Keeping any fingerprints or smudges intact. You should have taken this to the police." Rarity looked at Cara, who was now pale with concern. "Don't worry about it. We'll call Drew, and he'll pick it up."

She nodded as Jonathon walked closer with Killer. "I didn't know who to trust. Her sister says that the cops just want to keep the killer off the hook. I think she's wrong, but you can't tell Trish anything."

Jonathon leaned over and read the note. "You shouldn't ignore me?"

"Yeah. She kept getting these notes, but she said she didn't know who was leaving them for her." Cara pulled a folder out of her bag. "When the cops came by, I was in shock, so I didn't think of them. But here are the other ones."

Rarity tried not to gasp when she saw how many notes were in the file. "Did she ever report this to the police?"

"Campus police, but they said it was probably just someone trying to scare her." She reached down and rubbed Whiskey's ears. "I wanted her to go to the Flagstaff police, but she never got around to it. Then the notes stopped coming, so she left it alone. She threw away the notes, but I pulled them out of the trash. I just had a feeling."

Jonathon was on the phone, probably with Drew.

Rarity looked up at Cara. "Thank you for bringing these. Do you mind hanging out until our detective gets here? I'm sure he'll have some questions."

"I don't know what I can say besides what I just did, but I can stay for a bit. My first class isn't until two today. It's lab day." Cara glanced down at Whiskey. "You don't mind if he's in here, do you? I hate to leave him alone. He misses Janey. We usually rotated our classes so he wasn't alone a lot. Now, it's just me, and he notices. Janey did take vacations at times, so I'm guessing he thinks she's just gone for a few days. But as time goes on, he keeps staring at the door, waiting for her to come home."

Whiskey's situation reminded her of Killer's situation. He'd lived with Martha before she'd been killed. Then she didn't come home either. Drew had brought him to Rarity in a huge carrier, and he'd been so scared. But he fit in faster than she'd expected. Maybe it was the new surroundings, or maybe he'd figured out that Martha wasn't coming back. Whiskey would do the same, but it would take a while. At least he had someone who loved him. "He's more than welcome to hang out. Does he want some water?"

When Drew arrived, he looked at the notes, then chatted with Cara for a few minutes.

Jonathon came over to Rarity. "Since you have company, I'm going to grab us some lunch. What do you want from the Garnet?"

She gave him her order and reached for her purse.

He shook his head. "Don't worry about it. I've got it."

After Cara left, Drew stood at the counter, glancing through the notes. "This thing just keeps adding on layers. I asked her why she didn't bring these up before, and she said she'd forgotten. Her friend was being stalked for over a year, and she forgot about it?"

Chapter 17

When Archer came to pick her up, he stopped short when he saw Jonathon. "Hey, I thought you were only here until Caleb showed up."

"And that's still true. Caleb didn't show." Jonathon shut his briefcase. "I'm meeting some friends for dinner, so I'll see you both tomorrow morning."

"Thanks for hanging out, Jonathon. I appreciate you taking time out of your day." Rarity squeezed his arm as he moved toward the door and lowered her voice. Archer had gone to the backroom to find Killer. "You really don't need to be here all the time."

"According to Drew, someone is to be with you at all times. If you don't like the rules, you talk to my son. I'm not doing it. Besides, I've gotten a lot of words written this week. If I stay longer, the book will be done and ready for revision by the time I go home." As Jonathon left, he nodded to Archer who'd come out of the back room, holding Killer. "Like I said, I'll see you tomorrow."

"He's such a nice man," Rarity said after Archer closed and locked the door behind him. "I'll finish closing up, and I'll be ready to go."

"I thought we could do fish and chips tomorrow night for a Friday thing. I checked the fridge, and you've got everything we need." Archer chatted as she wandered through closing the shop up. "I didn't know what to make tonight, though. Thoughts?"

They decided on having sloppy joes with tater tots. Something easy for a weeknight.

"You know, when you're not around, sometimes I just eat soup for dinner. Or rice."

"You just eat rice?" Archer shook his head. "Maybe we should talk about us moving in together. Just so you don't starve or die from malnutrition."

"I'm not starving myself." Rarity laughed. "But if you want to talk about moving in, I'm ready to have the conversation."

"Whoa, girl, you're moving fast today. Maybe I want to be wined and dined first?" He must have seen the shocked look on her face, because he laughed. "I'm just kidding you. I think we should talk about what our next step is. But I want to do that on vacation, not in between all the day-to-day stuff."

"Okay." Rarity glanced around the bookstore, distracted. "We can do that."

"Don't sound so excited." Archer nodded to the back room. "Do you want me to go check the lock?"

"I'm avoiding it, aren't I?" Rarity felt her face burn. "I'm not afraid, I promise."

Archer squeezed her arms. "There's been a lot going on. Don't worry about it. I'll be right back."

When he came back to the front, he reported, "Doors locked and lights off. No scary face in the window watching for you."

"Now, see, I feel rejected. Where is he today?" She grabbed her tote and Killer's leash. "Let's get out of here. I'm ready to make some dinner."

* * * *

The next morning, Rarity was drinking coffee while she waited for Archer to get off the phone. He was setting up another weekend group guide session. When he got off the phone, she opened her calendar. "When do you need a babysitter for me?"

"That's not really what I'm doing. I just can't be here Sunday. Maybe Holly or Malia could come and hang out with you?"

"I'll get it covered. When will you be home?" She wrote the information in her planner, then tucked it into the tote. "I'll call around this afternoon and get someone over here. Don't worry."

"I do worry. Maybe you should call now?"

"Holly just got off work, and Malia probably worked at the Garnet last night. I'm not waking either of them up before noon. I'm not sure I even could." She went to dump her coffee. "We better get going. Jonathon's going to be waiting outside in the cold."

"It's not that cold." Archer hurried to get his jacket and bag ready for work.

Jonathon was waiting for them when they arrived at the shop. He stood and followed Rarity into the bookstore. "Drew talked to Janey's sister last night. She's saying as far as she knows, she's the sole heir and executor of the will. She was a little put out when he suggested that Cara might have a claim. Apparently when the trust was set up by their grandparents, it had a clause that reverted the money from one sister to the other in case of death. Of course, anything that Janey had already taken out of the trust would be hers to do what she wanted in the will. I'm thinking we'll find that the money isn't as cut and dry as Trish thinks."

Rarity put her tote on the counter and unclipped Killer's leash. "So I wonder how Trish's finances are without the influx of Janey's money. Do we know how much the trust was worth?"

"Drew's requested a warrant to get all that information, and he has a meeting with Janey's lawyer, Catherine Johnson. She stopped using the family lawyer, Allen Holbart, a few years ago. Cara said Janey thought he was cheating them." Jonathon opened his briefcase and took out his laptop. "It's funny how loudly Drew talks in his den. With the television on low, I can hear most of his conversations. Especially since he tends to put everything on speaker. Just a warning in case you call him while I'm around." Jonathon took out his notebook. "I think that's all I needed to report. Now back to work on this novel. I'm enjoying having this investigation going on while I'm writing about this fictional one. It's giving me all kinds of ideas for red herrings and characters."

"Like the ex-cop who knows too much?" Rarity teased. "I just hope there's not a beautiful and intelligent bookstore owner who feeds the PI information about the seedy side of selling books."

He laughed and then focused on his computer. "Of course not. In my story, the bookstore owner is the killer."

Rarity went back to her own computer and work. She needed to finalize next week's book order and do payroll. Which reminded her, she still needed to pay Janey for her last few days of work. She looked up Catherine Johnson's phone number, then called, hoping to get ahold of the lawyer. Catherine had helped Rarity with some legal issues when she'd bought the store. Maybe she could help with this too.

"Hey, Catherine, I'm glad I caught you." Rarity saw Jonathon's head turn just a bit, and his fingers stopped moving on the keyboard. At least she knew she was being listened to. Not like Drew, who didn't realize how sound carried in his own house.

"Rarity, so nice to hear from you," Catherine said. "I've got a few minutes before my first appointment arrives. What can I help you with?"

"I have a question. I have a check for Janey Ford for work she did for me before she died. I understand you were her attorney. Should I just send it to you? Should I make it out to the estate or something? We were planning

on doing direct deposit, but I haven't even gotten that set up yet for her."
Rarity hoped she might get more information from Catherine about Janey
besides where to send her final check.

"Oh, that poor girl. It's so sad for her to be gone so young." Catherine
must have been typing, as Rarity heard keys clattering in the background.
"Let's look at her will. I just took over her finances a few months ago. Oh,
yes, she signed over a power of attorney for me to deal with these issues.
Send the check here, and I'll include it with the final distribution to her
heir when the court releases the funds."

"Sounds good. Cara could use all the money she can get to take care
of Whiskey. I bet that dog eats a lot."

Catherine laughed. "He's a bruiser, that's for sure. I'm glad her sister
wasn't put in charge of Whiskey. That girl would have the dog put to sleep
if she had control over the estate. Thank goodness Janey had withdrawn all
the trust funds before her death. Now Trish has no recourse. I know Cara
would much rather have Janey back, but this will help her keep the house."

"When things slow down, I need to get in and set up a will. I need to
have arrangements set up for Killer, just in case."

"Well, you come down anytime. I'll get that added to your will. I
know it's a pain, but thank goodness Janey had the foresight to make
sure Whiskey was taken care of. I know they're just pets, but they mean
a lot to us." A bell went off in the background. "Sorry, I've got to go. My
appointment's here."

Rarity got off the phone and added a note to her murder notebook. She
looked over at Jonathon. "Do you think I should call Drew?"

He shook his head. "I'm pretty sure Miss Johnson's next appointment
was with my son. Maybe he should hear it from the horse's mouth. But it
does shine a bigger light on the sister, doesn't it?"

"Except she has an alibi," Rarity reminded him.

Jonathon shook his head. "Sometimes alibis aren't airtight."

Rarity put the murder notebook away and tried to focus on getting
stuff done. When the third call to Caleb went unanswered, she called
Shirley. "Sorry to bother you, but are you planning on coming to the book
club tomorrow?"

"With bells on. I just finished reading this week's book. Is Caleb running
the discussion, or am I?"

"I'm thinking it's you. Caleb called in sick yesterday, and today I can't
reach him to ask about Saturday. If you feel up to it, that would be a godsend
for you to run the event." A weight dropped off Rarity's shoulders. Shirley
was going to handle it. Unless he decided to follow through, and he showed

up. Rarity wasn't sure if he could. She thanked Shirley and made a note when she'd be at the store.

Jonathon was up, pacing the bookstore. "Everything all right?"

"Fine. Shirley will be here from open to close tomorrow, so if you want a day off, that would be the best day." She watched him walk back and forth. "Are you stuck?"

"What? No, I'm just stretching my legs. I get up every hour and walk for a few minutes. It keeps my mind fresh along with keeping my body from rusting up." He put his hands on the counter and did a few back stretches. "Shirley's really enjoying her new role here, isn't she?"

Rarity nodded. "I think she was so lonely when George went into the home. I would have asked her sooner, but I didn't think she'd want to spend so much time away from home or George."

"Home can get lonely when no one's there. I'm sure Edith is spending a fair amount of time with the grandkids. She loves those little buggers." Jonathon turned to go sit down. "Let me know when you're hungry, and I'll go get us some lunch."

"Better yet, I'll order and pay for both of our lunches when we're ready, and then you can go pick it up. And I'll even close the shop while you're gone." Rarity gave up. If so many people were intent on keeping her safe, she wouldn't be the one who made their work useless and put herself in harm's way.

"You're learning." He smiled and went back to writing.

Rarity went into the back to start some coffee.

Caleb sat at the table. He had a gun in front of him. He looked up and blushed when she came in. "I didn't think you'd be in this early."

"Caleb, what are you doing?" Rarity stayed in the doorway, frozen. She didn't want to get shot.

"I came here to end my life. This was the last place Janey and I laughed together. I know she was dating your friend's brother, but I've been in love with her for years. She's always seen me in the friend zone. But here, we had projects together. We worked together. I thought if I left this world here, maybe I'd see her in the next life. Stupid, I know."

"Caleb, you can't kill yourself." Rarity tried to keep her voice level and just loud enough that Jonathon would hear her. But she couldn't risk turning her head to see if he was listening. "Janey wouldn't want that."

He sank deeper into his chair. "I'm not sure she'd even care. I used to call her, time and time again. Once she said hello, I knew everything was fine, and I'd hang up. But here, I needed to be here to be close to her."

Well, that explained one mystery. Who had been her stalker. The calls had been from Caleb. The attention that Rarity had seen between Caleb and Janey had been one-sided. And now, a very disturbed man had a gun in her back room. She glanced at the window. "It was you the other night peering in the back window, wasn't it?"

He nodded, then wiped tears away. "I couldn't stop thinking that maybe somehow she had gotten stuck here, in the bookstore. I didn't mean to scare you."

"Caleb, Janey is dead. She's not here in the bookstore." She tried to keep her voice calm and reasonable. She didn't think Caleb had those parts of his personality anymore.

"I know. We were just happy here. Was that so bad?" He started crying, and Rarity moved closer. She took the gun and put it behind her on the counter. Then she grabbed a box of tissues and handed it to him. He took several and didn't even seem to notice that she'd moved the gun.

Soon Rarity heard the front door open and footsteps, then murmured voices.

Drew came into the back room. He saw the gun first and crossed over, picking up the gun and handing it to an officer who came in with him. The officer disappeared with the gun, and Drew stood at the table, his hand on the top. "Caleb? My name's Drew. Can we talk?"

And as soon as Drew sat down, Caleb dissolved into tears. Drew rubbed his back, then asked if he had any other weapons. Caleb shook his head.

"Do you mind if I check?"

Caleb held his arms out to his sides, and Drew patted him down.

Rarity stepped out of the room and sank into a chair by the closest bookshelf. Jonathon came over and rubbed her back, a lot like Drew had just comforted Caleb. "Are you all right? Should we close the store and I'll take you home?"

She shook her head. "He's just so sad. I don't think he killed anyone. He just wanted to be loved."

"Well, that might be true, but he's not in his right head. And no one can be involved in a healthy relationship when you're not healthy yourself." Jonathon stood and met Drew's gaze as an officer led Caleb out of the bookstore. "Everything okay, or does Rarity need to leave the shop for a while?"

"We're fine. He's admitted breaking in last night just before you left. He hid in the stacks and just sat here for hours. I don't think he really would have killed himself, but he does need some help. I'll take him over to Flagstaff Psychiatric, and they'll hold him for a few days to see if they can get him stable." Drew met Rarity's gaze. "Are you all right?"

She nodded. "I just feel so bad for him. He was lost without Janey. Even though they never dated."

"Do you have his job application? I'd like to call his parents or relatives if possible. Maybe he's already been in treatment, and the docs can use that to help him now." Drew shook his head. "Archer's going to be steamed. He's been so focused on making sure you had someone with you, and still you get involved in this."

"Caleb wasn't here to hurt me. He just wanted his pain to end." Rarity glanced out the window where Caleb was being put into a police car. "Come over to the counter, and I'll get you a copy of his job application."

Drew leaned on the counter. "Not to be a downer, but now you're going to have to hire again."

"Well, for one spot. Shirley's taking over Janey's duties. So I just need one part-time person who loves books and hopefully likes to work with teenagers." She pulled out his file and without looking at it made copies for Drew. "Let me know where I should send his last check, okay?"

Drew chuckled and took the paperwork. "I'm sorry your hires aren't working out."

"It happens, I guess." She rolled her shoulders. "Maybe I should add some pointed questions in the interview. "Have you been or are you currently a stalker? Does anyone want to kill you or has attempted it in the past? Have you ever been incarcerated, and if yes, what for?"

"If you asked me those questions, I'd have to decline any offer of employment from you," Jonathon said.

Rarity looked around the empty shop. "Yeah, probably not the best way to hire trustworthy employees."

Chapter 18

With all the chaos, Rarity realized she hadn't called Holly or Malia. It was already three, and if she didn't call soon, they'd both be gone to work for the night. She dialed Holly's cell first. The women were roommates, so if she reached one, the other was sure to be nearby. The phone was answered on the first ring.

"Hi, Holly. I have a favor to ask you."

"Are you all right? I just heard about Caleb when Malia and I had lunch at the Garnet. Did he hurt you? Are you at the hospital and need a ride home? We were just about to call and see what we could do." Holly rattled on a mile a minute.

Rarity smiled at her friend's concern. It was nice having people who cared. Scary at times, but nice. "Hold on a minute. I'm fine. There wasn't a problem. I can tell you all about it if someone will come to my house on Sunday to sit with me. Archer is doing a private tour, and Drew still doesn't want me alone." She felt like she was four hundred years old.

"I'll be there. Can I bring my laundry? I was planning on doing it on Sunday," Holly explained.

"Sure, that would be fine." She made a mental note to put her own laundry chores on Saturday's list. She could fold on Sunday, but the machines had to be clear for Holly. "Malia's welcome too. Or if you can't come and she can. Whatever works."

"Malia has a date." Holly started laughing, and after what sounded like a struggle, Malia came on the line.

"I have a study session on Sunday, but I'll be there as soon as I'm free. If you want me to come, that is." Malia offered an explanation.

"Malia, that would be amazing. But if you're busy, don't worry about it. Archer just doesn't want me alone." Rarity told her the time she needed to be there.

"Then you won't be alone." She sighed. "Holly wants to talk to you again. I'll be there as soon as I'm free."

"That's fine."

Holly came back on the phone. "See, it's got to be a date. She'd dump a study group faster than a load of rocks for a chance to hang out. Anyway, I'm getting the evil eye from our friend. I'll see you at seven."

The store started getting busy as soon as Drew left. She didn't know if all businesses worked this way, but it seemed like anytime a cop car showed up at her business, walk-in traffic would stop while they were there. Then after they left, they'd be swamped with customers. Most were looking for information on what had happened, but every one of them bought at least one book to have some time to chat with Rarity.

She felt a little bad about milking the attention, but as she saw it, at least they got a good book for their trouble. And anyone with that much curiosity needed at least one book to enjoy. At least that was her story. Jonathon kept himself busy, and if someone asked him, he feigned ignorance and sent them to Rarity to get their questions answered.

Rarity glanced at her calendar and saw that she still had the hair appointment tomorrow morning. She watched as Jonathon was packing up his laptop. "Any chance you want to drive with me to Flagstaff tomorrow morning so I can get my hair done?"

He closed his briefcase. "People are going to start to talk, even if I am old enough to be your grandfather, but yes, I'd be happy to go."

"You're old enough to be my father, and if you need me to call Edith and tell her why you're hanging out with me, I will." She got her own tote ready and sat to wait for Archer to arrive. "Archer's busy, or I'd make him go."

"I'm always busy. What am I getting out of now?" Archer came into the building and shook Jonathon's hand. "I hear you two had a busy day yourselves."

"Your girl here is taking me with her to get her hair done by Miss Ford's fancy guy. I'm going to start calling myself a bodyguard. It looks better on a resume." He chuckled and waved at Rarity. "I'll see you in the morning. Six at the house?"

"Yep, and I'll buy you breakfast for your trouble." Rarity came around the counter and sank into Archer's arms. "It's been a really long day. But you'll be happy to know that Holly and maybe Malia are coming over on Sunday when you're off hiking with your buddies."

"When I have a job, not hiking with my buddies," he corrected her. "Anyway, after what happened today, I'm not sure even keeping someone with you is enough. Maybe I should wrap you in bubble wrap and put you in a closet."

"Hey, not my fault someone broke in and decided to stay. Although I am rethinking my hiring practices. Janey would have been amazing, but Caleb, he has issues. So I'm at a twenty-five-percent failure rate." Rarity walked over to the back room and glanced around before she stepped in. "Just make sure the door is locked and turn out the lights."

"Does talking yourself through the steps help?" Archer stood in the doorway, watching her.

"Yes, for today, it does." She checked the lock and forced herself to look out the window to the alley. No one was there. She let out her breath and went over to turn off the lights. "I guess I need to walk through the bookstore too. He said he hid in the stacks last night."

"You can, if it will make you feel better. I think someone like Caleb hiding in the bookstore is kind of a one-off thing." Archer met her gaze. "But let's go through the exercise anyway. You take that side, and I'll go to the left where the bathrooms are."

When they met back up in the middle at the counter, she picked up her tote and handed Archer Killer's leash. "I'm surprised Killer didn't say anything."

"He knew Caleb. Why would he?" Archer leaned down and picked the dog up. "Having a guard dog only works if your intruder isn't someone he already knows."

"True." She rubbed Killer's head. "Sorry if I'm inviting the wrong sort into your life."

"I'm sure he'll deal with it." Archer set him down and nodded to the door. "Let's go make fish and chips. Unless you'd rather eat at the Garnet? We can do dinner out if you'd rather. I can drop you off there, then I'll take Killer home and come back. By the time I'm back, we should have food."

She felt worn out. "Do you mind if we eat at the Garnet?"

"I just offered, so no, I don't mind." He pulled her into a hug. "Do you have a book to read while you wait, or do you want to grab one?"

She tapped her bag. "I never leave home without one. Even to come to the bookstore. I need to do a 'staff recommends' for this month's newsletter, and I'm running out of staff to delegate the assignment to, so I guess it's me."

He laughed and turned off the lights as they stepped out. "The joys of owning your own business. Did I tell you I think I found someone to work part-time at the shop? He's a hiker and needs a 'real' job to support his habit. He's going to school in Flagstaff but lives here with his folks. And he's majoring in accounting."

"Sounds like a perfect match." She locked the door and stepped up to meet Archer. "What do you want at the Garnet?"

"I'm dropping you at the front door. So we have time to talk about that." Archer put his arm around her. As they walked to the restaurant, he chatted. "I'm thinking about a Sedona burger with cheddar cheese and fries. We can do fish and chips tomorrow night."

"Sounds good." She felt her energy increasing now that they were out of the bookstore. Maybe it had just been all the negative vibes from Caleb that had sapped her. Now that she was out in the cool air, she felt better.

"What about you?" Archer asked. "What are you having for dinner?"

"A glass of wine, and after that, I'm not sure. I'll have to look at the menu." She watched as Killer greeted everyone who passed them on the street.

"You've seen that menu more than a hundred times. You'll look at it, then you'll do the halibut with rice and a side salad or the chicken with mushrooms." He nodded to the crosswalk, and they crossed with the light.

"Like I said, I need to see the menu." She laughed at the look on his face. "Seriously, I don't know what I'm getting until I weigh my options. And I might see something that someone else ordered that looks better than what I was thinking about."

"You're a goof." He opened the door for her and kissed her lightly. "I'll be back. Order me a beer, will you?"

"Of course." She moved to the hostess stand and waited for the woman to greet her.

She looked up and then around Rarity. "Just one tonight?"

"No, Archer is on his way, so two. Can you seat me now?" The place didn't look that busy.

"Sure, I'll put you in Malia's section." The girl grinned and picked up two menus.

Apparently, the hostess knew her. She sat down and looked at her name tag. "Thanks, Jessica."

"No problem. I'll be at the book club next week before my Saturday shift. I loved this book. Whoever chose it was spot on. It really spoke to me about the problems high school kids deal with." Jessica saw the door open and turned back to the hostess stand. "Have a great dinner."

Rarity opened her menu and thought about Caleb. He'd chosen the next six months' of books for the teen book club. Hopefully Shirley could use the group to choose more. Rarity didn't read young adult, but she decided no matter what book any of the clubs were going to read, she would read them too. That way, if she ever needed to step in to help out, she'd be prepared. She took out her planner and put a note on tomorrow's to-do list. It was too late to read the elementary school choice before tomorrow's meeting, but she'd read it anyway in case there were follow-up questions. She opened her phone, pulled up her website, and wrote out all the books that the clubs were reading for this month and next.

Malia was standing there, watching her make her list. "That's a lot of books."

"I need to be prepared for these clubs, just in case Shirley can't do the meeting." She shut the planner. "I'm supposed to order. Archer took Killer home, and he'll be right back."

"The kitchen's running a little slow anyway, so I think you'll be fine. What can I get for you?" Malia wrote down their order, then took the menus. "And just one more thing. No matter what Holly says, this thing Sunday is not a date. We're just getting together to study for an exam."

"Okay, you said that, so why are you worried about me knowing it?" Rarity watched as the pink flowed into Malia's cheeks. "Wait, so you're worried that *he* thinks it's a date? Do you like him?"

She glanced around the room and leaned closer. "I do like him. And this is the first time he's asked me to study with him, so I don't want to read too much into it."

"So don't. Go and be prepared to study. If he asks you to do dinner afterward, just let us know you're not coming over. I don't want to worry." Rarity pulled out the book she'd been reading that week. It wasn't on any of the book club lists, but it was so good.

"I'll get this in to the kitchen. I'll hold off on Archer's beer, but do you want your wine now?" Malia nodded toward another table that had just been seated, letting them know she'd be right with them.

"That would be amazing." She leaned back and opened her book. When Malia came back with the wine, she also had a basket of fresh rolls and butter.

"To hold you over." She moved to the next table and greeted them.

She had been going to wait to eat until Archer got there to eat, but the rolls smelled amazing. She took one and broke it open, watching the steam escape with another fresh scent of warm bread. She slathered on some butter and took a bite. It was heaven.

When Archer arrived, the breadbasket was empty. He picked it up and turned it over. "Was it something good?"

"Oh, the bread was amazing. Ask Malia to bring you some." Rarity felt her cheeks heat. She hadn't meant to eat all of the rolls. She'd just been engrossed in the book. "How mad was Killer?"

"I'm going to say he was at a five, but he tried to be all chill about it. I gave him one of his stuffed animals, and he shook it hard, then threw it across the floor." Archer slipped onto the bench seat next to her and smiled as Malia came from the bar with his beer and another basket of bread. "You're an angel."

"I'm an attentive server." She picked up the empty basket. "It looks like your meals will be out in a few minutes."

"Thanks, Malia." Archer grabbed one of the rolls. "I'm starving."

"I hear Caleb tried to confess to Janey's murder," Malia said, "but he guessed the time and place wrong. He said he followed Janey onto the trail that runs to the waterfall, not the quarry, just about an hour before Marcus was supposed to meet Janey at the quarry. He shot at her, and she went running. He was sure he'd killed her."

"Wait, why would he confess to something he didn't do?" Rarity finished the last sip of wine.

"Because he's crazy? Anyway, rumor is he was stalking Janey even before they started working at your store. He's a nutcase." Malia pointed to Rarity's glass. "Do you want another?"

"One more and a glass of water." Rarity took one last roll while she thought about Malia's news. "I still don't know why he'd admit to seeing her, much less shooting at her. I guess he said he used the same gun that he had at the shop?"

"Crazy is as crazy does." Malia waved at a new customer that had just been seated in her section. "Sorry, I've got to go. Hopefully, I'll see you Sunday, or at least on Tuesday."

Archer watched Malia walk away. "I thought she and Holly were coming over Sunday. Are you hiding things from me?"

Rarity laughed as she tucked her book away in her tote. "Me? I'm an open book. Malia, on the other hand, she might have a date on Sunday."

"What do you mean, might?"

Rarity smiled after she finished her roll. "Don't worry about it. Holly's a definite yes. We just don't know if Malia will be visiting with us on Sunday."

"You've totally lost me." Archer leaned back as a server put his dinner in front of him. "And I'm too hungry to even try to figure it out. As long as Holly's going to be there, I'll be happy."

They ate dinner and then paid the check. As they walked back to Rarity's house, she thought about Caleb. "Did you notice that Trish and Janey look like twins?"

He chuckled. "They are twins. I was with Drew when he found out. They went to Flagstaff High, and he found their yearbook with their pictures. They really looked the same when they were kids."

"It must be hard losing your twin. You've been together all your life, literally. Even in the womb." Rarity was starting to feel sorry for Trish. Maybe that was why she wasn't so friendly with Janey's friends and coworkers. She was probably still grieving the loss of her sister. When they got home, Terrance was sitting on his porch next door. He waved as they walked by.

"Terrance is on the night shift this week. He says it's payback for him missing a meeting last week when he was on his cruise." Archer lifted his hand to wave back at the older man.

"One more person watching out for me. I think I'm going to be fine." Rarity unlocked the door. She was glad to be home.

"Until you consider, with all those people watching your back, someone still got into your bookstore with a gun." Archer followed her inside. "I know, he wasn't there to kill you, but what if he had been?"

Chapter 19

The next morning, Rarity sat drinking coffee at the table when someone knocked on the door. Archer had been in the guest bedroom, but before she could get up, he was at the door opening it for Jonathon. "Hey, come on in. You're right on time."

"Then I'm late. My mother always said to be ten minutes early." He nodded toward Rarity. "That coffee looks good. Do we have time for me to have a cup?"

"Of course." Rarity rose and got him a cup, and she and Jonathon sat down at the table.

Archer walked over and gave her a kiss. "I've got to get to the shed and warm up the bus. I'm picking the group up at eight in front of the shop. I'll see you at the bookstore?"

"I'll stay until Shirley gets there, if not longer. I don't want to kill the writing if I'm in a flow state." Jonathon waited for Archer to leave. "I keep slipping up and talking about writing in front of Archer. Anyway, I suppose you heard about Caleb's confession."

"Yeah. Has Drew talked to Trish yet?" Something wasn't adding up between the two sisters.

"I think so. Nothing more than that she thought she was getting Janey's part of the trust." Jonathon sipped his coffee. "Why?"

"You heard me talking to my attorney, who is actually Janey's attorney too, right?" Rarity knew she'd hit the button when Jonathon blushed.

"Yes, I'm ashamed to say I listened in on your conversation. Why?"

"So if Trish didn't know Janey had taken the trust money out and put it into her own accounts, she still might be a suspect. Just because what she thought would happen didn't, doesn't mean she didn't kill Janey for the money." Rarity put her head between her hands. "It's driving me crazy that I can't pin the actual murder on her, but I still feel like her motive is the strongest. Even though it wasn't in actuality."

"But if she thought it was..." Jonathon added.

"And now you're down the rabbit hole with me. Maybe I can get Roger Kamp to tell us that she wasn't getting her hair done that day." Rarity sank back down in her chair. "Even though the receptionist checked on the appointment and said she did."

"You really want Trish to be the killer, don't you?" Jonathon sipped his coffee. "Mind if I change the subject for a bit?"

"Go ahead. My head keeps spinning this same record over and over. Maybe having something else to think about will get me out of this loop." Rarity stood and refilled her coffee. She lifted the pot to offer Jonathon more, but he shook his head.

"I was wondering if you knew of any good writing books. I've come to find out that writing a novel is hard work. I'd take a class, but there aren't any at the local colleges on how to write fiction unless you want to get an MFA or go back for a second degree. And there, it's all about studying the masters." He sighed. "If I read all those classics, I'll be dead before I get this book done."

"Stephen King says you have to read a lot to be a writer. So let's put you on some type of plan. Maybe a writing craft book, then a book in your genre or one I loved the writing in. First you need King's *On Writing* book and a crazy-plotted book. I know, *Oona Out of Order.* She goes back and forth in time, so the plotting is amazing. I've got a copy of both of them at the store. Then I'll make you a list of what to read for the next few months."

Jonathon didn't answer, and when she looked up, she realized he was staring at her. "What? Have you already read those?"

"No, I'm just amazed that whatever problem gets thrown at you, you always have a book to recommend. Bookselling was always supposed to be your career." He covered her hand with his. "And now you're on your right path. Some of us take a little longer to find our perfect line of work."

"I'm happy to help." As she finished her coffee, she realized that was true. She *was* right where she was supposed to be. Maybe not in Sedona, but even that was turning out to be a perfect place to live a life filled with friends and activities. She glanced at the clock. "We better get going, or I'm going to be charged for a haircut I didn't get."

She drove to the salon, and Jonathon sat outside in the car. "Are you sure?"

"The women in those places look at me like I'm some sort of puzzle to be figured out. I can see you from the car. If you go back farther, I'll come inside to wait, but for now, I'm going to give Edith a call. I like to touch base with her before she starts her day." He held up the phone. "Unless you want me to go inside with you."

"No, I'll be fine. It will be refreshing not to have a shadow everywhere I go." Rarity went into the salon and checked in with the receptionist. It was a different girl than who was here the last time. "Rarity Cole to see Roger Kamp?"

"His Saturday morning clients tend to no-show, so I'm not sure that he'll be glad to see you. He's typically taking a nap in the back. I'll go let him know you're here." The girl, Salena, stood.

Well, that was interesting. Maybe Trish didn't show on that Saturday. Rarity held out her hand. "Hold on a second. What happens when someone no-shows? Do you take the appointment off the schedule?"

Salena shook her head and turned the computer. "No, we just put an *X* by the name. That way, the next time they call for an appointment, we know they didn't show for this one. If they get three *X*s in a row, they have to get the stylist to agree to see them again."

"Can I see the schedule for the first Saturday in September?" Rarity hoped Salena wouldn't say no.

"Sure, I know he had at least one no-show that day. He sends me out for muffins and pays if we get two in a row." She hit a couple of keystrokes, and there was Trish's appointment with an *X* by her name.

"So this one, for example. That's a no-show?" Rarity asked. Excitement filled her as she waited for a response.

"Yep. But let me tell Roger you're here so he can get ready." She reached out and touched Rarity's hair. "You really need a cut to get rid of those split ends."

Rarity thought about just taking off as Salena went to the back to get Roger, but maybe he had more to say about Trish. And as she pulled her curls toward her, maybe she did need some self-care time. She turned to look out the window and saw Jonathon watching her. She gave him a thumbs-up gesture, and he nodded.

"He's coming out. Please take this chair." Salena stood at a chair near the front.

Rarity headed to where Salena stood and, as she sat down, glanced over at Jonathon. He repeated her thumbs-up gesture, so he must have been able to see her clearly.

Salena put a cape over her and asked, "Do you want some cucumber water?"

"No, I'm good." Rarity leaned back and tried to relax.

"Probably for the best, I haven't made any fresh today. I can get you some coffee if you want," Salena whispered quietly. There was only one other customer in the shop, and they were sitting in the waiting room with a glass of water in their hand.

"No thanks. I'm doing breakfast after this, and I had two cups at home. I'll be shaking from the caffeine soon."

"Good morning. I'm glad you decided to come and not waste Roger's time," a male voice said, and Rarity met his gaze in the mirror. Roger was talking about himself in the third person. Interesting.

"I'm glad you could fit me in. My life is crazy, so doing this early really helps." Rarity smiled at him. "I run a bookstore in Sedona."

"Books are fabulous. I'm thinking of writing a book about my life. Of course, I'll have to change all the names, but you'd be surprised at what people will tell me." He ran his fingers through Rarity's hair. "You still want this in layers? I think it would frame your face better if we shortened it a bit."

"I'll leave it in your hands." She hoped she wasn't making a huge mistake. "I just don't want something too short or too labor intensive."

"I will make you look beautiful even if you just got out of bed." He winked at her and sprayed water on her hair. "So a bookstore, huh? One of my clients just found out her sister worked at a bookstore before she died. Trish was very upset that her sister had chosen retail work."

"That was Janey. She worked for me. She was so sweet and smart. I'm going to miss her."

"Well, she wasn't like her sister, then. Sweet and smart are not words I'd use to describe Trish. Demanding, pushy, mean. Those words are more accurate. Funny how twins can be so different." He picked up scissors and started cutting Rarity's hair.

She sent up a prayer that it would look okay and swallowed. "I didn't know they were twins."

"Yes. I knew their mother before she passed. The girls had both just started college. Trish went back east for school, but Janey, she stayed nearby. Mrs. Ford was very ill by that time, but she still came in weekly for a style. Janey would bring her to her appointment, but she didn't get her hair done. She didn't need to. She was beautiful. But I could have done more." He chatted about the family and their lives, at least before Mrs. Ford had died. "When Trish moved back after college, she started coming to me as well. She didn't like to talk about her family much, though. For her, it was all about the charity events."

Rarity listened as he went on and on about the different events she'd attended, and he'd done her hair to match her designer gowns. Finally, he turned her to the mirror. "So what do you think?"

Rarity reached up to touch her hair. It looked curly, healthy, and bouncy. She loved it. "It's great."

"Well, don't forget to schedule your next appointment. If you let it grow out, it won't stay that way. Beauty takes maintenance." He took her cape off. "Pay Salena and make your next appointment with her. I'm heading to the back to take a breath."

When Rarity got back into the car, Jonathon nodded his approval. "You look amazing."

"Thanks, but I have something better. Trish didn't keep her hair appointment on the Saturday that Janey died. And she wasn't happy with Janey working for me in retail." She started the car. "We still have time for breakfast. Are you hungry?"

"Starving." He held up his notebook. "And I got the next chapter plotted out, so when we hit the bookstore, I can keep writing."

* * * *

By the time they got back to Sedona, Jonathon had already texted Drew with the information about Trish's missed appointment. So much for having an alibi. Rarity was sure the Tuesday night group would have a lot to say about this new information, but she wondered if Drew wouldn't find the killer before the sleuthers' club even had time to theorize. Trish was her main suspect. The evidence didn't totally support her decision, but the motive fit. And now she could have done the deed.

She opened the bookstore, and Jonathon made his way to his table to set up his mobile office. Rarity walked through the building, checked the locks on the back door, and then reviewed Caleb's plan for the upcoming book club. By the time Shirley arrived at nine, she'd gone through most of the checklist. She handed Shirley the clipboard and a pen. "Here you go. I've checked off everything I've already done."

"Why is Jonathon here?" Shirley nodded toward his writing table.

"He's my bodyguard. Well, until you get here. Then you are." Rarity laughed at Shirley's face. "I'm joking. Drew just doesn't want me alone at the bookstore."

"That makes sense. Well, Jonathon, before you leave, please go out to my SUV and get the treats. There are two trays and a box filled with sodas.

I grabbed a bag of ice as well and a tub to put all the drinks in." Shirley pulled out a book-themed table covering. "Rarity, you can help me with this while Jonathon brings in the food."

"I live to serve." Jonathon threw the two women a hand salute.

Rarity laughed and elbowed Shirley. "Thanks, Jonathon. Shirley and I appreciate your help."

"Oh, yeah, thanks," Shirley muttered as she smoothed the cloth on the table. "I'm so nervous to lead a group of teenagers. Babies are easy. I feel like I'm walking into the lion's den today."

As the time for the book club got closer, people started coming in. A few parents came in and bought some books, including the next month's club read, but then they'd leave, telling their kids they'd be back in an hour or would meet them somewhere downtown. By the time the group started, the only people in the store that were over eighteen were Rarity, Shirley, and Jonathon, who was still trying to work on his laptop.

As Shirley started the group, he came over and leaned on the counter, watching the group. "It's a little loud in here to write."

"Do you want to use the back room? You'd be doing me a favor. I keep having to shoo couples out of there who think it's a great place to make out."

He snorted as he went to get his laptop. "I'll go play mall cop for you. I'm pretty sure one look at me would stop all those hormones fast. Maybe we should pair up this group with your Mommy and Me class so they can see what can happen if they're not careful."

Rarity laughed, and Shirley glanced over to see what was happening. She turned to check on Killer, who had tucked himself into the bed she kept behind the counter as soon as people started to show up.

"I'll stop bothering you so you won't get in trouble." Jonathon went around the counter and through the door to the back room.

Rarity pulled out the book that the group was talking about and tried to finish reading it. She only had a few more chapters, and before Shirley led the group in a discussion of the cliffhanger ending, Rarity had finished. She tucked the book under the counter and picked up next month's book. It was still considered YA, but this time, there was a mystery involved. She started reading the book and was surprised when she was interrupted by a young woman with a stack of books to purchase. Shirley's club was over, and the kids were either hurrying out or wandering through the bookstore. One couple tried to go into the back room but must have seen Jonathon, because they'd backed out and then went outside.

Rarity smiled at the girl standing in front of her. "Did you enjoy the book club?"

The girl shrugged. "My mom said if I went, she'd give me fifty dollars to buy more books with. So I came. She's always trying to get me out of the house. My sister, she loves hanging out with her friends, so Mom worries about me."

The girl was so honest, Rarity wasn't sure what to say. She decided to focus on the books. "Well, we're glad you came. And these are all amazing choices. I've heard good things about all of these, but I haven't had time to read them. Maybe you could write a review for our newsletter on one of them sometime."

The girl blinked. "You want me to write a review?"

"I'd love it. I don't have a lot of staff, so readers' reviews are hard to come by. I'd love to have a book club member reviewing books that we don't get to cover in the club." Rarity was making this up as she went along. Then she had a brilliant idea. "I could pay you with a book club credit. If your writing is good enough, that is."

"I always get As in English, and I've been reviewing on Goodreads for about a year. My mom always reads them before I post, just in case there's a problem." She handed over the fifty-dollar bill to pay for her stack of books. "You're not kidding me, right?"

"I'm not. It's a bona fide offer. I'm Rarity Cole. I own this place." Rarity handed her back her change and a receipt. " So what's your name?"

"I'm Staci Patterson. My mom was your real estate broker. I was so excited to get an actual bookstore in town. Before, I'd have to beg her to take me to Flagstaff or buy them online." She pushed back a curl that had fallen in her eyes.

"Nice to meet you, Staci. Come by when you have a review for me to consider." Rarity saw Staci's mom standing outside the bookstore in the courtyard. She waved at the woman she'd worked with to buy the building. "Your mom's here."

As Rarity finished up the last few purchases, Shirley came by and helped put books into bags and to say goodbye to the few remaining stragglers. Finally, the bookstore was empty. "Well, that went better than I'd expected. I was hoping Caleb would show up and help me, but I muddled through."

"Shirley, I need to tell you something." Rarity went on to tell her about Caleb and his last visit. As she was finishing up, Jonathon came out of the back room with his laptop.

"Rarity, I checked the back door, and someone had unlocked it. I don't know if they were just going out to smoke or something, but I relocked the door. You may want to think about that during your next club meeting. At least with the high school group. They were a little hard to corral. You may need several people to help on club days."

Chapter 20

On Sunday, when Malia joined Holly and Rarity at the house, Rarity brought up the issue she was having with the teen book club. "Shirley and I need help with our high school book club. I'll pay you for the two hours and buy the book for you if you want to read it, but mostly we just need chaperones to make sure the participants stay in the discussion area and to monitor the store and back room."

Holly raised her hand. "I love reading YA. Pick me."

Malia elbowed her friend as they sat outside on the deck. "I'll come too, as long as I don't have a shift at the Garnet. It's from ten to noon on the third Saturday, right?"

"Exactly. And I could use both of you." Rarity loved her group of friends. She knew she could count on them for help when she needed it. Even with this specific request. "Remind me to give you next month's book on Tuesday at book club. Are both of you going to be there?"

"Of course. I've got some dirt on Caleb. Apparently, he has a habit of stalking coeds on campus. One of my friends said he followed her around until she had a classmate tell him they were dating and to buzz off. All she did was be nice to him in class once, and she couldn't get rid of him." Malia dipped her chip into her salsa. They each had their own bowls of chips and salsa since Holly insisted that Malia often double-dipped, which Malia disputed.

"Interesting. Except, apparently, Caleb had the wrong place and time of death when he confessed to shooting at Janey. Even so, I think he's going to be staying at the psychiatric hospital for a while. They found pictures in his apartment of Janey and other girls. And he had his own darkroom. I guess he didn't like digital pictures." Rarity sipped her beer. She'd already swum today, so now all she needed to do was fold laundry and relax. The rest of the chores could wait. And with Archer temporarily living here with her, he took care of a lot of cleaning chores during the week. The guy was pretty close to perfect as a boyfriend.

They were having a taco bar for lunch, but they'd been waiting for Malia to finish with her study date or one o'clock, whichever came first.

"Speaking of guys at school, was that Dane O'Conner who just dropped you off in front of Rarity's?" Holly asked.

Malia flushed, and Holly laughed.

"I knew it. I saw you two talking at the game yesterday. He's a cutie."

Malia shook her head. "He's my partner for a sociology class project. Nothing more."

Holly held up her hand. "Fine, and I didn't see the two of you kiss anyway. What good is a secret romance if you're not even going to kiss?"

"Let's change the subject." Rarity was happy for Malia. The girl had kept herself closed off for so long, worried that the cancer would come back. Now she had a chance at love. She deserved it. "So Caleb probably didn't kill Janey. Who do you think did?"

"Her sister." Holly set her beer on the table. "She's entitled and wanted the rest of the trust money. She's probably already spent her inheritance and now needs her sister's money. 'What's yours is mine' kind of thing."

"Yeah, I'm thinking Trish too." Rarity picked up her last chip and dug out the rest of the salsa to go with it. She thought better as she ate. "She's just not a nice person."

"That doesn't mean she killed anyone. What about that lawyer who was at the funeral? He looked like a potential murderer," Malia suggested.

"He's too wimpy-looking to kill anyone, even Janey," Holly offered, but then she looked up and noticed Rarity and Malia watching her. "What? Don't tell me you weren't saying the same thing when you saw him."

"He doesn't look like he has any kind of workout routine," Rarity admitted. "But have we totally ruled out Marcus? I know Sam would hate me right now, but we don't have evidence to prove he didn't do it."

"His timeline. The coroner said Janey died at one thirty or after. He was on a Zoom call with his team during that time." Malia reminded them of how Sam had explained his whereabouts.

"One thirty California time or Arizona time?" Holly challenged.

"Is there a difference?" Rarity was confused. Time zones did that to her, especially when she was trying to catch a plane when she traveled. Well, when she had traveled when she'd been a marketing consultant.

Once, she'd missed a meeting because she thought it was an hour earlier than it was where she landed.

"I'll check it out." Holly glanced at her watch. "Can we start lunch? I need to be at work at five."

Malia nodded. "I'll stay until Archer gets back. We all need to sign up for one of his hikes next week."

"I work graveyard," Holly grumbled as they moved into the kitchen to make the ingredients for the taco bar.

"Then we'll do it early so it will be right after you're off work. You'll sleep great that day," Malia suggested. "Are we making homemade tortillas? They're the best."

* * * *

After the others had left and Archer was in the shower, Rarity pulled out her murder notebook. She'd had a few suspects listed, and as she reviewed the names, she felt like she could cross off most of them, except Trish.

Would a sister kill her own twin? She knew now that Trish hadn't been in Flagstaff getting her hair done. So where had she been? And this lawyer still bothered Rarity. He seemed way too familiar, at least with Trish. Had he been in on the murder too?

But if the lawyer had been in on it, that killed Trish's motive because he would have known that Janey had drained her trust. Unless he thought she hadn't made a new will. It was almost seven and too late to call Catherine to see if she'd talked to Allen Holbart about Janey's new will. He was helping Trish sue Cara. Would Catherine talk anyway? Or would that be attorney-client privilege? Would she need to tell the other attorney he wasn't doing her work anymore?

Rarity sighed and put the book away in her tote. Maybe Jonathon would know more about what an attorney would do in this situation. And why. She'd talk to him in the morning before he got involved in his writing.

"You look tired. Is the investigation getting to you?" Archer sat next to her on the couch. She hadn't heard him come into the living room. He pushed back his wet hair. "I talked to Drew when I was driving the bus back to storage. He's frustrated with everything. His dad keeps second-guessing his actions, Sam's still not talking to him, and now Marcus says that as soon as Drew tells him he can, he's moving back to California."

"Which means Sam's going to blame Drew for Marcus not staying." Rarity closed her eyes. "I am tired of this whole thing. The drama everyone seems to have in their lives is making me freak out. Seriously, this is nothing, and everyone's trying to make their lives the issue. A woman is dead. That's the issue. We should be focusing on who killed Janey, not whose feelings are getting hurt."

"Before this week, I would have put money on Caleb. He just looks like a stalker. Especially when he was around Janey. I only met him a few times, but he was suspect number one in my book."

Rarity turned and looked at him. "Because of the way he looked at Janey?"

Archer shrugged. "That and the vibe he puts out. He's all not a care in the world, then you see flashes of something under that carefree attitude. Like he was wearing a mask."

"Well, I guess I only saw the mask. I knew he was in love, in lust, in something for Janey, but I thought it was just one of those attractions." She stretched her neck. "I can't believe tomorrow's Monday. Having Saturday events makes the weekend go really fast."

"You might want to close on Monday and give yourself a full two days off," Archer said. "Of course, I do my paperwork on Mondays, so I'm still in the office. There's just not walk-ins since the sign says closed."

"I kind of do that anyway, with opening late on Monday. Not very many people walk in, but I'm there if a tour bus hits town." She took his hand in hers. "Who would have thought I'd be missing my Monday-to-Friday routine with corporate America?"

"Running a small business isn't for the weak. We work all the time, and when we're not working, we make lists of things we should be doing when we are." He squeezed her hand. "Do we have enough leftovers for a taco dinner?"

"Of course, but I'm making mine a taco salad." She stood and pulled him to his feet. "Want to help?"

"I was going to handle it and just bring you a beer so you could relax." He leaned in and kissed her. "You've had a busy week."

"I've had a crazy week. Helping you with dinner is a spot of normalcy I'd like to enjoy." She followed him into the kitchen and opened the fridge, handing him things as she found them. "I'm getting used to having you around all the time. I'm going to miss you when this is over and you go back to your apartment."

He didn't say anything. When Rarity looked up, he was watching her. "What?"

"That's the nicest thing you've said to me." He leaned into the fridge with her. "Did you make any Spanish rice?"

* * * *

The next morning, she swam while Archer made breakfast. She'd told him to go and do his work, but he said he could log in from his laptop and do most of what he needed to get done here. Then he'd walk her to the store, where Jonathon would be waiting to work on his book.

After they finished breakfast and did the dishes, she called Sam. "Hey, I'm just checking in. Did that woman ever come in for a necklace last week?"

"Oddly enough, no. I called her on Wednesday and told her when I'd be in the shop, but she never showed. Customers are flakes like that. That's why you need to get them committed when they first fall in love with a piece. If they have time to think, they may not buy." She sounded okay. Not excited, but not sad either. "I'm glad you called. I wanted to tell you that I won't be at the Tuesday book club until this is all settled. I don't want to stop you guys from talking freely. And any discussion around Marcus just makes me mad."

"Are you sure?" Rarity had her planner out and marked Sam's name down near the book club. "Everyone knows your situation. They understand when you get upset."

"They might, but I don't. And I don't want to be yelling at Shirley for her just stating a theory or her opinion. It's not fair to the group." She sighed. "Besides, Marcus will be leaving as soon as this is settled. He's going back to California. He says Arizona is just too small-town for him."

"I'm sorry, Sam." And Rarity was truly sorry. It seemed like whether or not Marcus killed Janey, he was going to be disappearing from Sam's day-to-day life soon. "Have you talked with Drew?"

"Not recently. I know I need to call, but I'm not sure what to say. Besides, he still has Marcus as a suspect. Until that changes, I can't even look at him without listing off all the reasons my brother couldn't have killed anyone." Sam murmured something to someone, probably Marcus, in the background. "Look, I've got to go and get breakfast made. Thanks for calling, and I'll talk with you soon."

When Rarity hung up, she saw Archer playing with Killer and pretending not to watch her. "That was Sam. She's not coming to book club until Janey's murder is solved."

"That's probably for the best. I bet it's really hard for her to hear people discussing it." He gave Killer a rub on the head and walked over to her. "I'm sorry this is hard on the two of you."

"I don't understand why she won't just talk to me. We used to talk about everything." Rarity stepped closer and let Archer wrap his arms around her. She felt the tears starting to well up. "We're best friends. Or we were."

"Give her some time and space. She'll come back. She's dealing with a lot," Archer said as he rubbed her back.

Finally, Rarity stopped crying and stepped away from Archer. She glanced at the clock. "Let me go wash my face and put my makeup back on. I'll be ready to go in a few minutes."

"No rush."

When she came out, she saw him finish a message on his phone. He tucked it away in his jeans. "Are you late?"

"No, my new assistant is early. I told him to go get us some coffee, and I'll be there soon." Archer grabbed his backpack. "I'm going to teach him invoicing and scheduling today. Or at least what I do. He'll probably have a new system set up for me by next week."

"Oh, I should text Jonathon and tell him we're on our way." Rarity reached for her phone, but Archer shook his head.

"Already done. He'll be there before we are." He handed her the tote. "Anything you need to put in there?"

She glanced inside and shook her head. "Nope, I'm ready. Killer? Are you ready to go to work?"

The dog ran to the door and stared at his leash. Then he turned and barked at her.

"I guess that's a yes and a 'please hurry up.'" She turned off the lights and went to put on Killer's lead. So much of what she did was automatic. She had a routine. Maybe that was the problem with this case. Since Janey was new to Sedona and the job and dating Marcus, all her routines had been upended. She took her phone out and started a text.

"I've already updated Jonathon." Archer took Killer's leash from her.

"I'm not texting Jonathon. I'm texting Drew." She finished her message, then looked up at Archer. "We're looking at this wrong. We need to know who knew where Janey was going to be that Saturday. Yes, it puts Marcus squarely in the crosshairs, but there had to be someone else. Her roommate? Her sister? Who knew she was going hiking to the quarry with Marcus that morning?"

Drew's text finally came back when they'd just arrived at the bookstore. It was short. She read it, then snorted.

"Okay, what did he say?" Archer held Killer while she unlocked the bookstore door.

Rarity switched on the lights and headed directly back to the register counter. She set her tote on the counter. "He said, 'Interesting question.'"

"That's all?" Archer laughed. "Man, he's holding his cards close to the vest."

"It must be my son you're talking about. I got a stern lecture this morning about eavesdropping and my guest room privileges." Jonathon set his briefcase on the table as he talked. "I guess I'm going to have to be more discreet. I'd hate to lose my free Sedona guesthouse."

"I asked Drew who else knew that Janey was going to the quarry that day. He said it was an interesting question." She unpacked her murder notebook and her laptop. Then she opened the notebook and wrote down the question on a clean sheet of paper. "I think the answer to that question will help solve this murder."

"And if the answer is only Marcus?" Archer glanced at his watch. "Don't answer that. I've got to run. See you in a few hours. Thanks, Jonathon."

He set Killer's unhooked leash on the counter and sprinted toward the door. Jonathon looked amused. Rarity put away the leash and met his gaze. "He's meeting a new employee."

"Calliope's not training them? I swear that girl knows Archer's business better than he does." Jonathon nodded to the break room. "Can I grab some ice for my water?"

"Sure. And Calliope's not working for Archer anymore." Rarity closed and put away the murder book.

Jonathon frowned. "Really? Well, she must have just been in the area last week when I ran into her. I just assumed. Do you want me to bring you something from the refrigerator?"

Rarity shook her head. "I'm fine."

As she opened her laptop and tried to work on the income spreadsheet for last week, Jonathon's words kept ringing some sort of bell for her. What had Calliope been doing in Sedona last week? She trusted Archer, and he'd said that he'd had lunch with his ex-admin assistant lately. So why was she feeling like she was missing something?

Chapter 21

The Tuesday night crowd was all there early. Archer had come at five and taken Killer with him to the house. He was making dinner, so as soon as the book club was over, they'd eat. Jonathon would be walking her home even though she'd insisted she could make it there on her own. When Archer threatened to ask Terrance to escort her, she'd given in. At least Jonathon would be on his way back to Drew's house once he dropped her off at her door.

"Besides," Jonathon had told her when Archer had left that afternoon, "I'm getting more walking in here than I do at home. I've already gone down a pant size. Edith's going to be so jealous."

She couldn't fight that. She just worried about Jonathon. The last time someone had been murdered, he'd been robbed for a set of journals that the survivors' club had been reading to see if they held any clues. She didn't want that to happen again.

Shirley had brought treats, and as they gathered by the fireplace at seven, everyone had coffee and a pumpkin sugar cookie nearby.

Rarity took her murder notebook and sat down. "I guess we should get started."

"Where's Sam?" Holly asked, glancing around the bookstore.

"She's not coming tonight. With this investigation being so close to Marcus, she felt like she couldn't be objective." Rarity hoped she was relaying Sam's message meaning without hurting anyone in the club. "So does anyone have any new information we need to add to the notebooks? I do, if no one else wants to go first."

Shirley pointed at the flip chart. "Rarity, you go, then I've got some gossip I heard at church."

"And Malia has some things she heard at campus." Holly nudged her friend.

Malia nodded. "With Caleb's institutionalization, it might be a moot point, but it's better to have all the information out there, right? You start, Rarity."

Rarity told them about Trish Ford not being at the hairdresser's like she'd told Drew. "So she no longer has an alibi. At least not one we know. She could have been sleeping in or having an affair or even shopping. But she wasn't where she said she was. And that's at least suspicious. I've told Drew what I found out, so he's looking into that."

She paused as people made notes. The week had been crazy, but she didn't want to leave anything out. "So Malia mentioned Caleb. Do I need to go over that? Jonathon was here, too, that day, so he can fill in anything I forget."

Shirley held up her hand. "I know we talked about it, but can you go over what happened again?"

Rarity went through the incident with Caleb and his pain. She added in her own feelings and observations. "I don't think he killed Janey. I believe he was her stalker and only took the job because she had been hired, but I think he was just trying to get her to notice him."

"You've got a kind heart," Jonathon said. Then he went on to talk about what he'd learned about stalkers and what he called "love" killers. "Caleb fits the mold of the killer's thought process. If I can't have you, no one else will. The fact that he couldn't go through with his own suicide after the fact doesn't mean he didn't kill her. And later he admitted killing Janey. Maybe he was lost in a deep fantasy."

"Yeah, but he got the details wrong. He said he saw her an hour before Marcus left her at the quarry. And on the wrong trail." Rarity tried to poke holes in Jonathon's theory.

"He shot at her. Or he shot at someone. He's my top suspect, just because of that. Drew's got some guys going down the trails to see if they can find this spot. If there's no blood, he could have followed her to the quarry, watched her and Marcus, and when Marcus left, finished the job." Jonathon had thought this out thoroughly. And since he lived with Drew, this might be one of the theories the police had been kicking around as well.

"But if he shot at her, wouldn't Janey have been upset when she met Marcus? Why would they hang out and swim if someone had just tried to kill her? Marcus would have taken her right to the police station to report the shooting." Holly shook her head. "Something's off. Either Caleb is lying and living in a fantasy world. Or..."

"Or the woman he saw and shot at wasn't Janey. It was her sister." Rarity ended her thought.

"Whoa. He shot at the wrong twin?" Malia nodded. "It could work."

"But it doesn't tell us who killed Janey," Shirley countered. She got up and refilled her coffee cup. "I'm going to regret this cup when I get home, but I've got some quilting to do if I can't sleep."

"Well, it might. If Trish was shot at. And if Trish knew Janey was meeting Marcus that morning." Rarity felt everyone's gaze on her. "And if Trish killed her sister."

"That's a lot of ifs. Typically, investigations take one piece of evidence and try to build a case. I think in this situation, we need to find something on the trail that proves Caleb isn't just making stuff up. Or proof that Trish went out to the trails that day. We know she didn't get her hair done. That's all we can prove. And if you can't prove it, it didn't happen." Jonathon stood and got another cookie. "We should see what else we have going on or who else has information. Maybe there's a clue in some of that."

Then Shirley told them what she'd heard at church. "Janey and her sister were orphaned just before they started college. Their mom was involved in all the local charities, even some here in Sedona. She had lost her husband years before, and she'd set money aside for the girls out of an insurance settlement."

"Okay, so we know where the trust money came from. And each girl handled the money differently. Trish went down the same road as her mom, doing charity balls and such. Janey decided to be a perpetual student." Holly looked up from her notes. "But that doesn't give us any clues to Janey's death, does it?"

"It shows a divide with the two women. At least in interests and opinions," Shirley said. "There's one more thing I heard. It's not flattering, but the rumors said Trish had been having an affair with Allen Holbart. He had a really messy divorce a year ago, and Trish's name came up several times in the court case."

"I knew that guy felt slimy," Malia said.

"He's got to be twenty years older than her." Rarity stared at Shirley. "Are you sure?"

"It's rumor, but yes. That was why his wife was so mad. When the affair started, the girl was maybe twenty." Shirley looked around the room. "I know it's legal, but it still feels wrong."

"If he was their family lawyer, it's manipulative at the least." Rarity rolled her shoulders. "And it may explain why Janey felt the need to get a new lawyer and take her money out from under his control."

"Before we end tonight, I want to tell you what I heard." Malia glanced at her watch. "I don't think it's earth shattering, but several of the women on campus substantiated the fact that Caleb was stalking Janey. They're all sure he's the killer and the cops just aren't pursuing it."

Jonathon sighed. "People like that always think they know exactly what's going on. It doesn't matter what the cause is, the mob knows better than the authorities."

Malia looked at him. "Sometimes people protect the status quo."

"True, but I guess the question then comes down to the people in charge. Do you know and trust my son, Drew?"

Malia blushed, but she nodded. "I do trust Drew. But what about..."

"What about the people who are working the case that you don't know?" Jonathon finished her sentence. Malia nodded. He looked at the group. "What I'm going to say may be old-fashioned, but what if we gave people the benefit of the doubt? That most people are trying their best and doing what they think is right?"

Holly nodded. "I was always an us-against-them type until I started working at the city. Getting to know people and the rules they're working under, that helped a lot with my distrust."

"Jonathon, I don't think Malia was saying that she didn't trust Drew," Rarity added. This discussion was getting personal. She realized maybe Sam had the right idea. When it was too close to the people you know and love, objectivity goes out the window.

"I definitely wasn't saying anything against Drew and the investigation he's doing." Malia met Jonathon's gaze head-on. "But the women on campus are feeling unsafe and think that Caleb is not only a stalker but also a killer. I think getting this case solved sooner rather than later will help."

Rarity agreed with Malia, but she wasn't sure the investigation was ending anytime soon. "Let's go back and look at our suspect list. We need to know if Caleb was telling the truth about that morning."

Shirley scribbled that on the to-do list they made at the end of each meeting.

"And we need to know where Trish was that morning," she added as Shirley nodded, still writing.

Malia held up a hand. "And we need to know if Trish knew about Janey pulling the money out of the trust. Have we totally ruled out Cara yet? She's the one with the most to gain from Janey's death, at least with the new will."

"I think someone should talk to Cara again. Maybe see if she has an alibi for Saturday." Holly looked at Jonathon. "I know Drew probably already has, but we don't have access to the actual investigation. Unless someone wants to sneak into the police station and get copies of the case file. I'm telling you right now that I'm not doing it. I need my job. And I kind of like it."

Jonathon held up his hand. "I'll see what I can find out, but Drew's already giving me warnings about eavesdropping on his conversations. Maybe if he accidentally leaves the case file at the house, I might be able to see something. But that's a long shot."

"And I've got to have someone with me at all times, which makes me less of a covert interviewer." Rarity glanced around the group. "Malia? Do you want to talk to Cara?"

She nodded. "I can do that. Especially if I use the campus safety angle. If Caleb was stalking her roommate, Cara should be open to talking about it. I could say I was writing an article about women's safety on campus."

Holly glanced at the to-do list. "Okay, that has one of the tasks marked off. What about finding out where Trish went that Saturday? I'm sure she's not going to be truthful if we come out and ask her. What about cabs or drivers? Does she even drive?"

"We need to talk to someone close to her. What charity was she working with most recently?" Rarity grabbed her phone and scrolled through the pictures online that came up when she typed in Trish's name. "Here's one. It's an animal shelter. I'll call and see what I can find out. If we can find someone who knew Trish and her schedule, then we can glean what we need from there."

"If there's more than one charity, let me know. I have connections in the community service arena here in the area. Someone I know should also know Trish." Shirley wrote Rarity's and her name by the "find out where Trish was" item.

Holly pointed to the first one. "I'll take looking at the trail. I'll get up early tomorrow and go around those trails near the quarry. Maybe one of the regular hikers heard a shot fired during their walk. I need to get some exercise in anyway."

Malia grabbed another cookie. "I'll go with you if I can. I've been eating too many of Shirley's sweets."

"Haven't we all." Jonathon chuckled.

And with that, the tension that had been starting to build with the club dissolved. Rarity thought Jonathon's message to the group, having a positive attitude, also meant believing the best of everyone. Even those who act on their baser instincts like Caleb.

Jonathon was quiet as they got ready to close the store and walk to Rarity's. She locked the door, and they crossed the courtyard to the sidewalk. Sam's shop was closed already, but that didn't surprise Rarity. She often closed before Rarity.

"Are you okay? Malia was a little tough on you today," Rarity asked as they started walking back to her house.

"I think I was the one who was tough on her. As a police officer, I knew every day I could be involved in something that could end my life. I can get defensive when people make overgeneralizations. We're not all bad cops out there." He pulled his jacket closer.

"I think your bringing it from 'they' to a specific person was brilliant. We can blame 'they' all we want. But when we start blaming people we know specifically, then you have to decide what you believe more. 'Did your friend act this way?' versus 'Did the general city management act this way?' We're all just people. Some of us are better people than others." Rarity bumped his shoulder with her own.

"I'm glad I'm hanging out with good people now. The book club is trying to help Drew out, whether he wants it or not." He waved at Terrance on his porch. "We all have to do our part to keep Sedona safe."

Rarity stopped in her driveway. "We didn't assign anyone to look into the lawyer, Allen Holbart. If he'd have an affair with a young woman he was supposed to be watching over, he might just kill if he thought the money should be under his control."

"Or if he used the trust money like it was his own. I'll do an internet search on him and see if he's done something like this before." Jonathon brightened. "It will give me something to work on when the muse is being stubborn and I can't write."

She opened the door. Killer came running to her. "Hey, I'm home," she called out to Archer. She turned back to Jonathon. "Do you want to come in?"

He shook his head. "I'm fine. I'm going to wander on home. Maybe Terrance needs to do a walkabout and I can get some company for the walk home."

"That's a great idea. I'm sure he's ready to stretch his legs." Rarity said goodbye to Jonathon and told him she'd see him in the morning. The house smelled like homemade chicken noodle soup. At least that was what she hoped it was. She called out to Archer, "Something smells amazing."

"I should hope so. I slaved all day over this hot stove." Archer came over and gave her a kiss. "How was your club?"

"Tense. I think everyone just wants this investigation to be over. They're seeing shadows in people we should be trusting." Rarity fell on the couch and brought Killer over to her lap to cuddle.

"I know the cure for that. Let's all go to the Lava River Cave on Sunday." Archer went to the kitchen and poured Rarity a glass of wine.

"Lava what?" She took her wine and scooted over on the couch to make room.

"It's a cave that was made from a lava river. It's really cool, but everyone needs to wear solid shoes and warm clothes. And it's completely dark, so we'll need several flashlights, just in case." He sipped his wine and nodded. "I go there when I need to think. It changes your perceptions on things. I always come out more focused and, if I had a problem, with a solution by the time I leave."

"Sounds interesting. I've never seen a cave like that." Rarity ran her fingers through Killer's fur. "Did you miss me, bubba?"

"We had too much fun without you. We went outside and barked at Terrance across the fence, then we wandered through the yard, checking the fence. And that was all after he helped me make dinner. He makes sure nothing stays on the floor if I drop it." He pulled out his planner. "I'm blocking off Sunday, and we're going. I'll call the members of your group and see if they want to go. The hike's not horrible, so Shirley and Jonathon shouldn't have any issues."

"How far is this cave?" Rarity liked having some decompression time on Sunday.

"Just over an hour, maybe an hour and a half. If we get there before the snow closes the road, we can take the shortcut." He was scribbling in his planner. "I'll make the calls tomorrow and see who we can get to go."

She watched him block off the time. "You love this, don't you?"

He grinned and shut the planner. "It's a good thing that planning and giving hiking tours is my job. We'll take the bus. That way you can all talk while I drive. Let's get dinner going. I've got a game I'd like to watch."

"Sounds great. I've got a book I need to read." Rarity had brought home the elementary school book club selection for next week. She was looking forward to this club, way more than she did the teenagers last week. But she was definitely participating as part of Sedona now. She'd met so many new people in the last month, just through the book clubs. And Sunday, she'd go to another tourist spot she could talk about with her customers.

Life was good. Or it would be if one of her employees hadn't been murdered just a few weeks ago. And her killer was still on the loose.

Chapter 22

Before Shirley's Mommy and Me class started, a young woman with a camera came into the bookstore and introduced herself. "Hi, I'm Beth Charters. I'm a reporter for the *Sedona Star*. I hear you're doing a few more book clubs starting this month. Can I talk to you about them? Maybe snap some pictures?"

Rarity held out her hand. "Nice to meet you. I'm Rarity Cole, owner of The Next Chapter. I'll be glad to talk with you for a while. Our Mommy and Me class starts in a few minutes. Do you want to sit in?"

Beth leaned down and petted Killer. "Do you want to be my baby so I have someone to read a book with?"

Killer barked at her and went back around the counter to lie in his bed.

Rarity smiled. "I don't think he identifies as a baby. That's Killer. I've had him for about a year now."

"He's adorable. I have a German shepherd. My boyfriend has a house with a yard, so I thought why not. I've always wanted to own one. We do classes once a month so he's well trained. And smart. I didn't know how smart dogs could be. My mom didn't want us to have pets." Beth was a rambler.

"So what did you want to ask?" Rarity handed her flyers for all five of the book clubs, including Tuesday night's. "I'm hoping to add a couple more adult groups once I get some employees hired. As it is, Shirley's here for all of the book clubs. Although she's a member of the club on Tuesday, not an employee."

"Shirley goes to church with my folks. She's always busy with one activity or another." Beth pulled out a notebook that had several questions already written down. She added in a few things they'd already talked about. "You're not a Sedona native. What made you move here?"

Rarity talked about surviving breast cancer and deciding to follow her dream. "My best friend, Sam Aarons, runs the crystal shop next door. She told me about the building being for sale, and the next thing I knew, I'd bought the building, my house, and I was moving to Sedona."

"That's brave." Beth glanced up at her from her notebook. "I've lived here all my life except for the four years I went to school in Tucson."

"Some people know where they belong early." Rarity smiled. "What else can I tell you?"

They got through Beth's questions right before Shirley started the Mommy and Me class. Rarity handed her the book they'd be reading. "Just in case you want to follow along."

"Thanks. Do you think it would be okay to get some pictures of Shirley as well as you and the bookstore? I won't take any direct pictures of the moms or babies, and I'll get releases from everyone who I do catch in a snap." Beth tucked her notebook into her tote bag and took out her camera. She took a picture of the book, of Rarity, and one of Killer, sleeping.

Rarity watched as the reporter moved toward the fireplace, where she sat so she could watch Shirley. She'd had reporters here when she first moved into the building, but she should have thought to send a press release about the book clubs. Another reason she needed some help at the bookstore. With the clubs, she thought she was selling enough books to be able to afford to hire someone in addition to Shirley. The school had been subsidizing wages for Janey and Caleb and probably would again for a new hire, but she thought she'd just put up an ad in the local paper and see what she could get. She'd make the first line of the ad "Must love books." Hopefully that would bring in the right kind of people.

She worked on a long-range to-do list that included the press release idea. She didn't have to send this one to the *Star,* but maybe the Flagstaff papers would be interested. And maybe her old hometown as well as her college magazine. By the time Shirley's class ended, she had a full page of ideas and a line of moms waiting to buy more books.

As the crowd thinned out, Beth came over and had Rarity sign a release for the photos. "I'm not sure when they'll publish this, but I'm going home to write it now. Maybe we can get more interest for your Saturday elementary school–aged club."

"That would be lovely." Rarity waved goodbye to Beth and the last of the moms. Then she went over to help Shirley clean up. "You did amazing as always."

"You were working on something. How do you know I did amazing?" Shirley handed her a cookie. "Does it look like a giraffe? The book was told in Gerry the Giraffe's viewpoint, so I thought it might be cute."

"It's adorable. And yes, I was working on some planning for the future, but everyone told me how much fun they had and what a great job you're doing." She bit into the giraffe cookie. "And we're getting some interest from the local paper. You're going to be famous."

"I'm sure they'll use your picture, or even Killer's, for the story. I'm just the club leader; you're the bookstore owner." Shirley arranged the last of the chairs. "Now what else can I do? I'm here for the full day today."

"Actually, I do have a few things. Do you want to write a press release or handle the counter while I do?"

"I'll handle the front, but send me a copy of the press release, and I'll try my hand at it for next month's featured books for the clubs." Shirley walked with her toward the counter. "Are we doing three or four Mommy and Me classes a month? I told them we might take off next week since we don't have a book club scheduled for Saturday either but that I'd check with you."

"I think that's a great idea. That way we can use the time to plan the next month's books."

"We should have a calendar that we can have available and people can take home. And one on the website," Shirley suggested.

"Hold on, let me write that down. So our first one will be next month, right? Do we have books scheduled yet?"

They worked together on the calendar first since the books had already been picked out by Janey and Caleb.

Shirley sent the draft copy to both Rarity and herself. "I'm going to play around with some graphics at home."

"Don't be working a lot at home. And tell me what you do so I can pay you for the time," Rarity reminded her.

"Of course." Shirley winked as she greeted a customer that had just come up to the register. "How can I help you today?"

Jonathon had left early, but he showed up at one with lunches for Rarity, Shirley, and himself.

"Oh, did Archer call you?" Rarity asked as she set down her sandwich.

Jonathon nodded. "I talked to him about an hour ago. I'm game for the Lava River Cave. I went a few years ago with Drew and Archer, but I haven't been back since. Shirley, are you going?"

"I think I will. Archer told me to wear my hiking boots and dress in layers. I'll probably bring a light coat too. I get cold easily."

"We'll load up at Annie's with coffee and treats for the bus ride," Rarity added. "I'm looking forward to doing something besides working and thinking about who killed Janey."

"After Tuesday night, I am as well. I think I was a little harsh with Malia," Jonathon said, then he changed the subject. "Shirley, when are you leaving? I have some errands to run if you're staying until closing."

"I will stay until Archer arrives." Shirley tucked her wrapper into her empty lunch sack. "We just came up with a few promotional items that we need to work on. I'm trying to make myself as useful as possible."

"You're kidding, right? You've been amazing." Rarity finished the last of her sandwich. "And this was just what I needed for lunch today. Thanks, Jonathon. Can I reimburse you?"

Jonathon shook his head. "I was going to tell you, but you actually already paid for this. I talked to the manager over at the Garnet. You have an account there now. She'll bill you once a week with the food itemized and labeled with who picked it up. You should do the same with Annie's. That way you don't have to deal with petty cash all the time."

"This must be 'upgrade The Next Chapter's business policies' week. Thank you." She pulled out her notebook and wrote down a note about the weekly invoice from the Garnet as well as a note to contact Annie's owner. "I should have thought of this earlier."

"You're running pretty fast lately. I'm surprised you have time to do anything besides keeping the doors open." He handed her a flyer. "This is the information for the business chamber for Sedona. I know it's one more meeting for your schedule, but I think you'd make a lot of connections that way."

"I hadn't thought about that." Rarity put the flyer in her calendar. "I promise, I'll check it out as soon as things slow down here a bit."

He shook his head. "Now, see, that's the problem. You think things are going to slow down. From what I know from my friends who run their own businesses, you have to make time for the important things. And with that last piece of advice, I'm going to put my errands off. I'm going to get back to writing."

When Archer came to get her, Rarity was just closing up the bookstore. Shirley and Jonathon left together as soon as Archer came into the shop. He said his goodbyes, then walked over to where Rarity was putting things into her tote. "Do I know how to clear a room or what?"

"I appreciate them being willing to hang around. Although it does make me feel a little helpless." She clicked the leash onto Killer's collar. "So how was your day?"

As they walked home, he told her about his hike and the group he'd taken out that morning. "Oh, and I got ahold of all the survivors' club members, and they're all in for the hike. Including Sam and Marcus. I figured you wouldn't mind if he tagged along."

"No, that's fine. According to Sam, he's leaving town as soon as he can, so he definitely needs to get out and see at least some of what Sedona has to offer as far as natural beauty." She looked up at the darkening sky and took a breath. "I'm glad you had a good day. I had a reporter come and interview me about the new book clubs. Shirley was so nervous. But then after we finished the event, she stayed around and helped me with some marketing projects I'd been meaning to do."

"I bet she loved that. She's so creative." Archer moved closer as they walked toward the house.

Rarity nodded. "Hey, have you ever gone to the business chamber meetings? Jonathon gave me their flyer."

Archer groaned. "I went once, but then Calliope took that task over. I haven't been back, but I guess I need to start up again. Why? Are you thinking about joining?"

She waved at Terrance, who was reading on his front porch. "Jonathon thinks I should. And if you're going, that's an added benefit. I won't feel like the new kid where I don't know anyone."

"I've got the next meeting on my schedule. I get emails from them. When we get home, I'll pull it up and send it to you." He paused for Killer to sniff a patch of grass. "I hate going to things like that, but if you're going, I'll brave the dragons."

"Is it that bad?" Rarity unlocked the house and reached in to turn on the outside lights. Her foot hit something as she stepped toward the door. "Wait, what's that?"

Archer squatted down and looked at the box by the door. He glanced at the label. "No shipping information again. Should I call Drew?"

She sighed and pulled out her phone. "Set it down. I'll call Drew. Can you put Killer in the house?"

They stayed out on the porch, waiting for Drew.

Terrance leaned over his porch railing and called out to them, "What's going on?"

"We got another package. Did you see anyone drop something off?"

He shook his head. "But I've been here on the deck except for from noon to two when I did lunch and walked the neighborhood. And then another walk from four to five. I'm supposed to be off shift tonight at ten. The next guy's coming on then."

Terrance's neighborhood watch team was extreme. The men who ran it were all prior military or law enforcement. So they had a schedule and a process. She appreciated the commitment but sometimes worried that it was overkill. But the package had made it onto her porch without being seen today. Maybe whoever sent it had known the watch's schedule. Or had waited for Terrance to leave his spot. It could have been coincidence when they dropped off the box, but Rarity didn't think so.

"Drew's on his way. He'll probably want to chat with you."

"The city needs to put up those video cameras they have on Main Street. Then we'd just have to check the feed to see who's doing this." Terrance nodded toward the road. "Your friend's almost here."

She looked up and saw Drew's truck coming down the street. A little too fast for the speed limit. She didn't agree with having cameras all over Sedona as a general principle, but right now, she thought it wouldn't be such a bad idea.

"You know, I could install a video doorbell system." Archer was studying her door setup. "It wouldn't take much. And I think you'd be happy with the results."

She nodded. "It's not a bad idea. Especially since I'm seeming to get caught up in these murder investigations. It might help Drew catch the culprit faster."

"I guess we need to find out if one of our suspects, besides Marcus, was in town today. We know where he was, at Sam's." Archer watched as Drew parked his truck in front of the house. "Hey, buddy. Rarity's getting more presents from this secret admirer. I wish you'd catch him. I'm feeling a little competition heating up for Rarity's attention."

"How do you know it's a him?" Drew nodded to the package. "I take it you weren't expecting something? We're not going to open this and find a box of Shirley's homemade fudge."

"I'm not expecting anything, and Shirley was at the bookstore today, so she would have just given it to me." Rarity sat down at the deck table as Drew put on a pair of gloves and brought the package over.

"You may want to get back." Drew put a mask on as Rarity stood and moved to the opposite end of the deck. "Just in case it's some sort of powder or poison. It's pretty light."

"Now you're freaking me out just a little," Rarity said.

"Just being cautious." Drew turned to look at her, his eyes twinkling over the mask. "Here we go."

He turned back, and using a knife he'd taken out of his pocket, he slowly opened the box. He leaned back when he opened it, but no puff of air or powder came out. He leaned over and pulled out a photo. "Well, this is interesting."

Now Rarity stepped forward. "Who or what is it?"

Drew took a photo of the box and took a picture of it with his phone. Then he turned to let Archer and Rarity closer. "It appears that your secret admirer really wants Marcus to be focused on for the murder. It's a picture of him and Janey at the quarry. I guess the sender thinks I'm not seeing the forest for the trees."

Rarity leaned forward. Marcus had the word *Killer* written on his chest in red Sharpie. "They weren't looking at the camera. They didn't know this picture was being taken."

"I think our friend has given us a clue that they didn't think they were giving. Someone was watching them at the quarry and took at least one picture." Drew tucked the photo into the box, put it into a large bag, and sealed it. Then he took off the gloves and leaned on the counter. "I'll check, but I'm pretty sure Caleb is still in the hospital, so it couldn't be him."

Rarity met his gaze. "What about Trish? Or Cara?"

"I'm not sure. But I'll find out. It's too bad that pictures aren't developed professionally anymore. Now, anyone with a good home printer could do that without leaving a trace." Drew glanced at his watch. "I've got to get this back to the station. I'm meeting Dad for dinner in a few minutes."

"Thanks for coming by, Drew," Rarity said as he picked up the sack. "I'll be really glad when this is done and no one's leaving me presents anymore."

Archer faked swiped a hand over his forehead. "Whew. I guess I'm off the hook for any future gifts."

"I didn't say that." She lightly punched him in the arm. "Tell Jonathon thanks for everything."

"He's enjoying having something to do rather than hanging around the house. I could do without his snooping for information for your sleuthing club, but it's been nice having him around." Drew walked toward his truck.

Rarity and Archer went inside, where Killer was sitting at the door, watching. Rarity picked the little dog up and went to the couch. "Is it just me, or is someone invested in making sure that Marcus is the main suspect here?"

Archer went to the fridge and opened the door. As he studied the options for dinner, he called back, "I think you're reading the message exactly as they want you to. The question now is who?"

Chapter 23

The rest of the week went by fast for Rarity. There were no more surprise packages left on her doorstep. Drew hadn't gotten back to her about any conversations with either of her priority suspects, Cara or Trish. Not that she expected him to update her, but she would have thought he might have caught one of them on some sort of street camera on Main or someone might have seen them.

Saturday morning, Shirley was already sitting on the bench in front of the bookstore. She looked up at Rarity with tears in her eyes.

Rarity's breath caught. *Please don't let it be George,* she prayed as she met Shirley at the door. "Are you all right?"

"You haven't seen it, then." Shirley pushed in front of her and Archer as soon as Rarity unlocked the door. "You have to see this."

Shirley unfolded a paper and pointed to a picture with a large headline: "Sedona's Own Grandmother." The picture was of Shirley reading a book at the Mommy and Me class. "I don't think I've ever seen anything so sweet in my life."

The tears were joyful. Rarity felt her body starting to work again. She'd been bracing against the news that something bad had happened. Instead, Shirley was being honored for her work. Rarity picked up the paper and read the article. It wasn't long, but it painted not only Shirley but the bookstore in a positive light as a welcome addition to Sedona. There was even a list of book clubs and their schedule in a sidebar article. "This is amazing. I bet our traffic today is going to be crazy. At least from the in-town folk."

"I've never been in a paper before." Shirley beamed and took the paper back. "I'm going to show this to George tonight. I wasn't going to go to the home today, but he really will want to see this. I know it."

Archer and Rarity exchanged a look, and she realized he'd been thinking the same thing. He'd been worried about her concern being for George too. "This is great, Shirley. You should get a second copy to send to your daughter. I bet she'd love to see it."

Shirley's eyes widened. "You're right. I need to go to the store and pick up another copy now. Do you mind, Rarity?"

"Go on. I'll be fine." Rarity laughed at her over-the-top joy. "The club doesn't start until ten, so you have time."

"I'll be right back."

Archer watched Shirley spin around and leave the shop. He glanced at his watch. "Let me text Mike and let him know I'll be late. I'm taking him with me on today's tour so he can get a feel for what we're doing here. I still need to pick up the bus."

"You go ahead. Jonathon will be here any time. We talked yesterday about his writing hours today. And he's so excited about visiting the tubes tomorrow."

"Lava River Cave, not the tubes," Archer corrected her. He looked outside at the nearly empty street. "Are you sure? I hate to leave you alone."

"I won't be alone for long. And I'm pretty sure the killer is focused on getting us to believe Marcus is the real killer. He's got to be thinking that we're taking the picture he dropped off seriously."

Drew had called her last night and said he'd brought Marcus into the station to make it look like the picture had worked, but instead, he'd just tried to get him to remember anything about the day at the quarry.

"Drew's been playing it up. I'm pretty sure Sam's still mad."

"Well, just don't take any chances. If someone comes in that looks scary, run. Or sic Killer on him." He glanced at his watch again.

"Leave. Jonathon will be here at nine. We were early getting here." She pushed him toward the door and started to shut it. "I'll keep the door locked until then."

"Okay, fine." He leaned in and kissed her. "Be careful."

She locked the door, making sure the closed sign was still turned. Then she went to the counter and unpacked her tote. Killer had found his bed by the fireplace and was already back to sleep. He'd move as soon as the kids started piling in the store for the club. He didn't hate children, but Rarity thought they must scare him. Especially since they moved so fast.

As she got ready for her day, she realized she was smiling. Having Shirley recognized in that manner was heartwarming. She'd have to do something special like bringing a cake for her at the next survivors' club meeting. After the last one went so poorly, this would be a way to bring the group back together. She'd tell Holly and Malia during the hike tomorrow.

When the knock came at the door, she hurried over to let Jonathon in, but he wasn't at the door. Instead, it was Trish. Janey's sister. Rarity left the chain on the door as she opened it just a little bit. "Sorry, we're still closed."

"Oh, this won't take but a minute. I just wanted to give you something that Janey had made for you. I found it on her desk when I went over to clear out her office at the school. It's sweet. I thought you might like it." Trish dug in her purse. "I just had it."

Rarity wasn't sure what Janey might have made for her, but this might give her some time to talk to Trish and see if she could find out where she'd actually been the morning Janey was killed. She went to unlatch the chain lock, and as she was doing it, she saw the gun that Trish was pulling out of her purse. The chain dropped, and as Rarity struggled to grab it and put it back in its place, Trish aimed the gun at her through the narrow slit of the door.

"Let's not make this a problem, okay?" Trish met Rarity's gaze, and Rarity realized that there was no life in Trish's eyes. They looked dead.

Rarity stepped away from the door and raised her hands. Hopefully someone would see Trish force her way into the shop. Jonathon was coming any time. And the kids. The kids and their parents would be showing up soon. She needed Trish to say what she needed to say and leave.

"Okay, come on in. What do you want from me?" Rarity moved to the table. She glanced over, and Killer wasn't in his bed by the fireplace. He must have moved behind the counter.

"Well, I tried to get you to point that policeman's attention to Marcus, but you didn't listen. And now I find out that my friends are being asked about my whereabouts. That won't do. I'm a big name in supporting charities here in Arizona. I can't have people thinking I killed anyone, especially not my sister. That doesn't seem very generous, now does it?"

"I'm not sure how this gets you cleared. If I'm dead, they're going to be looking for someone who killed two people. And killing a bookstore owner, that's just being mean." Rarity glanced at the clock.

Trish hadn't noticed that the door was still unlocked. From the way Trish looked, Rarity thought she wasn't noticing a lot of things. Her makeup looked like it had been put on at clown school. And the mascara on her eyes showed she'd been crying. There were still some feelings there. Maybe Rarity could use it.

"I brought his coat from his car and cigarette butts. Can you believe he doesn't even lock it? What does he think, Sedona's small-town enough for no one to steal from him? Men, they're idiots."

"His car?" Now Rarity was just confused.

"Marcus's car, idiot. He thought you were getting too close to finding out that he killed Janey, so he came over just to talk. When he realized what you knew, he killed you." Trish looked at the gun. "The gun is clean. No attachments to any other murders. At least that's what the nice man on the corner of Flagstaff Avenue and Eleventh told me when I bought it from him. It's surprisingly easy to get a gun these days."

Rarity wondered if getting into a spirited conversation about gun rights would at least delay Trish from shooting her until Jonathon figured out how to save her, but she doubted Trish was in any condition to argue logically. The woman looked like her sister's death had pushed her over a cliff that she wasn't coming back from anytime soon. "I'm surprised you didn't use Caleb. He seemed like a more likely fall guy."

"You mean suspect." Trish waved the gun at Rarity. "Where should I shoot you? In the front or in the back?"

"Are you asking if I want you to shoot me in the front of the store or in my front? I'm a little confused right now." Rarity thought she saw the door opening, but then it stopped. Had Jonathon seen them? Seen the gun? She could hope. All she had right now was hope. She'd survived breast cancer, and now she was going to be shot in her shop by a crazed twin? Life wasn't fair.

"Wait, what?" Trish rubbed at her eyes, then went into a full-on yawn and used both hands to rub her face. "I'm so tired. I can't sleep. I just keep seeing Janey's face. But I get this done, and it will be over. Marcus will be arrested, and I can focus on going after the money Janey's roommate thinks is hers."

"You won't be able to break the will. I talked with Janey's attorney. She'd written you totally out of her will. What happened? Did the two of you have a fight, so Janey went and changed the will? Or did she find out that you and the lawyer were playing footsie, so she dumped all her money into her own accounts and broke ties with the sneak?"

"Allen isn't a sneak. He's a good man." She rocked from one foot to the other. "If you would have just stayed out of this or took that photo to the cops like I told you to do, this would be done by now. He killed someone when he was a teenager. Who wouldn't believe he killed Janey?"

"Marcus didn't kill that other girl. She overdosed. If you would have done your homework, you might have known that." Rarity shook her head.

She needed to keep Trish talking just a little bit longer. "And I'm sure Allen's wife doesn't think he's a good man, or hasn't he told her about you?"

"Ex-wife. Besides, what's going on in my personal life is not your concern." Trish pushed back her hair. "As soon as I get this money back, he'll come crawling back to me."

"Oh no, he broke it off with you? Don't tell me he's trying to go back to his wife? I feel so bad for you. Not." Rarity saw the door start to swing open. Hopefully it was Jonathon and not a kid or their mother coming for the event. "You had to realize it was going to happen, right? Men never leave their wives for the flavor of the month."

"You witch." Trish pointed the gun at her, and Rarity dove behind the counter. She saw Killer lying there and hoped a random bullet wouldn't hit him. She should have run for the back room instead. She was getting set to do just that when she heard her name being called.

"Rarity, are you all right?" Noises were coming from the front of the bookstore. She prayed it wasn't any of the customers, or worse, the kids for the book club.

She peeked around the counter from her place on the floor, hoping she wouldn't be staring into Trish's gun. Instead, she saw Trish being led out of the bookstore by a deputy. Her gun and Marcus's coat were on the table that Jonathon usually occupied. Rarity glanced upward and saw Drew come closer and kneel down to meet her gaze.

"Drew?"

"Yes, it's me. Are you okay? Where's Killer?" He glanced around the area. "I don't see him. Did you leave him at home?"

"No, he's right here with me. He hid from her. I guess he could tell she wasn't much of a dog lover." She stood up and dusted off her jeans. "How did you know?"

"Dad called me. He heard voices but saw that the closed sign was still up. It felt wrong, he said. So he peeked in and saw you with a gun pointed at you. He guarded the door and called me. Apparently, there's a bunch of kids out there waiting to get inside for the club. I've got what I need. I'll take a few pictures here, but then you can probably open in about thirty minutes. If you want to. No one's going to judge you for not opening today."

"Besides the kids who are waiting for the club to start. The show must go on, right? I'm not the one who will be in front of the kids. I think I can handle some sales. Shirley's having such a great day with this Sedona's Grandmother label, I'd hate to cut it short." Rarity walked over and picked up Killer. She turned him from side to side. "Are you okay, boy? I was so worried I'd given away your hiding place."

He whined, then licked her face.

She pulled the little dog closer. "I know, I love you too."

By the time Shirley got back, most of the police had left, including the one who was dealing with the yelling and screaming Trish. Shirley looked around the bookstore. Rarity was sitting at the table with Jonathon and Drew.

"What's going on? Drew, I saw your truck out front. Do you have news about the murder?"

"Yes. We found the killer." He smiled at Shirley. "Congrats on being Sedona's Grandmother. It's a fitting title."

"Well, I don't know about that." Shirley blushed as she patted the newspapers in her tote. It looked like she'd bought more than just the one she'd said she was buying. "So where did you find the killer?"

Drew pointed to the floor. "Right here. And she gave us a full confession. We'll have to get another one when we get to the station, but at least I have a recording to work from."

"A recording?" Rarity didn't realize Drew had been recording the exchange.

He nodded. "Yep. Dad had his recorder going from the time he got off the phone with me. We still have some missing information, mostly why she thought it was necessary to kill her sister."

"Money. It's always money. I wish someone would fix the world and make money obsolete." Rarity leaned her head back and closed her eyes. Then she leaned forward. "It's after nine thirty. Are we doing the book club or not?"

"I'm fine to run it, if that's okay with you. I don't want to disappoint the kids. I might be old, but I have enough gumption to do this. I hate that she came to our happy place." Shirley squared her shoulders and turned to face Rarity. "Is it okay for me to run it?"

"Sure. I just want to make sure you're okay." Rarity rubbed Killer's back. She might never let the little dog out of her arms ever again.

Chapter 24

Rarity pulled her coat closer. She was glad she'd listened when Archer had nixed her first choice of a cute sleeveless bubble vest as her overcoat. The cave temperatures must have been hovering near freezing. She stepped closer to Archer as he paused in front of the lava river tunnel they were getting ready to step inside. The cave was amazing and scary at the same time.

He put an arm around her and turned toward the others. "Okay, so here we go. The tubes circle around, and we'll come back out here, but don't wander off. I'd hate for you to take a wrong turn and your flashlight go out. It's dark in here."

"I hate the dark," Sam complained as she gripped her flashlight tighter. "Maybe I should go back to the entrance."

"No way. This is the one and only time I'm doing this, and you're coming with me. Someday we'll tell the story to my kids, and they'll want to know that Aunt Sam wasn't a scaredy cat." Marcus grinned at his sister. He was back to his fun, over-the-top personality. The one Rarity had seen that night at the party.

Sam took a step forward, but Archer held up his hand. "Hold on a second. Shirley? Jonathon? Are you two ready for this?"

"I just talked to a group of kids yesterday. Don't play with me. I can do anything. I'm Sedona's grandmother." Shirley grinned.

Jonathon nodded toward Shirley. "I'm with her."

"Okay, then. We're putting the past behind us at this point." Archer met Rarity's gaze. "We're putting our fears, our insecurities, and our negative words on a shelf here on the wall. Then when we come back, they will all be gone. They will have sunk into the stone. We'll walk out of here as positive, optimistic people who care for our environment."

"And social issues," Malia added.

Archer smiled. "Yes, those as well."

"We should say something about trusting each other," Marcus said, looking straight at Sam.

"And something about understanding when others are in a tough spot," Sam shot back to him.

"Okay, so with that, I think we've finished the ritual. Just think positive thoughts, and this should work. If something happens, just call out to the next person in line. Then we'll all stop and make the next decision together." He glanced around the crowd. "Now, are we ready?"

"Onward and forward and all that," Rarity said as she stepped into the tube with Archer. She didn't know what was going to happen tomorrow or when they stepped out of the cave, but that was the fun of life, right? Not knowing where they were going?

Recipe

As I'm writing this, I'm getting ready for my first neighborhood Halloween bonfire. I always freeze up when I think about what I'm cooking for others. I want it to be perfect. I know that's a lofty goal, but I like being prepared and feeding people. It's a trait I got from my mom. She wasn't perfect, but she was probably the best cook I've ever known.

I love making brownies. They were always my go-to cookie as a kid since we always had the ingredients on hand.

Enjoy the brownies.

Lynn

Marbled Pumpkin and Chocolate Brownies

Preheat the oven to 325 degrees and line a 13x9x2 pan with aluminum foil. Then spray the foil with spray oil.

In a mixing bowl, beat together the following:

3 oz softened cream cheese

1 tbsp butter

Then add and beat until smooth:

½ cup sugar

Add the following and mix together:

1 egg

1 cup canned pumpkin

1 tsp vanilla

½ tsp ground cinnamon
¼ tsp ground ginger

Stir into mixture, then set this bowl aside:
1 tbsp flour

In a small bowl, mix the following ingredients, then set aside:
1 ¼ cups flour
¾ tsp baking powder
½ tsp salt

In a small saucepan over medium heat, melt the following together and cook until smooth:
6 tbsp butter
1 1/8 cups cocoa

Then add the below and cook until smooth:
¾ cup butter, cut up in cubes

Remove from heat. Pour the melted chocolate into a mixing bowl, then gradually add the following:
2 ¼ cups sugar
4 eggs (add one at a time, beating well after each)
¼ cup milk
2 tsp vanilla

Beat in the flour mixture until combined.
Spread the chocolate mixture into the prepared pan, smoothing it even. Then drop several mounds (using all) of the cheesecake mixture onto the chocolate. Using a knife, swirl the pumpkin into the chocolate to get a marbled look.
Bake 60 minutes or until the center is just set. Lift the brownies out of the pan with the foil. Then cut.
Store in fridge for up to three days, layered between sheets of wax paper.

Acknowledgments

To the fans who brought Rarity into your hearts and loved her as much as I do, thank you. It's been a challenge to bring a cancer survivor heroine to the pages, and you welcomed her with open arms. To all those who wrote me about their own health journey and the friends and family who walked me through mine, I can't thank you enough. Thanks to the Kensington crew for taking a chance on this cozy with a serious side. Michaela, Esi, Alex, Larissa, Lauren and everyone else who championed the idea. Thanks for seeing past the c-word. As always, I send thanks to my agent, Jill Marsal, for walking this path with me and challenging me to reach for the next rung.

Also by Lynn Cahoon

Are you over the moon about Lynn Cahoon?
Don't miss *Two Christmas Mittens, a Kitchen Witch Novella*
Featured in *Christmas Mittens Murder*
Coming soon from Kensington Publishing Corp.
Turn the page to enjoy a sample chapter...

Chapter 1

The Lodge Culinary Department holiday party was the one event that Frank Hines allowed to be catered by an outside company. Unfortunately, a larger catering company out of Sun Valley had been given the contract instead of Mia's Morsels. Mia sighed as she watched the trays being passed around the large, dimly lit ballroom. She adjusted the black slinky halter dress she'd let Christina talk her into wearing tonight. Mia had to admit, it made her hairdo work, especially with the jeweled hair combs she'd slipped into the updo. A matching necklace and black heels finished the outfit. Now, all she had to do was hang out with her coworkers for the next two hours and try to have fun and not judge the food Frank had contracted.

As the lodge's new catering director, Mia had been part of the decorating team that had planned the festive decorations that went up right after Halloween every year. Now, a month and a half later, the Santa and friends décor would need refreshing after this weekend before the Christmas parties started in earnest. She'd suggested three different décor setups. One for a more general holiday theme for the Thanksgiving groups, one for Christmas parties, and then a refresh between that and the New Year events. But Frank had vetoed her suggestion for the large ballroom. Just like he'd vetoed Mia's Morsels as the caterer for this event.

Christina Adams stood next to her and took a stuffed mushroom from the server. Christina was Mia's roommate and worked with her at Mia's Morsels when she wasn't finishing her schooling. Christina shone in her silver dress with a large tulle skirt. With her blond hair down and pulled away from her face, then topped off with a small tiara, the girl looked like a princess tonight. She had plenty of appropriate party clothes since she'd never worn anything twice when she was under her mother's roof.

"We would have rocked the food at this party. Probably for less than what this place charged."

"I know, but Frank was concerned about my connection with Mia's Morsels. He thought it might look like I had the inside track." Mia shook her head at the mushroom tray.

"Our proposal had better food and a lower per-person cost. So instead of choosing us, he hires the catering company where his new girlfriend works." Abigail Majors also waved away the tray. Abigail was currently managing Mia's catering business while Mia worked for the lodge. "That seems fair. Not."

Mia smiled at Abigail, who not only worked for her, but she was also Mia's boyfriend's mother. Sometimes in a small town the connections got a little close. Especially when you added in the fact that Magic Springs, Idaho, was also where the members of the local coven outnumbered the number of normal people in town. Even tonight at the lodge's Christmas party, Mia recognized many of the coven members. Most had tried already to bring Mia and her grandmother back into the fold to rejoin the coven. Mia blamed her work schedule, but that excuse wouldn't work forever. She needed to make a decision. And soon.

Abigail had on a burgundy pantsuit that shone in the twinkling lights. She pulled her phone out of one of the front pockets and sighed. "It's Thomas. He's checking up on us. The boys are supposed to be scouting new tour sights for his company, and yet he has time to call just when the party gets good. He's afraid I'm going to fall for one of these business suits and leave him."

Mia laughed. "I don't think so. He probably just wants to see how beautiful you look tonight. Let's make sure we get a picture of all four of us in front of the tree. If we can pull Grans away from that guy she's been talking to all night."

Abigail stepped away from the group to take the call out in the hallway.

Mia scanned the room. Everyone seemed to be having a good time, but very few of the trays were being emptied. She'd been right about the food. It was subpar. Next time she'd insist that Mia's Morsels be given a fighting chance. Maybe have a tasting contest before the contract was decided. No one in their right mind would choose this garbage.

Christina pointed to a man near the doorway. "That's one of my professors, Geoffrey Meyers. He knows your boss from when they went to school together. He says Frank's a tool."

"He's in the culinary department?" Since Christina went to school in Twin Falls, a town about two hours away, Mia hadn't met any of Christina's professors.

"Hospitality, actually. I guess he used to manage a bunch of hotels before he took on the teaching job." Christina waved at the man, and as he recognized her, she waved him over. "I guess he's coming over to meet you. He's super nice."

"Okay, just make sure he knows I didn't cook this food." Mia grinned and turned to meet Christina's professor.

"Well, at least the company is entertaining tonight." Geoffrey waved away the catering staff person who was now trying to get them to take a cocktail wiener on a stick. "Frank always was about going with the cheapest bid. Although, I've heard that most of the lodge's events serve top-notch food."

"That's because Mia is usually in charge." Christina took Mia's shoulders in her hands. "Professor, I'd like you to meet my boss and friend, Mia Malone. She owns Mia's Morsels and is the lodge's catering director."

Mia held out a hand. "And no, we didn't cater our own event this year. A mistake I hope to not repeat next year."

"Well, not expecting staff to work during a staff party is at least a good notion on Frank's part." Geoffrey shook her hand. "I've heard great things about Mia's Morsels. Why did you take on the unfortunate position of working for Frank?"

"You know how small businesses are at the beginning." Mia tried to skirt the issue and not badmouth her boss. Geoffrey was doing it enough for both of them. "Christina talks a lot about you and the program. I'm afraid she's going to graduate in June and be swept up by a much higher-paying job as soon as they know she's available."

Geoffrey hugged Christina and spilled a bit of wine from his drink on her skirt. "She's the best student we have. She should bring in amazing offers."

As he wandered off to refill his glass, Christina dabbed at her skirt. "Good thing he drinks white wine. I think the drycleaner should be able to get this out. I've never seen him tipsy."

"I would hope not. I hope he got a room nearby tonight and won't be driving back to Twin." Mia watched as he went over to the open bar. The bartender who worked for the lodge shook his head and offered the professor a cup of coffee. At least he wouldn't be getting any more alcohol at the party.

"Oh, Professor Meyers has a house in Sun Valley. His wife works at some Hollywood film studio. Everyone says he works just to keep busy."

Christina dropped her voice a little. "Mom keeps harping at me to invite him to the Boise house to meet Dad. She's looked up their investments, I guess."

"Well, if they have a house in Sun Valley, then your dad is probably dying to get him and his wife as clients."

Christina's dad was a lawyer, and her mom was always on the lookout for new, wealthy clients. Unfortunately for the Adamses, both of their children had gone into the hospitality field, with Isaac, their oldest, being a culinary director for the most prestigious hotel in the Boise area. And now, Christina worked for Mia. A job her mom would say was beneath her. But people had to eat, right?

Her gaze caught her grandmother moving her way from across the room. "Here comes Grans."

"I'll grab us a couple more drinks. White wine again?" When Mia nodded, Christina hurried away toward the bartender.

Mia watched as her professor moved away from the bar headed out the door. Apparently being cut off had made it the end of the party for him. Mia threw a blessing at him and got a vision from the Goddess back, showing her that he had a car and driver sitting out in the parking lot waiting for him.

"You can't worry about every drunk driver," her grandmother said as she followed Mia's gaze to watch Geoffrey stumble out of the room.

"Maybe not, but if he hadn't had a driver, I would have asked one of the staff to drive him home. We don't need that on our roads. Especially on snowy nights like this." The snow had just begun to fall when they'd come into the lodge an hour before. "I'll use my power for good, as long as they let me."

"Okay, Glenda, I just wanted to tell you that Robert is taking me to Sun Valley for a late dinner. He'd assumed that since you catered the last lodge staff party, the food would be edible, not this crap." Grans shook her head at the trays being passed.

A waiter frowned at them as he tried to push a tray of undercooked egg rolls.

"I wasn't in charge of making that decision." Mia waved Abigail over. "Before you leave, let's get a picture of the four of us at the tree."

Abigail hurried over, and then Christina met them at the tree. They took several pictures, including one of Mia and Grans. Grans was in a little black dress with black heels. She still looked younger than her actual years—a magic spell gone wrong—but at least she looked closer to her age than Mia's.

Abigail showed them the last picture. "You two look like sisters."

Mia grinned as Grans shook her head. She handed Abigail back the camera. "Not now, but we did."

"And I liked it that way." Grans gave her a kiss on her cheek. "We should have gotten a picture of the two of us when we did look like sisters. I'll call you tomorrow."

Mia watched as her grandmother rejoined Robert, who stood by the door with her coat in his arm. Mia had met him once before when they'd stopped by the school. She liked him. He seemed to fit in well with her grandmother's life. And since he was involved in the local coven as well, nothing had to be hidden from his view. Hiding her witch life wasn't something her grandmother did well. Especially since she tended to make potions in her bathtub.

Abigail tucked her phone back in her pocket. "I haven't seen Robert this happy since his wife passed several years ago. I mean, since before she passed. They were a cute couple, and it was obvious that they were still in love. I hope Mary Alice and Robert find the same joy."

"Mia's Morsels may be catering a wedding soon," Christina teased and then pointed toward Mia. "Oh, my goodness. You should see your face. You look scared."

"I'm not sure who I'm scared for, Robert or Grans?" Mia nodded to a table. "Let's sit for a bit, then as soon as eight hits, let's get out of here. I've got lasagna ready to warm up in the oven, and if you want to stay over, Abigail, I've got a few bottles of wine in the house."

"Sounds like a real party." Abigail sat down and slipped off her shoes. "My feet are killing me. We used to do the party scene probably twice a month when we ran the grocery store. Now, it's rare for me to get dressed up unless I'm catering, and then I'm in sensible shoes."

Mia giggled at the older woman's gripes. She liked spending time with Trent's mom. His dad, he still was an unknown, but his mom was fun.

"Since the boys are all gone, we should have a sleepover. I'll make brownies, and we can watch rom-coms until we fall asleep." Christina sipped at the wine she'd gotten from the bartender. She kept looking at the door, distracted.

"Are you waiting for someone?" Mia asked.

Christina turned back and shook her head. "No, I'm just a little worried about Professor Meyers. I know Sun Valley isn't that far, but his place is up in the mountains, and the roads aren't the best."

"He had a driver," Abigail told her.

Mia turned to her. She'd thought she'd been told that by the Goddess, but sometimes the messages weren't totally clear. "How do you know?"

"Kate insists on it when she's out of town. Geoff has an issue with alcohol. It's been a problem for a while." Abigail saw the shocked look on

Christina's face. "Oh, I'm sorry. He's your professor, isn't he? Just because someone has a drinking problem doesn't mean they're not a good person. He's just troubled."

"How do you know his wife?" Mia figured the answer was obvious, but she asked it anyway.

"She's a member of the coven. He's not. Not a magical bone in his body, so to speak, but Kate's quite adept at magic. It's probably why she's so good at her job. She makes magic in the movies for mortals."

About an hour later, Mia had made her final rounds at the party to say good night to her employees. She met Abigail and Christina at the ballroom door. "I'm ready to go whenever you are."

Abigail dangled her keys. "The designated driver is at your service. I've already told Thomas that we're having a girls' night at your house. He says to expect a delivery from the grocery store when we get there."

"What is he sending?" Mia asked as they got their coats from the coat check and bundled up. Now that they were heading home, she pulled a beanie over her head, tugging it down over the updo. She pulled on her warm gloves.

"I'm not sure, but you two can stay inside while I get the SUV warmed up." Abigail pulled on her hat and winter gloves too. "I'd hate to see you fall in those dresses."

For the first time that night, Mia envied Abigail's pants. The fabric wouldn't be the warmest, but it was thicker than the tights she wore under her dress. "We're not that far, and the lodge keeps the sidewalks clear. We'll come with you."

"Definitely," Christina said, but her tone didn't sound as certain.

"Okay, then, stay close." Abigail walked through the sliding doors and into the night. The snow was still falling, but it hadn't worked its way into a strong storm or blizzard, yet. It looked lovely, wafting down in front of them to land on the still-black asphalt.

Mia just hoped the surface wasn't hiding black ice. They went around to the back where employees were directed to park, and she watched as Abigail remote-started the vehicle. She'd still have to clear the windows, but the inside might start getting warm as soon as they climbed inside. "I call shotgun."

"That's not fair. I would have if my teeth weren't chattering so much," Christina said as they moved as a group toward the first row of cars. Abigail's car was in the second row, so they didn't have far to go. Christina paused and reached down, picking up something.

Mia paused as she turned to look at Christina's find. The item was a mitten knitted in a bright Christmas red. A knitted picture of Santa's face was in the middle of the mitten.

"Look, someone dropped a mitten." Christina held it out for Abigail to see.

Abigail turned, and a small scream popped out of her mouth. "Don't pick up that..."

Christina froze, holding the item in front of her. "It's just a mitten."

"It's not just a mitten." Abigail stepped toward her and groaned. "You've already made contact."

"What do you mean?" Now Mia was worried about Trent's mom. It was just a mitten. "We should get in the car. I'll take the mitten to the front desk for lost and found."

"No. Don't touch it too." Abigail dug in her tote and pulled out a plastic bag. "Here, put it in this. The mitten has powers."

"Oh, it's magic? Am I going to be a witch, then?" Christina followed Abigail's direction and looked up at her hopefully. "Is it a Christmas wish mitten?"

Abigail carefully sealed the bag and put it in her tote. Then she carefully stepped toward the car. "We need to get out of here."

"Okay." Mia shrugged and shook her head at Christina, indicating they should follow Abigail.

Then Abigail stopped and pulled out her phone.

"What are you doing?" Mia asked, trying to look around her. "Is there ice on the road?"

"So much for leaving," Abigail muttered. Then she spoke into the phone. "I need to report a dead body. Please send out Mark Baldwin to the lodge. We'll be inside the lobby waiting for him."

About the Author

Photo by Angela Brewer Armstrong at Todd Studios

New York Times and *USA Today* best-selling author Lynn Cahoon writes the Tourist Trap, Kitchen Witch, Cat Latimer, Farm-to-Fork, and Tuesday Night Survivors' Book Club mystery series. No matter where the mystery is set, readers can expect a fun ride.

Sign up for her newsletter at www.lynncahoon.com.

Turn the page for more from Lynn Cahoon!

Printed in the United States
by Baker & Taylor Publisher Services